SHARDS

BRUCE BAUGH

Book One of the Clan
Lasombra Trilogy

author	bruce baugh
cover artist	john van fleet
series editors	philippe boulle &
	stewart wieck
copyeditor	jasmine d. milberger
graphic designer	aaron voss
cover designer	aaron voss
art director	richard thomas

More information and previews available at
www.white-wolf.com/fiction

ISBN: 1-56504-865-2
First Edition: February 2002
Printed in Canada

White Wolf Publishing
735 Park North Boulevard, Suite 128
Clarkston, GA 30021
www.white-wolf.com/fiction

To Frances, for a most unexpected return and for doing so much to make this possible.

SHARDS

prologue

Monday, 1 November 1999, 6:40 AM
Hotel Vista del Castillo
Zaragoza, Spain

Sunrise was only four minutes away now, and the ghosts were leaving before All Hallows' Eve became All Saints' Day. Lucita turned her head occasionally to watch them fade out of the lands of living, but her attention was focused on the spires of the Aljafería, the capital of Aragon when it had been a kingdom and not just a Spanish province. Her hotel was almost a dozen miles west of the palace, on an uninteresting strip of commercial road. Its one redeeming feature was its height: tall enough that the upper stories looked out over the modern mass of Zaragoza and offered an unobstructed view of the hilltop crowned by the palace. Her suite occupied half the top floor, and she'd put the room's most massive wooden chair directly in front of the windows. Full sunlight wouldn't strike her, but light was already glaring off of the office and car windows catching dawn's first rays.

The palace's silhouette had changed in the nine hundred years since she drew her last breath there. Unfamiliar shadows fell across the palace's walls. There'd been no great civic towers, let alone skyscrapers, in the Aragon she'd known, and the new buildings surrounding the Aljafería loomed like conquering soldiers of a mightier empire.

But still…there was the window where she'd watched her father argue with her uncle about Uncle Ramiro's abbot. There was the battlement where she'd paced and said the orisons her confessor (*May he rot in Hell*, the thought intruded) assigned. There was the little shrine erected in the memory of her grandfather, a Moorish-embellished monument to the warrior who died fighting Moors.

It was still her home.

She felt the prickling across her skin from reflected sunlight. She wasn't burning yet, but it was just a matter of time. It took all her strength to hold herself in the chair. The curse within her made her tired. The bed looked so appealing. Day was no longer her element. Like Jacob of old, she wrestled with an angel of the Lord, but there'd be no blessing for her, no moment when the tormenter would say, "Well done, good and faithful servant," and depart. A few wisps of smoke wove through the layers of blanket, toward the smoke alarm she'd disabled during the night.

Ghosts had never been common in Lucita's experience, but even very rare events happen over the slow dark centuries. She knew a fair amount of the etiquette suitable for addressing the restless dead, modes of inquiry likely to draw out useful answers and modes of address unlikely to provoke attacks (or, worse yet, later vengeance). She knew that at times ghosts were frequent in the lands of the living, though not why, and therefore wasn't particularly surprised to find herself thronged on this All Hallows' Eve. She *was* surprised to find one of the ghosts both familiar to her and capable of making itself—himself—tangible long enough to hold a meaningful conversation.

He had been a retainer to her family only two generations after Lucita's time. He remembered the tales about "the poor lost one," the promising young lady who wasted away so tragically. They'd reminisced about the old ways—nothing consequential, just the routine of life in the lost age. Now he walked up to stand beside her, very carefully not obscuring her view, and pointed at her bare hands and face. "Milady, don't you think it a bit presumptuous to court stigmata this way? It isn't seemly for you to lay out your flesh so that the mark of Caine becomes the image of Christ's wounds, and that's what will happen if you don't put them under cover."

Lucita didn't turn to look at him. "These hands have spilled more blood than I can imagine in one place. These eyes have looked on countless sins. These teeth have drained the gift of life again and again. I told myself for a thousand years that I was all the things my sire wasn't. But I was just like him: I have preyed on others for my own ends. God won't take the curse away, but I must atone as I can. It's baptism, if you want to call that. I'm going to let fire strip off what water can't."

The ghost looked doubtful. "Milady, you were educated in the classical manner, and it's my duty as a tutor to point out that you are speaking in the absence of authority. Which of the blessed fathers tells you that cooking yourself removes sin?

You're confusing an accident of your condition with its essence. This is a stunt, not genuine penance."

This time she did turn look at him, briefly. "Are you forgetting your place? You were a servant, and now you're just a ghost. Who, exactly, are you to judge me?"

"I am a servant, milady. I saved my masters from embarrassment with private wise words. Should I stop doing so now, when a daughter of the royal family is once again in need? You put on a martyr's appearance, but it's for your own guilt rather than the glory of God or a true witness. God is not mocked."

6:44 AM. Lucita's travel alarm clock chimed one second before direct sunlight struck the highest tower of the Aljafería. Her hands began to smoke, and she felt the skin of her face beginning to wrinkle and crack. Sunlight crept down the palace's red walls. With her inhuman eyes, Lucita could clearly see constantly shifting patterns of shadow in the courtyard as sunbeams shone through layered geometric lattices built when she was a child.

The outer layers of her skin now drifted around her as a fine ash. Smoke—some columns black with vitae, others white with vampiric flesh—filled more of the hotel room, and its haze obscured the topmost foot of the windows. The pain was unbearable, and her strength continued to fade. Soon, she feared, she would collapse into fearful frenzy and flee like any neonate coward to the safety of some dark corner. She started to cry, but stopped as soon as she felt the bloody tears sizzle and burn on her cheeks.

Lucita had seen sunlight less than a dozen times in the last nine hundred years, and the reflected glare made it nearly impossible to see. She willed blood to her face, strengthening the burning tissues and restoring some measure of supernatural clarity to her vision. After a few rapid blinks, she could make out people walking in front of the palace. Memory peopled the landscape with servants, messengers, farmers delivering food, soldiers on their way to battle. The men and women who actually moved along the familiar roads, though, were none of them. They were not servants. They were *employees*, bound to their superiors by contract and economics rather than by oath and faith.

Realization broke upon her with an almost physical pain— she actually did drag her focus in for a moment to see if the windows had shattered. The palace she had known was as dead as her family, as dead now as the darkling priest who'd made her a vampire. The shell remained, but its soul had gone wherever souls go. She remembered a particular hollow tree in which she and dead departed Anatole had sheltered, in their walks along the Danube road. The palace was like that. The mortals who went around and through it were as irrelevant to the old place as she and her mentor were to that tree. It served them, but only because it no longer lived the life intended for it.

The ghost was right: there was no point to this. Her pain would not bring back her lost Aragon. She might act the part of its lady, but nobody now would serve as they'd served then. This was a delusion.

As her eyes began to crack, Lucita's vision grew more and more impaired. Within just a few seconds it was no better than any living person's, and in a few more she was nearly blind. Her world now consisted of the window, a bright rectangle, and the pitch blackness of everything else around her. Her hands no longer held firm; her body trembled in the chair, and if she had her full strength, the arms of the chair would be splinters now. She couldn't see her hands, but she could hear the click of bony fingertips on wood.

Finally her resolve failed. She managed to avoid full-blown panicked flight, but she had to stand and walk with all the dignity she could muster toward the bed and darkness. Her last step ended in a stumble—she hadn't remembered the count just right, and she ran into the footboard. The mirror above the bed smashed with the force of her impact, and she felt pieces of glass drive into her burning skin and tinkle onto the bedspread and floor. She drew the blankets and bedspread around her, feeling the power inside her healing her wounds, knowing that in just a few nights no sign would remain of her act of self-mortification.

The ghost spoke from somewhere near the window. "I go, milady. You have made yourself hurt, and to what end? You are no wiser or better than you were. You are still yourself. As the prophet Jeremiah said, 'The harvest is past, the summer is ended, and we are not saved.'" With a whisper of inrushing air, it was gone. Lucita slept.

part one: accusations

Monday, 1 November 1999, 11:30 PM
Somewhere beneath Mexico City

Trasaric watched the cardinals pace across their chamber, and once again he admired the inhuman proportions within their various outfits. There was always something new to see in the service of the coming kings.

The room was not ideal for Trasaric's viewing pleasure. It was a converted temple, built by devotees of the old gods after European lords stamped out expressions of un-Christian faiths on the surface, and taken over by vampire priests sometime later. The chamber was carved like the inside of a stepped pyramid, a hundred feet square at the base, sloping in three feet with each step. The lowermost step was a full nine feet off the floor, and even the tallest Tzimisce could walk underneath it; after that the walls slanted in every three feet. The flat red ceiling was less than half as wide as the floor. Illumination came from lanterns hanging on chains attached to the underside of steps chosen, as nearly as Trasaric could tell, purely at random. The shadows were chaotic and the light dim, so that he had to fill in details with his imagination.

Trasaric himself stood as motionless as possible in one corner, along with a few other chosen retainers. None of the others were familiar to Trasaric. He'd heard the one cringing next him referred to as "Niccolo," and looked disdainfully at the grease-stained coveralls he wore. Clearly, some driving fear prevented this pathetic figure from changing out of stolen sailor's garb. The cardinals could move freely around the obsidian altar in the center of the room. (No sacrifice graced the altar tonight. Discussion tonight, not action.) The single stone door was shut, though not barred, and Trasaric could hear the exotic ghoul guards' claws clicking in the corridor beyond.

As the senior Tzimisce present ranted on, Trasaric regretted the tensions that kept him from more frequent encounters with that marvelous figure. What a challenge it would be to clothe a form so subject to change! Not that the

Lasombra elders he usually clothed offered *no* scope for his art, of course. It takes a real craftsman to arrange a suit or gown with openings for all the shadow tentacles a vampire might wish to conjure up without the garment looking like a cobbler's vest or some patchwork salvage. Likewise, there is a specific art to the design of an entire outfit that collapses gracefully when its wearer turns into intangible shadow (and chooses to leave clothes behind rather than take them along), and which can be readily gathered up and put on again when substance returns. But mostly it was just tailoring, putting the right clothes on a form that stayed largely fixed. So unlike the opportunities the Fiend offered.

This particular evening, Cardinal Vykos obviously wished to emphasize its differences from the Lasombra with whom it argued. The features it usually wore were gone beneath elaborate ridges of bone and cartilage, with spiny protrusions that turned as the cardinal's eyes did. The body was tall, the limbs proportioned for speed, as if it expected conflict. The hands each bore an extra finger with a triple-tined claw, now holding the sleeves of a robe that reminded Trasaric of Byzantine vestments.

The cardinal's high voice had a timbre that suggested polished metal rather than a fleshly throat. "I find it peculiar that you refuse to discuss the matter. The bitch Lucita cost *you* position and influence. If I were to proceed purely on the basis of self-interest, I'd say, 'Let her run free.' What keeps you from acting?"

The eldest Lasombra present was a dour little man Trasaric had never cared for. The man seemed perfectly content to slouch around in just anything at all, from hermit's cloak to castoffs taken from last night's prey. No sense of style at all, thanks to an unshakable confidence in the power of manipulation. Trasaric had actually heard Master Timofiev say, explicitly, "My will clothes me." What could you do with that sort of attitude? One could understand too readily how vampires concerned with their place in the world had once risen up en masse to slaughter their elders.

Timofiev spoke with a deep basso rumble that didn't match his frame. "With all due respect, Cardinal, the affairs of the Lasombra clan are not yours to judge. Cardinal Monçada was one of us. So was his destroyer. Her punishment will unfold as we deem appropriate. I am sure that you will respect our desires as you would wish us to respect yours were some upstart Tzimisce to go astray."

Vykos snarled. It was a captivating action, involving the shifting of bones on each side of its chest and the tensing of muscles that seemed to run from neck down to dual sternums. Then the voice came again, calm and unruffled. "Cardinal, you know the power of precedent as well as I do. Do you really feel the need to fight the battle over the Code of Milan all over again? We established once that the 'freedom' we tell the masses about must be limited by the needs of the sect, which is to say by *our* needs. You heard the same report I did." Vykos pointed at Niccolo. "Even one incident of one of our followers glorifying your problem childe is too many. Shall we ask the Regent what she thinks?"

Timofiev's aide, a stately androgynous figure who shared Trasaric's passion for elegance, made a small gesture at its master. Timofiev stopped, listened, and smiled. "Thank you," he said very softly. Then he pointed up at one of the terraces, where old blood laid out a brief scene in pictograms in Aztec style. "Cardinal, the Paladin has reminded me of the story there. Can you see it, or should I refresh your memory?"

The Tzimisce stared up. Small ripples ran down its arms. "Thank you, and thank your Paladin. I remember the incident."

"Then you must recall that at that time we agreed that a rebel among your clan, whose actions only affected members of the same clan, was properly the affair of your clan. That was true in 1762 when one of yours attempted to build a brood in the wilds of Pennsylvania, and should be just as true now. I am sure you wish us to respect your precedent."

Vykos turned its head to look at the Paladin. Razor-sharp thorns extended from the carapace around Vykos' left eye, which the Paladin knew perfectly well were intended to literally "look daggers" in situations where direct violence wasn't feasible. The Paladin would do well to be elsewhere before the next time Cardinal Timofiev met with Vykos. With a single nod, Vykos strode out of the chamber, the other Tzimisce following closely.

When only Lasombra remained, Timofiev and the Paladin spoke softly with Niccolo. The Paladin held him aloft with one hand and two shadow arms while Timofiev used only his bare fingers to peel off long strips of skin from Niccolo's legs. "You remember nothing else, are you quite sure?"

Trasaric listened with great curiosity to the story Niccolo gasped out between moans. As nearly as the tailor could make out, Niccolo was the youngest of four childer traveling with their sire, an ambitious Italian Lasombra whom Trasaric remembered vaguely from previous years' Grand Balls. The other three had, like a great many Lasombra, discussed the significance of Monçada's destruction and the possible fates waiting for Lucita. Rosa, the eldest childe, felt that they weren't getting anywhere interesting as attendant childer. She proposed to destroy their sire, then go seek out Lucita as the proper leader of a sort of Second Sabbat, revitalizing the sect's abandoned roots in diablerie and the revolt of the young. Teodor, Matteo, and Niccolo fell in with her.

Niccolo chickened out (one of Trasaric's favorite modern phrases) at the last moment, not that the raggedy childe would admit it. He simply said that he felt increasingly unconvinced of the merits of Rosa's cause as they and their sire sailed from Portugal to the United States. He took no more part in the actual act of destruction than he had to, and as soon as the ship docked in Miami, he stole a sailor's uniform and made his way south, looking for Sabbat enclaves. A coastal pack found him somewhere along the Gulf and brought him to Mexico City.

"You see what trouble you have made," Timofiev said calmly. Rip. Rip. "We can certainly manage another confrontation with the Tzimisce, but how much better it would have been to avoid all this fuss." Rip. Rip. "You weren't clever enough to stop the disobedient childer in the first place, nor clever enough to at least make sure that only Lasombra heard the tale in the second place." Rip. Rip. "Paladin, explain the punishment."

Timofiev stepped back as the Paladin tossed Niccolo up in the air. The Paladin made sure to catch Niccolo with its sharpened fingernails right where Timofiev had cut most deeply. "You didn't scream. You've earned the right to survive. For now. Your sentence is to find your rebellious siblings and report back to us. We'll assign you some companions. If you survive them and return, then you may consider yourself in good standing once again."

The Paladin dropped Niccolo onto the ground and ran one boot along exposed nerves. "You'd love to slaughter us both. But you've got sense to keep the thought inside. You may yet amount to something." Niccolo looked up through the ribbons of vitae trickling down from his hair and kept silent.

Timofiev remained a few paces back as the other Lasombra gathered around to look down at Niccolo.

Trasaric recognized Cardinal Mysancta by the cardinal's lack of substance. Mysancta was a dedicated student of the mysteries of the Abyss, and prone to tedious harangues about the masteries of darkness possible only to those who forsake the flesh. She (at least Trasaric remembered the cardinal as having once been a middle-aged woman) spent as much time as possible in shadow form, extruding semi-tangible paws to push around a silver frame on which servants draped cardinal's robes. Trasaric occasionally came in to adjust the robes to suit Mysancta and her evolving notions of stylistic or dramatic appropriateness. The spiraling wires supporting the cardinal's glass crown chimed softly as a shadow paw pushed the headpiece forward in imitation of a human's bending gaze.

Cardinal Mysancta only worked with one aide on a regular basis. Skiapena remained distinctly male, but was in the process of getting his entire body tattooed a uniform black. For this occasion he'd adopted shadow form; Trasaric knew from private meetings that in his flesh, Skiapena had an inverted Tree of Life spread across his face. Trasaric had copied the design for ceremonial robes for last year's grand ball. The tailor suspected that one night Skiapena would disappear in a "regrettable accident" over his choice in clothes, which ran to mirrored finishes. The aide took a perverse pleasure in confronting his clanmates with their lineage's curse and seeing who might flinch, even once, after too much staring at the absence of reflection. Those who showed weakness always ended up convicted by one of Mexico City's Courts of Blood for some offense or other. The tailor devoutly hoped that one of those victims would survive and subject the aide to the same treatment, but it hadn't happened yet.

Cardinal Menuven, now. Trasaric wasn't entirely sure there actually was a distinct identity to which the title "Cardinal Menuven" could properly be affixed. There were half a dozen designated templars and pack priests chosen from among the cardinal's subjects to attend him, or her, or it. Each of them was trepanned at the start of their year of service, and thaumaturgically created carbon rods inserted into each exposed brain. Shadow tendrils constantly flowed between the rods. All six aides spoke with the same voice, a whispery tenor, for the duration of their service, and showed common mannerisms in addition to their own distinctive behavior. They showed mastery of the heights of shadow manipulation that they didn't have before and wouldn't have later. Trasaric suspected that the story about Menuven as a creature of pure Abyssal intellect was cover for something else, but he'd never had the chance to investigate it thoroughly.

Lord Greyhound was something else again. Trasaric found the lord almost as frustrating as Cardinal Timofiev, though for different reasons. Greyhound championed what he called "the rational existence" approach to vampirism. He wasn't a fool, and certainly didn't deny the supernatural element to his condition—he just didn't care about it. As far as Lord Greyhound and his followers were concerned, what mattered was tangible existence. He took active pride in having no aptitude whatsoever for shadow manipulation; he set out to be the clan's best at feats of strength, both physical and mental. To make sure that others never forgot his prowess, he habitually went around naked, wearing only decorative jewelry taken from fallen enemies and rammed into his flesh, where it would stay until expelled in healing slumber. He encouraged his disciples to study shape-shifting disciplines, and had them constantly re-shape his flesh to emphasize this feature or that.

As always, a small mob of sycophants clustered around Lord Greyhound. Half of them went naked like their master; the others combined modern athletic garb and ancient armor in various combinations Trasaric found appallingly trite. They looked with carefully practiced scorn at Niccolo's thin, ragged form and murmured condescending remarks to each other.

Not many vampires of Trasaric's acquaintance felt comfortable near Timofiev's Paladin and its bland, blank façade. One of the few who did was Heydar the Small, an Arabian boy Embraced eleven hundred years ago. As nearly as Trasaric could tell, Heydar was constitutionally incapable of finding anything disturbing. It was all just data, which he would sift through for patterns he could compare with his own experience and historical studies. Heydar refused all rank and title, but there was usually at least one cardinal with the sense to appreciate his insights. At the moment, Timofiev supported him and covered the costs of the boy's investigations. Heydar contributed little to any discussion, but afterwards he'd report to his patron about any warning signs of insurrection in the young: Heydar had solemnly helped slaughter elders once, in the Sabbat's creation, and intended not to perish the same way himself.

The gathered crowd spoke quietly. Timofiev disapproved of loud noises in preliminary discussions, and nobody present cared to risk his anger. Perhaps this pack member, responsible for alerting a police officer to an ambush by his carelessness. There was a pack leader in disgrace in some Chicago suburb after his whole pack failed a simple fire-dancing challenge. That bishop had spawned an unsuccessful brood, and the last two were looking for some way to prove their usefulness. This would-be templar had proven too weak for the job, but her speed was good. This one knew of a refugee from the Camarilla, who of course couldn't be trusted in the midst of the Sabbat but might serve for this sort of peripheral mission. As the discussion continued, those who could conjure images or impress them in the minds of others added their feats of will to verbal descriptions.

The most inhumane participants, the ones who most thoroughly mastered the Sabbat's engineered paths of morality, suffered most from the effects of the sun, and some had to retire for slumber an hour or more before dawn. They pushed for resolution before they had to leave, cutting short rambling digressions and repetitions. Niccolo remained on the floor, trying his best to heal himself inconspicuously. Shortly before 4 AM, the Paladin picked him up again. He shook in those strong hands, tossed back forth a time or two.

"Are you paying attention?" the cool voice asked. Niccolo nodded as vigorously as he could; he tried to speak, but the gashes on his neck made it hard to form sounds. "Good. We have chosen your companions. Sleep now, here. After sunset you will begin."

Gradually the gathered crowd dispersed. The last thing Niccolo saw, before the curse forced him to sleep, was the Paladin still standing calmly over him.

Monday, 8 November 1999, 10:15 PM
Sheraton Hotel
Seattle, Washington

Lucita sat bolt upright as she dialed. She'd sent a necessary fax, and now it was time to wrap up the last loose end of business. The client couldn't see her (unless he were much more adept at psychic affairs than she realized), but she preferred to conduct herself as if he could. So she wore one of the suits she'd bought at Sea-Tac Airport and had her notes arranged neatly on the hotel room's desk. Their tidy pattern shone back at her from the mirror, and she made sure to handle them carefully so that they seemed to rise and fall in an orderly manner rather than as if simply blown by the wind.

The phone rang three times. A man answered, speaking slightly bored-sounding German. "Bitte."

"Herr Wiscz, please."

The man switched over to English with a smoothly generic middle-class English accent. "Mr. Wiscz is unavailable to callers at this time. You may leave a message, and if it is a matter of business warranting his attention, he shall return your call when feasible."

"This is Katherine Scott." She gave the name she'd accepted this contract with. "Inform Mr. Wiscz that it is necessary to invoke the termination clause of our agreement. He may verify the return of funds with this number." She recited an access code for her Hamburg account. "Should he have any further questions, he may...."

"Excuse me, please," the man interrupted. His calm was gone. "Perhaps Mr. Wiscz is available after all. Please hold while I confirm."

Lucita waited. She'd hoped that the ghoul might simply set down the receiver so that she could listen to background sounds, but he retained enough presence of mind to actually put her on hold. So she reviewed her notes on the client and watched a late-night ferry cruising north up Puget Sound.

Two minutes and twenty seconds later, the client answered the phone. He sounded perfectly composed, with the arrogance of the elder who has been accustomed to obedience from others for four hundred years. "Miss Scott. My retainer informs me that you are canceling our contract. This is very disappointing."

"Mr. Wiscz, the world is full of disappointments. I am sure that you will be able to bear up under the grief of this loss."

"Miss Scott, I am not paying you for efforts at comedy. I am paying you to retrieve my missing childe. Are you admitting your inability to do so?"

"I am declaring that the termination clause is now in effect. This means that I have not finished the assignment and that I will not be proceeding with the matter."

"I demand to know—"

"Our contract does not include any provision for you to demand any knowledge. There's a provision to notify you with evidence upon completion, and there's the termination clause. Review the document you signed."

"This is *extremely* disappointing. I shall—"

"Take out a complaint with my sire? Best of luck finding him. Complain to your superiors in the order? I'm sure they'll be very sympathetic to your plight. We both now how much they approve of hiring independent operatives. Take it up with the Sabbat, perhaps, or the Monitor of Prague." She smiled at the silence on the other end. "If anything, Mr. Wiscz, I should bill you for the information you received."

"What!" He raised his voice for the first time.

"You now know four suspected aliases your childe isn't using. That information has value, since your next operative can proceed that much more quickly. Be appreciative that I don't charge you for the service."

Wiscz sputtered incoherently.

"Thank you, Mr. Wiscz, that's all. Please, feel free to take your business elsewhere in the future." Lucita put down the receiver and quickly replaced the scrambler attached to the phone jack with a different one. She didn't really believe the stories of blood magic that could pick up on the sympathetic resonance of a completed circuit of hardware-and-user, but she did believe in not taking chances. Just to be on the safe side, she unplugged the receiver and set it across the room, making a note to herself to pick up a replacement from some other hotel phone later.

Lucita looked down at the rain-flecked streets and thought about strolling along them corporeally, but something inside her warned of trouble. She put on a coat and took along a new umbrella just in case, then turned off the room's lights and stepped into a corner shadow.

The passage through the Abyss, the realm beyond shadow, was as free of sensation as always. No temperature, no wind, no motion, nothing to stimulate any of her senses. *Awareness* flooded in to her well-trained mind: of her location relative to the material world, and of the inhuman forces far away in the depths. She had never encountered any of the independent shadow-creatures spoken of in Lasombra folklore, only the unthinking entities conjured up by some vampire's own force of will. Or at least that was true until that final encounter in Madrid, when *something* had risen in her sire's lair and nearly destroyed them all.

Lucita did feel very sure that her sire was truly gone. She could find no trace of his influence in her mind or soul. There might be some still-embedded command, but she thought not. She'd demonstrated to her own satisfaction that her will was her own, at least for the present moment. His undead hand did not stop her from making the pilgrimage home, nor from then immersing herself in her calling.

On a whim, she stepped out of the shadows onto the roof of an apartment building somewhere north of downtown. The clouds lifted for a moment, showing her the dark waters of Puget Sound and a few lights in the distance. The neighborhood around her gave off a faint smell of blood; she suspected that some vampire had fed nearby. Sabbat? Camarilla? Independent? She wasn't altogether certain of the state of affairs in Seattle, and decided not to risk a nuisance encounter. One step took her back into the shadows.

As she drifted, she laid out her recent actions as if she were someone else, treating herself as the target of one of her operations. Reason must prevail.

shards

The target had recently lost her sire, with whom she'd had extremely hostile relationships. The target had then attempted to retreat into juvenilia with a return to the mortal home. After an unproductive act of masochism and an argument with resident ghosts, the target flung herself into a frenzy of very un-mortal activity, accepting the sort of routine job from an unpleasant client that she'd usually reject. Less than a week after *that*, she abruptly broke off the contract and put her primary point of contact on indefinite suspension.

The pattern was obvious. The target is in a state of panic, suffering from identify confusion. It is very likely that if she does not find a stable foundation, she will engage in increasingly self-destructive actions until she meets true death. It's an old story, one that the observer had often exploited to make assassination easier.

But where might stability lie now?

Willa Gebenstaler examined the fax on her desk for signs
of hoaxing. While her communications links with Madame
Scott were as fine as she could make them, nothing material
could be totally secure against supernatural manipulation. If
this was a hoax, it would be the…she paused to count. Yes, it
would be the fourth since Willa took this position, and the
second this century.

The fax itself was clear and simple. It had instructions for
paying off the recent contract with Wiscz in Prague and the
longer-term one with Kamedov in Istanbul, and a separate
paragraph reading, "Accept no contracts. Take no messages.
Inform all callers I am unavailable. Apply Reserve Fund B until
further notice." The last part worried Willa: Reserve Fund B
had been set up at the very beginning of her term for use in
the event that her employer was destroyed or permanently
incapacitated. If it was genuine, then Willa was at liberty to
dive into three and a half centuries' accumulated interest and
set-aside funding and occupy herself very comfortably indeed
until such time as Madame Scott chose to resume their
relationship. Fretfully, Willa held the fax front and back to
her glass desktop, as if hoping to see a secret message reflected
there.

Officially, Willa knew nothing of her employer's identity,
and in point of fact Madame Scott had never let anything slip
which could point to her identity. She'd always spoken a pure,
accent-free German to Willa and avoided discussing anything
specific about the past except with reference to a current
assignment. Still, given time a careful observer notices things,
and an intelligent office assistant puts the pieces together.

To begin with, the name was fake, and so were the facial
features. Willa knew that the custom of disguise was pretty
well universal among elders who didn't maintain permanent
residences in affiliation with one of the big sects. (She hadn't

known that in 1642, but then she hadn't known much of anything about Kindred society then.) The name wasn't particularly clever, though. "Scott" meant "Shadow," if you traced it back to Greek, and that immediately suggested either the Lasombra or someone deeply concerned with darkness. There weren't that many elder Lasombra known to be without permanent havens. "Katherine" suggested, among other things, one of the queens of Aragon, and that merely confirmed Willa's speculation.

She suspected that Madame Scott *wanted* people to figure it out, with just a little effort, and then feel that extra touch of awe at realizing who they dealt with. She'd never asked Madame Scott, of course. Nor had she ever mentioned her speculation to anyone else; she was fairly sure Madame Scott would be able to read the thoughts or emotions associated with such a betrayal, and in any event she enjoyed her position and wished to keep it.

Ever since those long-ago days of Protestant revolution, Willa had maintained an office somewhere in the Hamburg area and made it known discreetly that she was the contact for an experienced, unaligned vampire willing to perform potentially messy operations for suitable fees. For most of that time, the Camarilla court of Hamburg recognized Willa as a quiet, scholarly individual of unfortunately clanless origin—how she hated the sect's preferred term of Caitiff—who nonetheless earned her right to survival through timely research and administrative services. Unofficially, of course, the prince usually knew what she really did; every so often she even arranged a (completely deniable) contract on behalf of the court. As long as her visitors didn't create trouble, the court didn't care.

Thirty years ago Willa moved into a corner of the basement of the Museum of Labor and Technology. Madame Scott assisted her from time to time in applying mental leverage to the museum staff, and nobody ever, ever noticed Willa or her office. She tapped into the museum's communications, which now included permanent high-speed Internet connections, to retrieve messages from multi-layer cover and redirection systems. Deals with Hamburg's Tremere secured her network against most intrusions, but there was always someone out there with more raw power, skill, or both in a position to try something she and her consultants failed to anticipate.

Most of the time, Willa's work was very routine. Individuals would make tentative contact, following leads which suggested ways to get an assassin or fixer. There were apparently abandoned mailboxes in Berlin, formats for newspaper ads in Vienna and Zurich, phone numbers in Brussels which were re-routed through encrypted satellite systems—a whole constellation of avenues for approach, whose apparent geographical center was somewhere in the Rhineland in the far western reaches of Germany, just as another bit of misdirection. Willa would send back information on more securely anonymous channels, and from there negotiations would proceed. Madame Scott would take the case (or not), and the funds would move, and the work would be done, and Willa would deliver the proofs of completion.

Every so often, things got a bit livelier. Madame Scott sometimes went into seclusion, or into frenzies of activity. She had some pet projects which she'd pursue to the abandonment of normal assignments, making extra work for Willa and spreading bad rumors which could dim business for decades at a time.

These last few months had been strange, even for Madame Scott. There was the summer of furious activity when Willa could scarcely reach her employer. (Willa knew perfectly well that Madame Scott maintained other points of contact under other aliases, but preferred not to think about it. She was jealous of her employer's divided attention and felt distrusted when out of touch.) Suddenly Madame Scott was in Spain, Willa learned, and traveling mostly out of touch. Then came the almost frantic phone call from Zaragoza at the start of November. Madame craved work, *now*. Willa found the request from Wiscz at the top of her stack, and Madame accepted it without nearly her usual caution. Off to the New World to hunt a lost childe!

Now this.

Willa had worried before that Madame might be approaching the point of no return, where she'd either commit suicide directly or keep plunging into too-dangerous assignments until she was destroyed. In the past, Madame had managed to calm down with the help of colleagues and associates, whom Willa did not know how to reach. Madame was out there among the Western barbarians—for Willa, the New World remained a haven for savages and malcontents, many of whom no doubt went through life with tribal paints and tattoos—and out of touch. The punishment for Willa contacting her now would be extreme, perhaps even final. Reserve B threw Willa onto her own devices.

She very much hoped that some night she would hear from her mistress again, but she feared that the association had come to its end. Her pace, as she walked toward her prepared sleeping chamber in a large converted file locker, was slow and sad.

Thursday, 30 December 1999, 10:10 PM
Diablo Amarillo Tavern
Bahía de Los Angeles, Baja California, Mexico

The tavern was an oasis of light and noise in the midst of a dozen blocks of darkness. Two fires within a week of each other had taken out a whole series of transformers. The Yellow Devil remained lit because its builder had been a paranoid survivalist who aimed for self-sufficiency. More than thirty years later, the current management carried on the tradition, and tonight they reaped the rewards once again in windfall business. There were a *lot* of people in there, sending out scents and noise into the night.

From his vantage point on the roof, Andrew Emory could hear the conversations echo up through street-level windows, kitchen stove vents, air conditioning intakes, and a dozen other ways through the tavern's walls or ceiling. With a little concentration he could triangulate in on any particular knot of conversation. Every few minutes he shifted slightly to better concentrate on a different part of the main room below. Some of the exchanges sounded promising.

"So, Jerry, who'd you rob this time?"

"No robbery, boys, this was one flush customer."

"Oh, God, here we go again. 'Dear Boat Rental Forum: I never used to believe your stories were true…'"

"Laugh all you want. Really. But she had a lot of money, and such particular needs."

Andrew stretched forward over the closest vent. This sounded like a classic vampiric ploy.

"This one came in looking like your typical bitch in heat, all done up pretty. She started preening herself in the mirror…."

Andrew stopped listening. He was hunting experienced Lasombra, who would neither expose their lack of reflection carelessly nor, given their circumstances, engage in casual use of mental domination to make mortal targets think there'd been reflections. On to other conversations.

"Man, I woke up this morning feeling sooo fuckin' drained."

"No kidding. You look like you been seeing ghosts all night in your sleep. If you just ever fuckin' *washed*, you'd be pale."

"Aw, shut up. I'm serious, man. Three days running I been just totally tapped out all day. Wake up feelin' like shit, don't get no better, don't sleep well. This sucks."

Andrew concentrated again. He personally wouldn't prefer to feed on someone who sounded so obviously like a junkie, but then some vampires got a thrill from that kind of thing. The complainer and…two, make it three…friends sat in one of the booths on the harbor side, and Andrew could easily lean back against the façade and hear them clearly.

"Show us your arms, Mike."

"Uh?"

"Don't 'uh' me, you fuckhead. You're on the needle again. You got all the signs. Show me your goddamn arms."

"You're full of shit, man."

"Show 'em or I'm gonna pull 'em out myself and break up your little game of pocket pool."

"Gimme a fuckin' break! I'm sick!"

"I'll give you two. Show."

There was a moment's silence. Andrew readily imagined the foursome staring at two outstretched arms.

"Okay, Mike, sorry." There was another moment's silence. "Wait a sec. Maybe you're shootin' up somewhere *else*."

"Fuck you! You got me stickin' out here so you can do the junkie test in front of all these people, ruinin' my goddamn reputation, which I have been working hard to fix, fuck you very much, and *now* what? I ain't bending over for you to poke nowhere else."

"Shut up. I remember last year with the legs trick. That actually got you onto that salvage job, remember? Boss didn't think to look anywhere, and if you'd been smart enough to keep the damn wet suit on until he left, he wouldn't ever have seen the needle marks in your ankle."

Andrew wished he could get a look at the scene, clear though the descriptions were.

"Mike, gimme your goddamn leg or I'm gonna take it off at the hip. If you're really clean, then you got some weird shit, and we're gonna help. But if you're having us on again, you're gonna regret it."

"Swear to God, man, I ain't doin' nothin' that could make me sick like this."

"Take off the sock, Mike, or it ain't gonna last the night."

"Jesus H. Christ, man, if I wanted some foot fetishist, I'd go over to…"

"Mike."

There was another silence.

"Mike, I'm gonna kill you. What the *hell* is this shit? Those don't look like no needle marks, but you're sure as shit on something. Talk. Now."

"You know the old ladies at the salvage place?"

"Yes." Andrew appreciated the controlled anger in that voice. He made a note to have someone check up on that one; if he kept it up, he might make a fine vampire some night, or at least a very useful bit of cannon fodder.

"You know the one who's all bald on one side?"

"Yes."

"Okay, well, one night I saw her lying on the dock. This was a couple weeks back, when I was down there to, um, you know…"

"Steal anything that wasn't nailed down for your damn fix."

"Aw, man, you make it sound so *tacky*."

"Talk."

"Okay, so she's lying on the dock, and she's got *ants* crawling all over her ankles. They was crawling over these little piles of broken glass with somethin' white sprinkled on it. I go to brush them off, and she says, no, no, leave them. I ask here what for. She says, I show you, and quick as anything puts one of them on my wrist. There's this bite, and then wow."

"Wow."

"Yeah. Wow."

"What the fuck does that mean?"

"I felt *good*. I mean, I could see that kind of double-ring thing like down there, but I had about two seconds of being

shards

really about ready to upchuck and then just this pure white bliss."

"An ant."

"Yeah."

"A fucking ant. You shithead, you been spending two weeks letting fucking bugs bite you?"

"Well, yeah, but it's not like…"

Andrew tuned out the rest of that conversation, too.

Bahía de Los Angeles wasn't Andrew's idea of a good place to spend some time. He didn't like the desert, or the industrial ambience of the port. By preference he wouldn't have been in Mexico at all—his pack operated out of Portland, Oregon, and he spent most of his time there. But in recent months there'd been a steady flow of refugees from Sabbat enclaves in Central and South America, with stories of mass slaughter and mysterious predators. The Cardinal for his region decided that the new Bishop, Andrew, would be just the right one to lead an investigation.

So here he was, with three of his pack spread out along the waterfront. They'd worked their way down the major trail of panicked vampires, through California's Central Valley (with a detour over to the Mojave Desert), into and out of the mess in Los Angeles, down into Baja California. It looked like a few refugees came in at just about every port along the Gulf of California. Someone on the scene, Andrew suspected, was doing fairly sophisticated coordination of covers and transportation. Andrew wanted very much to find that person and have a nice long talk about the desirability or lack thereof of dumping large numbers of upset, scared vampires into a country still recovering from a major Sabbat/Camarilla conflict and other disorders.

Andrew really wanted whoever was doing the coordination destroyed, painfully if possible. Then he could….

The middle-aged woman in expensive "resort" clothes and her younger male companions in obviously new suits, standing near a mooring post half a block away, caught his eye. They didn't look like revelers. Andrew couldn't be entirely sure from this distance, but he thought that they weren't actually breathing. In a minute he had confirmation of his suspicion, when the Yellow Devil's doors swung open. A fan of smoky light lit up the lightly rippling bay, and there were sharp reflections in the water.

The trio did not reflect.

Andrew pushed the button on his walkie-talkie, sending two bursts of static to his own companions. "Converge. Follow my lead," the message meant. He jumped down from the tavern rooftop, curling his useless legs under him with the aid of a shadow tendril, while a spongy mass of conjured darkness slowed his fall. He pivoted to a stop with two swings around the post holding up a bilingual stop sign in the alley behind the tavern.

His regular wheelchair would be a dead giveaway, but he'd stashed the cart on which a beggar had pushed himself until Andrew drank him dry the night before, just in case he had reason to appear mortal. Andrew lost the use of his legs in a car accident—one rigged, he learned later, by his sire-to-be as a test of character—fifteen years before his Embrace. Twenty-nine years and a month, as of the 31st. Thanks to superhuman strength and the Lasombra gift for control of shadow, he didn't ever really need his legs, and most of the time he kept them strapped up and out of his way as much as possible. For cover, though, there was little better. Since they remained genuinely incapable of sensation, he didn't have to worry about accidentally revealing himself to be fit and able-bodied.

With smooth, practiced moves he settled himself on the cart, twirled a ratty blanket around his legs, and splashed cheap tequila across his mouth. He couldn't drink the stuff any more than most vampires, but if his prey were any good at all they'd smell it and assume he was drinking. He slouched over and pushed himself out of the alley, across the waterfront street toward the trio. They were clearly not Hispanic, though a little darker than the typical American tourist. "Alms, sirs and madam? A little charity for an unfortunate victim of industry?"

The three turned with near-perfect synchronization. Andrew immediately diagnosed a high degree of Vinculum bonding, that peculiar tie of mutual dependency created by the Sabbat rituals of blood sharing. These three had been together a while, likely longer than Andrew himself had been a vampire, to become so close. Whether they liked each or hated each other, they'd have to defend each other, possibly even at the cost of damage to themselves. (Whoever that unknown ritualist inventor had been back in the late Middle Ages, he, she or it had hit on something impressive.) That made matters more difficult. Andrew was hoping for a coalition new enough that they wouldn't have had time to form strong Vinculum ties. Damn. Two more squawks on the walkie-talkie: simple code for "Caution. Watch before moving."

The woman clearly seemed in charge. The men constantly looked at her, wherever else their eyes might roam, and they stood half a pace behind her. They may not have been aware of their deference, though Andrew would bet heavily that *she* did and encouraged it. She looked up and down at Andrew. When she spoke, it was an accent he didn't quite place. "What good would it do to reward you? Surely my money would only help support one more loser? I should better give it to whoever is responsible for your injury, since they came out ahead."

"Is there no compassion in your heart, madam? Would you not want someone to aid you if misfortune came to you, wherever you lay your head when not gracing our fair city?"

"I would want someone to put a bullet through my addled brain. Why do you cling to life in that condition? What can you possibly hope for or strive toward?"

Andrew feigned horrified recoil, while inwardly applauding her directness. "Madam perhaps has too narrow a definition of what makes life worth living."

"Perhaps Madam understands better than you what's worth living with and what isn't. Perhaps Madam should show you." Andrew suddenly realized that she'd been wearing an illusory complexion. As she glared at him, her features shimmered, revealing a very different face underneath. The mask was matronly, smooth and arch. The reality was younger and distorted by barely controlled rage. Andrew recognized the signs of the Beast, the self-destructive voice growling inside every vampire, in almost complete control. In this light it was amazing that she hadn't simply attacked him outright, or for that matter run amok on the boardwalk hours ago.

She continued to glare. He felt the probing pangs of an effort to manipulate his mood. But he was better at that game than she was. As he repelled the assault, he began flooding his body with extra blood, forcing strength into the muscles. The insight struck her. "What are you?"

Andrew didn't bother answering. He gave one push on the walkie-talkie—"Attack"—and leapt at her. He aimed for a point just over her shoulder, and made it. His left fist plowed into her face, snapping her jaw in two places, while his right crushed a rib halfway down her side. He rolled over and past her, hitting the ground with a solid thump (he'd have to tend the damage later), and twisting around into position for a second attack.

Then all the lights went out. It was one of the most rudimentary tricks in shadow-manipulation, a completely amorphous mass of thick shadows. Andrew knew that none of his pack would be foolish enough to do it, and he didn't think any of his targets would have had time to prepare it. An unfamiliar voice with an accent similar to the woman's shouted out, with echoes flattened by the dark cloud, "Surrender, Rosa! Neither you nor your allies can oppose the will of the Sabbat in this matter!"

What the hell? Andrew drew himself up into a tight crouch and slid halfway around the targets' last locations. Who was this new arrival, and was he actually as big an asshole as he seemed?

The woman—Rosa, presumably—made some quiet sound in her throat, then spoke up. "Not a chance, Niccolo. I can still take you blind, remember. Take your best shot. You won't get a second."

The man shouting didn't answer her directly. "I speak with the authority of the assembled Cardinals! This woman and these men are my prisoners, to be taken for trial in Mexico City! Interfere with me and you risk the wrath of the Sabbat!" Andrew wondered if the schmuck had been sent out on the equivalent of a snipe hunt, if some elder had gone berserk and started handing out assignments to the terminally incompetent, or what. While he considered, he continued to slide right up behind one of the men accompanying Rosa (the damn fool was tapping his foot, making it easy to home in).

In one continuous motion, Andrew withdrew a knife from its pants sheath, cut both of the man's hamstrings, and re-sheathed the knife. One of Andrew's shadow arms clogged the man's mouth and cushioned his fall. Andrew's fangs tore out veins as the man fell, and the feeding began before the remains hit the ground. Andrew watched just long enough to verify that the wound was ragged enough to keep draining for a while and that the target would stay down while healing, and turned back to the rest of the fray.

He'd hoped Rosa would continue shouting, but no such luck. He could hear her coat rustle as she tapped the other man's shoulder and her whisper, "Stay here, Leonardo. Niccolo's going to make himself a target." Then her torso turned toward where Andrew's victim had been. "Teodor? Teodor?" She went quiet. *Dammit.* Andrew felt pretty sure she realized what he was doing. Silence.

Andrew probed through the darkness with a trio of tendrils while Niccolo blustered some more. The fool was closer now. "Surrender, Rosa! Submit and survive! Resist and perish!" The thought of just immobilizing the fool and giving him lessons in rhetoric for a few years had some charm, but Andrew decided that a quick resolution would be better. He still couldn't find where Rosa had gone; he expected to have heard her move, but he only brushed up against thickened points within the darkness, no flesh or vitae.

Rosa settled his uncertainty by dropping on his back, a mass of spiny shadow extrusions piercing his skin in half a dozen places. Andrew cursed himself for not having realized what she'd done: he used the same trick himself, after all. Hoist yourself off the ground on many small shadow tendrils and keep them moving, fading in new ones and letting old ones dissolve, and you'd leave no constant presence on the ground. Fortunately for Andrew, her aim wasn't quite good enough to immobilize him. He flipped on his side, grabbed her arms, and pulled. In a fraction of a second, both her shoulders were dislocated. The pain distracted her.

He'd intended to keep flipping end over end on his way out of the darkness, in what his pack liked to call the "break-dancing stealth curve," but his wounds got in the way. He had to physically pull himself toward where he thought the edge of the darkness would be…and it wasn't there. He must have gotten turned without realizing it. He could hear the snaps as Rosa forced more blood into her arms to speed the healing. The other man, Leonardo, was silent; Andrew feared another dropping assault.

Niccolo was *still* shouting out there. "You must acknowledge my authority, or I shall—" He gave one choking sound and fell silent. The darkness fell as well.

Andrew froze and surveyed the situation. Two male vampires were closest, one kneeling and clutching at a badly cut throat, the other straddling him and holding claws outstretched. It wasn't hard to guess that this must be Leonardo standing, Niccolo kneeling. Behind Andrew, the sounds of Rosa's accelerating healing continued. Half a dozen or so vampires cowered in the next alley over, many of them groping their surroundings as if blind. Andrew's own packmates watched them calmly, occasionally poking one of the crew with a claw or rusty nail. One of the guardians, Milly, smiled at Andrew, and he smiled back. She traced her lineage to the Ravnos *antitribu* and clearly her dark skills in creating illusions had come in handy once again.

Rosa took one step, then another. Andrew didn't look behind him, just unleashed a solid wide punch of concentrated shadow-substance. To his satisfaction, she actually screamed as it impacted into her not-yet-reset jaw, and then into her arms. They dislocated again, and Andrew thought he might have heard a hip snap as well. As she fell over, he stood up and *then* turned to face her. She wasn't going anywhere.

Leonardo heard the sounds of Rosa breaking and also began to turn, still clutching Niccolo. He wasn't nearly fast enough. Andrew threw himself forward and performed two flips, the second ending with his steel-tipped boots precisely aligned with Leonardo's eyes. In an instant, those watery gray orbs filled with vitae. This time Andrew completed his maneuver as planned, angling to the left and sideswiping

Leonardo's nearest leg. A simple grab sufficed to topple the target, with Niccolo trapped underneath for the moment.

Two of Andrew's packmates stepped forward to shackle Niccolo and Leonardo. Rosa was going to be unconscious for a little while, and immobile because of her injuries after that. The riff-raff were still blinded, and if they began to recover, there were plenty more flash grenades to throw.

As Andrew feared, Niccolo's shouting hadn't gone unheard. A few random bystanders—mostly would-be drug buyers, from their looks—had drifted in from outside the blacked-out area, and there was a small crowd coming out of the bar. Andrew gathered his reserves for some acts of will-bending. It hurt. He had burned a great deal of blood and would have to feed again soon, just at the moment he most needed not to give any vampiric impressions. He hitched back onto his cart and forced his features into a semblance of calm.

"No trouble here," he waved at the bystanders. "Just a few more Northern drunks. My friends the officers have them in hand." He pointed at his packmates, and was relieved to see them stand straight, just as officials should. He looked intently at each onlooker in turn, shoving an attitude of boredom and slight fear of the authorities into each frail mortal mind. "We should let the officers get on with it. We certainly wouldn't want the police to think that they should spend any more time looking for matters requiring their attention here, would we?"

The crowd broke up with gratifying speed. Humans were so easy to manipulate. (Andrew sometimes felt a touch of shameful regret at his own mortal days, and hoped that he at least hadn't been quite that sheep-like.) The vampires had the street to themselves again.

Andrew looked down at the bound Niccolo. Kicked him twice in the face. A shadow tendril rolled the captive over to look into Andrew's angry glare. "What *are* you doing with all your shouting? You can't tell me any lord of the Sabbat instructed you to behave like a damn fool just because you've learned the first art of shadow control."

Niccolo sputtered helplessly for a moment. Then he looked more carefully at Andrew. The battle scars (almost completely healed, but still visible to someone who knew to look for the forms of Sabbat combat), the obvious mastery of disciplines well beyond Niccolo's reach…Niccolo had crossed the wrong vampire's path. "Um. I do come from Mexico City. In my pocket is a warrant for the bitch and her men."

"You stay there." Andrew reached his own hand into Niccolo's pants, found the warrant, and withdrew it. Sure enough, it was a declaration of judgment on three fugitive packmates, with the technicalities needed to secure aid from local Bishops and Archbishops while the bearer pursued the rogues. Code phrases suggested the invocation of old debts or reminders of who held the balance of power where. "Did you get a lobotomy with this?"

"I was excited." Niccolo licked his lips. Andrew noticed badly healed scars and wondered what the fool had been through. "I've been after them for weeks, and suddenly they swerved from the San Diego harbor to down here. I think they were planning to meet with someone. Then I thought you were that someone, and so I thought I'd take them all."

"Who are they?"

"My siblings in the blood."

"And?"

"They devoured our sire."

"And you ran and got the big boys to back you up."

"How dare you speak about our leaders that way!"

Andrew snarled. "I speak however I like to fools and losers. You speak to winners with respect, or you lose more pieces. I don't like to repeat myself."

"Yes." Pause. "Yes, I escaped from them in Miami and made a man take me to Mexico City, where I met with our clan's leaders, and a few of the rest. They gave me this mission."

"Do you have any idea what you've done with your fool stunt?"

"I understand that you've kept me from capturing my rightful prey!"

Andrew flipped into a handstand, one of his comfortable thinking positions, and stared at Niccolo. "You've blundered in like the stupid oaf you are, risked alerting the whole waterfront to our presence, and completely shattered any chance of my completing an investigation which is far more important than your rogue hunt." Andrew balanced on one hand long enough to pry up a strip of boardwalk. He jammed it into Niccolo's heart. "Let your posse carry you home, and you can explain to your elders that the Bishop of Portland is not amused by their choice."

The jet could carry up to fifteen passengers. For this flight it had only two, at least only two who were capable of thought or speech. Corpses occupied the other seats. The pilot didn't mind; he had had his olfactory nerves cauterized years ago.

Andrew sat in a window seat, his legs drawn up and braced against the edge of a low table. His wheelchair was folded out of the way, across the plane. When he wanted to move, which wasn't often, he summoned a small shadow tendril and gave it some of his own strength. Mostly he was content to look out at the lights below, little oases of life in a largely unsettled expanse, and ponder all the ways a town could perish at the hands of a few dedicated vampires.

From time to time he looked up at the woman opposite him. She liked the name "Conrad," and when pressed said simply that her original name was no more pronounceable by most Westerners than it was relevant. As usual, she wore a maroon silk suit, tailored in a mid-century style, and accessories that would have been perfectly in place on Lauren Bacall or Greta Garbo. "It's a Western world," she said when asked, "and I use the tools the world provides." Her poise gave no hint of the fury Andrew had seen her unleash.

She met his gaze each time tonight with a perfectly calm expression. He knew better than to try to read her emotions: she really had taught him everything he knew about the art, and hammered home the lesson that the teacher must always remain ahead of the student. Finally he worked up the courage to ask. "I have a procedural question."

"Yes?" Conrad's voice was slightly husky, consciously patterned after lounge singers she'd enjoyed. Andrew had sometimes heard her shout in a pure high tone that might or might not resemble the voice of her mortal days. "You sound so formal, Andrew."

"Am I going to be executed?"

Conrad's expression didn't change. "Before I answer, let me ask a question in return. Why do you ask?"

"Two things." Andrew held up fingers and counted off. "First, there's the matter of Niccolo in Baja California. I assumed he was some random victim of self-grandeur. I've since learned that he was in fact transported back to Mexico City, and that he seems to be under the patronage of one or more clan elders. Trasaric doesn't make suits for just anyone." He waited for a reaction from Conrad, but didn't expect any. She didn't surprise him. "Second, there's our travel tonight. A charter flight with one of the Cardinal's personal pilots, in the company of chosen bodies for thaumaturgic experiments of the sort that I don't officially know anything about.

"And you, of course."

Conrad shifted her head slightly, examining his face from a different angle. "And what about this suggests an execution to you?"

"Are you serious?"

"You've seen me being jovial. Draw your own conclusions."

He did. He decided that it was almost certainly a test of some sort. The odds still seemed good that he'd be ash on the wind in a few nights. But just in case not, best to show as much of his vaunted cleverness as he could muster.

"*Everything* suggests an execution trip, beloved sire. I've helped arrange enough of these trips myself. You remember that thing with the Other Razor, and that was in my own pack, working against the Vinculum all the while. I know that it can be done, and how to do it. And I know that part of it is a detachment reinforced with a little ritual. You created me, but I don't for a moment think that means you'd hold off destroying me once you thought it was necessary.

"There's straightforward psychology at work here. This is for cases when you need information out of the victim before you burn him, bury him, sink him, whatever. You could, of course, just nail me down and rip it straight out of my head, but for some cases that's not as effective as getting a confession that is in some sense 'voluntary.'

"You're my definitive authority. I may know just how many levels of authority there are above you, but it's your blood and fangs that took me out of life in the first place. The fact of your presence is reassuring; the fact of your manner isn't.

"The environment," Andrew said with a gesture at the cabin, "is also calculated for effect. It's got luxury, which you know I respond to favorably. The corpses necessarily remind me of alternatives to cooperating with you and whoever's behind you on this one. 'You remember the ovens, I think.'" For the last sentence he made his voice gravelly and deep.

"Then there's the timing." Andrew gathered his thoughts for the next point.

Conrad raised one hand. "Thank you, Andrew, that's enough. I see that you've thought carefully about your circumstances."

"And?"

"My instructions do not include transporting you to your impending demise."

"What, then?"

She closed her eyes for a moment. Andrew knew the signs of a message going directly from one mind to the next. "Look up, Andrew." She pointed at the TV screen at the front of the cabin. With the push of an armrest button, she flicked it on. A roar of static gave way to a muted buzz and rippling forms increasingly evocative of a human head.

There were very few things Andrew hated as much as this sort of communication. The symbolism that pleased or amused a vampire powerful enough in the mental arts to send thoughts long distances was pretty well guaranteed not to be pleasing for the recipient. He also knew better than to do anything but stare intently at it.

In a moment the head was fully recognizable: Cardinal Timofiev, who'd presided over the rites confirming Andrew's rise to bishop rank.

"Hail to you, soldier and commander in Caine's army."

Andrew waited.

"Your name and deeds are known to your elders, who have fought this war from its beginning."

Andrew spoke quietly as calmly as he could. "Thank you, Eminence."

"You fear for yourself."

"I do." There was no point in lying about it.

"Do you know who I am?"

"Yes, Eminence. I met you and your brood at the Grand Ball two years ago."

"Your mind remains alert. Do you know who this is?" The static flared into a fresh outline. Andrew recognized the fool he'd staked in Bahía de Los Angeles.

"Yes, Eminence."

"Describe him."

Andrew began his answer even before consciously realizing his intent. He spoke angrily, and drew on alchemical symbolism of the sort he knew Timofiev would understand. He laid out one of the classic doomed-soul configurations: too much impatience, the attention of superiors, lack of vision, ambition not united with the proper selfish drive to survive. Blind and falling.

For what seemed like many minutes, no response came. Andrew tried to isolate and bury his fear, knowing the futility of the effort and the possibly redeeming factor of his determination. Finally the cardinal's head appeared again. "Do you think that there is a fate written in the stars?"

"Yes, Eminence." Andrew retained most of his mortal skepticism about mystical matters, but there's something about seeing blood magic and oracles work to wear down some resistance. "I believe that the world shows us signs, though we must put the meaning into them."

"Do you believe in approaching Gehenna?"

Andrew thought about it. In the sense Cardinal Timofiev meant it, no, he didn't. He had no more use for holy books and their prophecies of a nocturnal apocalypse simply because the authors were undead than he'd had for such works in life. On the other hand, in the time he'd been of the Blood, he'd seen a steadily escalating curve of conflict intensity. There were things active out there now that had slumbered when Conrad stalked him. Haphazard rumbles had given way to something much more like actual warfare. It was a more hostile world now, and becoming more so. "Yes, Eminence. I believe that the battles for which you and your peers created our sect are approaching."

"What do you know of Monçada's childe, Lucita?"

That one confused Andrew. What did that bitch have to do with anything? Nonetheless, he composed his thoughts and drew out another astrological diagram in his mind's eye. A point of power, submission to the great, rebellion, the loss of direction, stasis, impending destruction.

"I see. Tell me, when is the destruction of one's sire warranted?"

A trap. In theory, the Sabbat was dedicated to the notion of absolute freedom and the perfection of one's vampiric nature. Of course, in theory, the Sabbat was equally dedicated to the destruction of all foes, and to the disciplined, organized war against them. In practice, Timofiev himself was one of the great rebels and diablerists, and would not want his actions portrayed as illegitimate. In practice, anyone who destroyed a sire now without sanction would be asking for the worst trouble.

"The destruction of a sire is justified always and only in one condition: when it succeeds."

A harsh sound, like the laughter of breaking glass, echoed in Andrew's mind. "Explain, childe of Conrad."

"Gratiano destroyed our Antediluvian because he could. The universe didn't intervene to stop him, anymore than it did when the Tremere found another one to suck dry, or when Lugoj and his pack took down the Tzimisce progenitor. Other rebels proved themselves unworthy by failing."

"How do you account for the judgments laid down by Courts of Blood, or by tribunals of the Sabbat?"

"Success and failure don't happen at once. If they did, a war would always be over after the first battle, and sieges would be meaningless. Success happens over time. If I destroyed Conrad, and got caught for it ten years from now, and were given to my captor for the approved destruction, I would be a failure."

"So if some Methuselah rises from its tomb and slaughters the founders, is the Sabbat a failure?"

"If that were to happen, yes. Until then, you are a success. You've outlasted all rivals and challengers for centuries. You remain. They don't. You demonstrate by your continued existence that you deserve to continue existing."

"Lucita and her sand rats destroyed Monçada. They continue to exist. Do they prove themselves worthy?"

"No."

"Such confidence. Explain yourself."

"Lucita survives because she doesn't face worthy opposition." Andrew wasn't aware of his sentences becoming increasingly colloquial; for reasons of his own, the Cardinal chose not to comment on it. "None of us knows whether she deserves success until she's tested against a credible foe."

"You know of Bishop Talley's encounter with her in the American war last year?"

Andrew froze. Talley was one of the hardest cases he'd ever met, and he had precisely no desire to incur Talley's hostility, under any circumstances. "Eminence, I don't know enough about that encounter to assess it. I trust that since my elder still holds a position of honor, our mutual superiors find his conduct satisfactory, and therefore that circumstances I don't know kept it from being a sufficient challenge."

The broken glass laugh erupted again. "Very clever."

"I wouldn't be any use as a dullard, Eminence."

"True." There was no humor at all now, and Andrew was very acutely aware that a vampire twice as old as the United States was drawing pictures in his head. "Do you believe yourself her worthy rival?"

"Not alone, certainly."

"What makes you unworthy? Did Conrad fail in her duties, or did you fail in yours?"

"Neither. Eminence. No teacher can make a vampire a thousand years old in fifteen."

"True. As far as it goes. Tell me of your weaknesses, and of what might repair them."

From there it all got technical.

Thursday, 13 January 2000, 11:30 PM
Somewhere beneath Mexico City

Barry Morn waited in darkness, suppressing shudders. The darkness terrified him—that was why he embraced it. After the horrors of the last two years, he'd decided that he would master the darkness, become one with it, or perish in the effort.

Even with concentration and his best efforts at sensory enhancement, he couldn't make out the words being spoken on the other side of the heavy oak door he leaned against.

He already knew who was there, or all but one of them: Cardinal Timofiev, the cardinal's favorite paladin, the Bishop of Portland, and the ancient ghoul Trasaric. Barry had met each of them at least once, and knew Bishop Andrew pretty well. There was someone else in with them. Just one person, Barry thought from the voices and footsteps.

The hall Barry waited in was a simple affair, crudely smoothed stone. The lower half was all carved directly out of solid rock, the upper half mostly big slabs of rock bracing against packed earth and loose debris. Water trickled through in…Barry paused to count…yes, in three places. The old Lago de Texcoco might be centuries gone, but there were still plenty of subterranean streams to wear through less than perfect construction. Barry tilted his head to catch small currents in the air and identified half a dozen solvents and other pollutants, presumably washed out of some buried dump site. The single bench was bolted or perhaps shoved into the wall where slabs met the continuous rock.

There were no lights. This was Lasombra territory, and the clan's Mexico City packs took great pride in flourishing in the dark. They'd never willingly display vulnerability in front of the Tzimisce and the rabble. So Barry fought his Beast silently, turning each urge to flee or at least strike a light into a tally of revenge owed to the arrogant bastards responsible for his suffering. He knew enough Sabbat history to know that it's hard to survive for too long close to the throne unless you're right up next to it. In time, he could pick off the offenders one way or another, and show their tormented shades how to do it right.

He repeated some of his lessons, sometimes muttering quietly ("under his breath" didn't mean much to a vampire), sometimes simply thinking them and tapping out a rhythm with the fingers of one hand drumming against the other. "The practitioner of the Path of Night is the subject, not the object. You act. Others react. Whatever you can do, you may do. You are the vessel of the night. Let it flow through you into the world. Anyone who falls to you deserves to, and is your rightful prey. There is no law except the duty to act in darkness and as darkness."

As he reviewed the phrases, Barry felt the fear within him ebb. He wasn't Barry the Newbie anymore, Barry the last survivor of one of those poor packs shredded in the great Sabbat "invasion" of the East Coast. Now he was a student of the night, agent of his clan's great lords, and most assuredly a confident master of darkness.

At least, he hoped so.

Precisely at midnight, muted bells rang throughout the catacombs. As the last stroke died away, the door opened. Bishop Andrew stood, or rather floated, there. "Come on in, Barry. It's time to fill you in."

Barry walked behind Andrew. The bishop was apparently a young man, Embraced while still in his twenties. A car crash in his mortal days smashed his legs into useless flinders, and the bishop delighted in using various combinations of innate vampiric strength and control over shadow to move himself along in exotic ways. Tonight the trick was a writhing cluster of shadow tentacles that resembled an octopus, swaying in response to slight air currents and carrying the bishop's torso along a perfectly level path. Barry liked the Bishop and respected his prowess, but sometimes wished Andrew would be a little more prosaic or at least repetitious in his gait.

The meeting chamber was an irregular cube forty feet on a side, full of ledges and crevasses on all surfaces. The cardinal sat on an outcropping ten feet up, directly over the paladin. She (at least Barry thought she was a "she") held a vampire of about Barry's own apparent age in one hand. The ghoul Trasaric paced in a semi-circle, flashing robes that might have been the height of fashion sometime before the founding of the Sabbat.

The cardinal nodded to Barry and traced a sigil that Barry now recognized as an evocation of the Path of Night. Barry bowed solemnly and made a counter-sign before bowing in turn to the paladin and bishop. He nodded at Trasaric, then looked curiously at the other vampire.

"Good evening," the cardinal said in his calm voice. "Does the new year enter with good omens?"

Barry thought that one over for a moment. "Yes, Your Eminence." The experience had petrified Barry. He'd known in an abstract way that signs and portents sometimes struck Cainites, but it had never happened to him so powerfully. He hated to talk about it and hated to hide it.

"Share your omen with us."

"Two nights ago I fought a man behind the city cathedral. He was a bodyguard, out to stop me from feeding upon the woman in his charge. I threw him against a wall. His head hit a spike and flew apart. When his body slumped down, I could see the spray of his blood in the perfect image of our crown, the crown of the Keepers. Our power was already inside him, he just didn't know it yet."

"Let me see." Barry would much rather have denied the cardinal this, but he knew that the choice wasn't between preserving his mind or letting the cardinal in, only in whether it hurt and how much of himself the cardinal might leave behind. Barry bowed his head and felt the no-touch of the cardinal's will. The memory blazed in Barry's eyes and ears. "It is good. You bring me a good sign." The cardinal smiled, a twisted crack across his lower face that suggested decomposition more than good humor. "Now, fortified by your sign, I must give you a task."

The cardinal gestured to the paladin, who held up the other vampire well off the ground. "This," the cardinal said, "is Niccolo. He is the last surviving offspring of a Keeper who no longer keeps anything. The sire's other childer turned against him in the delusional desire to recreate our great act of rebellion, or so this one says. He came to us seeking refuge."

The cardinal rotated in place to look directly at Niccolo. "But we are not in the business of sheltering fools indefinitely."

Barry remembered the second lesson in the Path of Night: do not accept the superiority of another. So he spoke up. "Do you want me to keep track of him, then?"

"Not quite. No, I have another task for you." The cardinal watched Barry fight down panic. "Your bishop speaks well of your devotion to your new Path. He says that you shed the mortal coil more and more with each turn of the moon, and that you are a credit to your instructors. Do you agree?"

Lesson number two again. Confidence. "Yes, Your Eminence. I'm glad to be leaving my old self behind. I find the Path hard sometimes, but I'm working at it, and I think it makes me a better, more useful member of the Sword of Caine."

"Good. Then I give you a greater challenge. Do you know of the childe Lucita?"

Of *course* Barry knew about her. She was the great object lesson in how to be a bad Lasombra, the rebel and troublemaker and pathetic figure. "Yes, Your Eminence."

"Good. You will take Niccolo, and other companions which we will assign. You will form a new pack, which Bishop Andrew will consecrate. And you will find the childe for us."

No time to think. Act. "Your Eminence, is this punishment? Do you think I've done something that I need to pay for with my skin?"

"Not at all. This is a challenge. The odds against your finding the childe and returning to us with the news of her haven are great. But it is not an impossible task. The omens speak of our triumph this year, and of the reunion of fragments. With my own eyes I watched shattered canopic jars re-form at the end of the sermon. It is time for the childe to return to us, to be judged as one of us and punished for her sins as one of us. And you, with your omen of inward power bringing victory, are the one who will lead the seekers. You will succeed, and then those chosen to pull her in again will follow you."

Barry's imagination conjured up endless scenes of his passing: in combat, in sunlight, at the hands of some rival pack, and in countless ways at Lucita's hands. In his mind she was a demon towering overhead, her features formed into a seamless obsidian mask betraying no emotion. This was the beginning of the end for him, and all that he could do was agree, for now. "Your Eminence, I'm honored. I hope I'll prove worthy of your trust."

"The omen vouches for you. Trust in the signs the world gives us in the language of fate."

"Of course, Your Eminence."

"Now go with Bishop Andrew for further instruction."

Sunday, 16 January 2000, 3:20 AM
Biblioteca del Instituto de Investigaciones
Filosóficas
Universidad Nacional Autónoma de México

In the middle of the night, the philosophical research library was quieter than most tombs of Simon Peter's acquaintance. Tombs were seldom altogether silent. The ground shifted, and small living things burrowed through it. This place, on the other hand, occupied one wing of the university's new departmental library facility, and it had been built specifically with an unstable earth in mind. Beneath the basement, springs and braces dampened any ground movements, and each of the research library units had been insulated so as to allow the occupants of any one the freedom to be noisy without disturbing those in others. Some incautious student had accidentally disabled the heating system in this wing several days ago, so nothing disturbed the air except for Simon Peter himself and his...colleague.

Simon Peter looked like the geek he'd been in life: thin, arms and legs too long for his torso, eyes still weak enough to need thick corrective lenses despite several fleshcrafting treatments. Roxana looked like a wrestler, even though in life she'd been just as much a nerd in her own right. She was half a foot taller than Simon Peter and at least a hundred pounds heavier, most of her bulk very solid muscle. When they first started pursuing their studies at the university, carousers sometimes heckled them for the stereotype—brainy American boy looking for more real woman than he could get from his anorexia-enamored girls back home, big Mexican girl looking for a meal ticket to the States. A little judicious intimidation quieted the hecklers, though both Simon Peter and Roxana could read some of the just-barely-suppressed thoughts around them.

"Okay, now squeeze," Simon Peter said. To his enchanted eyes, the flow of electricity around him sparkled like raindrops moving in and out of narrow beams of light. The mixture of blood and mud he'd painted across his face three hours ago obscured material things, letting energy shine forth. In particular, the 220-volt lines he and Roxana had pulled across the main reading room floor glowed with continuous cascades.

Roxana lacked his knack for technological insight, but she had exceptional finesse when it came to shadow control. She pulled a more active blackness out of the simple absence of light and wrapped it around the cables. Simon Peter watched as the Abyss's essence compressed the cables. He could hear an occasional grunt from Roxana, subconscious physical effort matching her spiritual labor. The insulation around the cables started to fray, then broke in a dozen places where the Abyss pressed in. Sparks flew out, but didn't last long: they hit the Abyss and fled into other realms. The current itself continued to flow with nearly full strength until it couldn't flow at all, when the cables became hopelessly mangled.

"Done?" Roxana asked. "I can't feel anything much left of the cables."

"Thanks, that's plenty," Simon Peter answered. There was a soft whisper of wind as the opening to the Abyss closed up. Roxana stood up to stretch, while Simon Peter jotted a few notes to himself.

"So what did you see, anyway?" Roxana's voice sounded from unexpectedly close behind Simon Peter. She was getting better at moving quietly. He still remembered their early times together, when it seemed she could scarcely walk down a hall without finding something to run into. Of course, he had to remind himself, that was almost a decade ago now, and unlife had changed them all.

"Same as last time. The current flows pretty much without disruption until it becomes physically impossible."

"Hmm." She paced, more noisily now, then paused to prod the smoking remains with her bare feet. "There's something I still don't understand about this, then. Energy and matter convert into each other, right? They're pretty much the same thing at heart?"

"Right."

"So why does energy escape the constriction? It *should* get choked down just as much as matter does. From the point of view of the Abyss they're scarcely distinguishable. Soul is more different from either of them, and *it* suffers like matter. I don't get it." Roxana sighed, a carefully cultivated gesture she'd picked up from friends in Lord Greyhound's retinue.

"Beats me," Simon Peter said honestly. "It's always possible that there's something my ritual doesn't show, of course." He hated to admit that, but Roxana wouldn't abuse his confidence. The fact was that this technological sorcery was very much a raw, unrefined matter. Simon Peter's sire had taken a lot of information, some of it ripped from their still-living minds, from a little cabal of mortals practicing something they called "the Coiling Path" and adapted it to the demands of vampiric blood-magic. Simon Peter had worked with his sire until the old man perished in a foolish fight against mortal witch-hunters. But he wasn't really anywhere near ready to engage in fundamental innovation, and he was very much aware of the gaps that must exist in his existing lore.

His contemplative reverie ended with both their cell phones ringing simultaneously. They both answered, and heard a brief recorded message. "Bishop Andrew Emory requests your presence at the Chamber of Regrets within the hour." A living person had spoken it, presumably one of the ghouls the Sabbat employed for such purposes.

Simon Peter looked over to where he'd last heard Roxana and said with a touch of frustration, "Well, shall we go?"

Roxana clearly shared his frustration. "Yes. And we'll let His Holiness take care of the cleanup."

***

As always, Simon Peter chuckled briefly when they turned onto Avenida Insurgentes. Roxana didn't look away from driving. She liked the big sedan they'd taken after slaughtering both a band of kidnappers and their English hostages a few weeks earlier, but it took a lot of concentration to handle properly. "Same old joke?" she asked.

"Same old," he agreed. He didn't want to bore her with repetition; it's just that he kept thinking that the urban planners had no idea what real insurgency could be like. He hoped that some night he might show them, and once again reminded himself to find out just who was responsible for the street names around here and if they were still alive. "Carry on."

They headed south toward San Angel. Behind the quaint little shops and cobblestone streets tourists love was plenty of outright squalor, very suitable for concealing entrances to the sewers and the catacombs beneath them. Any locals out at quarter to four in the morning would take the car as an official vehicle, or as the property of some criminal secure enough to amount to the same thing.

Nobody got in their way as Roxana steered through a warren of increasingly narrow alleys to their garage. It still bore a few traces of the ground-floor apartment it had been before all the interior walls were removed and replaced with some heavy-duty reinforced beams. Simon Peter no longer gave the remaining bloodstains much attention, but he appreciated that they were there. It was good to remember that his kind flourished at the expense of humanity—predators who mistook themselves for primary producers could get into a lot of stupid trouble.

Down a flight of preexisting stairs into the basement. Down a ladder through a hole chipped in the floor, into the storm drain running alongside the street. Through it for a couple of blocks, then down a connecting tunnel to the bigger conduit for the neighborhood. Through that for a half dozen more blocks, then down an unofficial tunnel to the power access tunnel just above the Metro Line 3 extension. Back the way they'd come, only deeper now, and then into the top of one of the small network of caves. Along a clean, smooth slope down, past now-vacant antechambers, and then into the Chamber of Regrets.

The Chamber itself was a perfect cube twelve meters on a side. Roxana told Simon Peter once that one of her contacts said it was an act of contrition by some old-time war party leader who screwed up his, her, or its tactical estimates and got a bunch of potentially useful grunts slaughtered. The Chamber was certainly a monument to mathematical precision, from its overall dimensions to the decorations which wrapped all its surfaces: actual equations, perfect spirals constructed according to various systems, and more esoteric math-based art.

Bishop Andrew waited for them, standing on shadow-born legs next to his wheelchair. Simon Peter had only met the bishop in person once, but knew of him by reputation—Andrew was in his way as much a technological experimenter as Simon Peter, and that put them into something of a shared subculture within the Sabbat. Shadows cast by oil lamps down the hall told Simon Peter that at least two more people waited in one of the smaller chambers further down, close enough to hear any loud noises in the Chamber of Regrets but not precisely part of the conversation here.

"Excellency." The magician and the mystic spoke in unison.

The bishop was given, so Simon Peter had heard, to sustained bouts of bitterness. It was indeed one of his lingering attachments to mortality, though he'd deny it—nobody could get worked up in quite that way about injustices unless they still believed in justice. Certainly he was in a sour mood tonight, his customary dour look even more pronounced than on the last occasion he'd spoken with Simon Peter. "I've been talking with, among others, Bishop Francisco of the Old City," he began.

"Oh, shit." Simon Peter looked startled, wondering if he'd blurted it out himself, then realizing that Roxana had done the job for him. Blood suffused her cheeks, and the magician could see her rocking forward and back ever so slightly, trembling on the brink of frenzy.

The bishop's expression didn't change. "You don't think that's a good idea? Explain why, please, Roxana."

"He…." She stopped. Simon Peter saw her arms and legs tremble as suppressed the urge to attack, or flee, or do almost anything other than answer. "We…." She paused again, and a neglected mortal reflex made her gulp for air. The magician winced on her behalf, realizing that in denying herself the frenzy she was sinning against the version of the Path of Night she practiced. "He was our ductus, from 1989 to 1993."

"Yes." The bishop's voice flattened even further. "And." It wasn't even a question.

"We…." Another pause. "He had no talent for magic, and he was interested. So we tried to teach him some, and to share the experience with him through the Vinculum."

"Yes. And."

"And after a few years of this, he thought and we agreed that he seemed to be getting the hang of it. So he decided that what he needed was more research material. He…."

"Yes. And." The bishop's features slowly sank into uniform shadow. His eyes remained distinct and flickered constantly. Simon Peter realized that the bishop saw as much or even more of Roxana's struggle than the magician did himself.

"We suggested that he raid a Tremere ship on its way from Europe to the United States, bringing some flunkies and a backup copy of one of their big archives. We'd had a defector tell us about it earlier, and as near as we could tell, it was true. So...."

This time the bishop didn't say anything at all. His shadow-wrapped head merely nodded.

"We put our pack together with another one, up in Miami, and made plans for a big pirate attack. We launched the assault. It...." Again she struggled to maintain control. "It was a trap."

"Oh?" A question for once.

"They were waiting for us with fire and wards. Only the three of us—Simon Peter, Francisco and I—got away, and all of us were badly injured. It took us three nights to get back to shore, spending the days down deep and swimming along as best we could."

"And?"

"And Simon Peter and I took the blame for not having examined the defector thoroughly. He'd been conditioned with his story, and as soon as he heard that the raid had gone off, a mind bomb of some kind destroyed him on the spot. So we couldn't even examine him to find out who'd done it. The psychic traces were distorted by our questioning, and we took the blame for that, too."

"I see."

"But the bishop must have told you all this himself, if you know enough to ask. Your Excellency." There. She'd managed to get past the worst of it now. If she could just avoid compensatory arrogance, she'd survive to see the next night.

"Yes, he did, in fact. I've been given a project, and Cardinal Timofiev suggested that I speak to him. He gave me a full account. But it was necessary to see whether you'd be honest about it."

Simon Peter spoke up. "What kind of project, Excellency?"

"I'm— we're going to be hunting someone, and I wanted at least one magician along with me, since that's a weakness in the target."

"Has someone important gone rogue?" Too late, Simon Peter realized how bad that could sound.

Andrew seemed not to care about the implications, to Simon Peter's great relief. "Yes. Or rather, someone important *went* rogue, around 1200."

"1200..." Simon Peter paused. "You want us to help you hunt a Methuselah? Isn't this a job for the Courts of Blood, or the Black Hand, or someone *trained* for it?"

"Oh, that's been tried. Now, in this case...."

"Shit!" Simon Peter suddenly made the connection. "Beg pardon, Excellency, but are you taking a bunch of kiddies up against *Lucita?*"

Andrew smiled. "I am. And you're in."

"Um. Suppose I refuse?"

"Then we stake you out someplace with a nice view of the sunrise."

"Um. I see."

Andrew paced back and forth. "I'll be honest with you. This is a punishment assignment. You've both been waiting for the other shoe to drop since 1993. It can't have escaped your attention that neither of you is getting anywhere important, despite obvious talent and dedication." He nodded at Roxana. "You did very well there just now. A touch less control and I'd have had to rip you apart on the spot. Clearly you've learned lessons, but frankly nobody who could sponsor you into more important roles quite trusts you.

"This is your chance to clear your records." He saw Simon Peter beginning to speak again, and raised a warning hand. "No, let me finish.

"I'm being punished too, for this one. I have to go with you. I believe that we're not particularly expected to survive, despite a few bits of good signs from oracles. More about that later. But here's the deal. I believe that we *can* survive, if we do this right. And I propose to come back to be covered in glory. I'm willing to share it, too. Work with me, and we can get somewhere with all this.

"Now let me introduce you to the other members of our new little family."

Monday, 14 February 2000, 11:48 PM
Somewhere beneath Mexico City

Rosa hung in agony, her remaining arm bolted to a cast-iron cross dangling from leather cords attached to the craggy ceiling far above. Her remaining eye gazed on a narrow chamber, left almost entirely in its raw original state. Candles just bright enough to fill the space with shadows rather than pure darkness burned on the floor; if she swung her feet just right, the flames would lick her boiled soles and reopen last month's wounds.

At first they'd questioned her. Then they'd left her there, coming by once or twice a week with just enough blood to keep her going and a knife or tool to mess her up a little more. She was beginning to wonder just how long it could last, and to ponder just how many separate pieces of the vampiric body there actually were.

"Rosa." The voice came from somewhere nearby. And it was…

She forced blood into her throat to heal scarred vocal cords. "Niccolo, you little shit. We should have killed you along with dear Papa."

"You probably should have." He stood in front of her surrounded by unfamiliar vampires. Three male, one female, and a very mixed lot they were. "But you didn't. And I'm not here to kill you now."

"You pathetic worm. You wouldn't even be here now to speak to me, even with me at this disadvantage, if it weren't for your special friends."

He flinched, slightly. She saw that the others noticed. "Maybe not. But that doesn't matter. The fact is that they are here. I'm just here to ask you one question."

"Yes."

"Yes, what?" He looked genuinely puzzled.

"Yes, I still despise you."

"Oh." He laughed. "That's fine. You just do that. My

question is, why Bahía de Los Angeles? What made you go there?"

"Shit for brains. What makes you think I'm going to tell you that?"

"My special friends do." He nodded and stepped back.

The woman reached up and took Rosa around the waist, and hoisted her slightly. She was a strong one, probably a wrestler or something in life, Rosa judged. The twisted-looking guy grabbed Rosa's left leg and tore the hip and knee loose from their sockets without breaking the skin, and shoved the resulting dangling mess back behind Rosa. The woman then let go again. The other two men pressed Rosa firmly against the cross.

It was the most intense pain Rosa had felt yet. Even the burning didn't compare to it. Her body reflexively poured blood into efforts at healing, but it didn't work. There was no way the limb could heal while stuck in that position. So, before she could exert conscious control, reflexes drained all the blood available out of the damaged limb and cut off most sensation. Now it was limp, ready for amputation.

Rosa nearly passed out, but the man who'd pulled her leg gave her enough blood from a chalice to forestall that. She shook on the cross, trying to find a position that might be a little less miserable, but the two held her firm, and the pain dragged on and on. She tried to speak but couldn't.

"That's enough, I think," said the leg breaker. The two let her go. Her leg, now a third thinner thanks to the loss of blood, dropped back down to dangle beneath her. "As Niccolo said, why Bahía de Los Angeles?" He spoke in that annoying flat accent Rosa knew was common in the western United States. The pronunciation was good, but it had no soul. She despised him even as she feared him.

"Lucita, of course." She was startled to hear herself say that, but something in her was ready to talk. Perhaps there could be an end to it all?

"What about her? What's she got to do with that particular town?" The leg breaker pressed on.

"I don't know *why*," Rosa said, and then had to break off to heal her vocal cords again. Her body's futile attempt to fix her leg had drawn too much blood from everywhere else. "I don't know *why*," she repeated, "I just know that she has been there at least once."

"Tell us."

"She was there in 1983, for sure."

"How do you know?"

"Read it in a book." Rosa paused to gather her thoughts as best she could. "Book about diving. I was reading up on places we might go to hide after destroying Rudesi, I didn't even know how I'd go about searching for Lucita yet. The book fell open to this page where a man talked about how he'd gotten into the boat rental business. She was his first customer. The description matched. And I felt something as I read it."

"You felt something." The leg breaker was clearly skeptical.

"I felt something," she repeated. "It was…a sense of rightness. I had to go there. But before we did the deed, I read up on the history of the place, to see if she'd been there before."

"And what," he asked in an overtly mocking tone, "did your scholarship reveal?"

"Nothing."

"I see."

"I think she may have been there in 1822, on a ship carrying some visiting Spanish nobles to distant relatives in California. But there's not enough to tell. And I didn't get that sense of rightness from it."

"Thank you, then. That will be all." The leg breaker tossed his head, and shadows gagged Rosa. He turned to the others. "It's time to consecrate the bond, I think. Barry, the chalice, please?"

One of the two who'd held Rosa down produced a second chalice, more ornate than the one she'd drunk from a few minutes ago. He also had a butcher's knife, decorated with coats of arms from early Sabbat nobility. He offered them with a slight bow to the leg breaker.

"Thank you, Barry. I stand in the office of ductus of this gathering. I choose our brother in blood Barry Morn to stand in the office of priest. Barry, please proceed."

Barry gulped. "Er, as you wish, Excellency."

"For this purpose, Barry, I'm your brother in blood, Andrew."

"Yes. Andrew. Very well." Barry held the chalice more firmly, and gave the knife to Andrew, as the leg breaker was apparently called. "Brothers and sisters, as the blood is the life for things that breathe, so blood is the unlife for those of us that are dead and yet live. Our blood is our self. Through blood we may bind one to another. Through blood we measure our strength. Through blood we transmit our legacy from one generation to the next. The Vaulderie calls on us to give up some of our blood, that we may become a new thing, at once our selves and another, the combination of our selves into a single purpose. In the resulting bond, the Vinculum, we share our strengths and our weaknesses. We make windows into the walls of our selves, and see into the places that others keep separate.

"This is a serious duty. And yet it is also a glad time. For it is in this act that we show ourselves most truly what we are. We are not the living. Nor are we those who envy or fear the living. We practice this act which is distinctively ours. Our enemies do not and cannot have the bond we form. They are trapped within themselves, and before our united strength they scatter like dew before fire. In this bond we forge ourselves into weapons, bodies and minds joined for the tasks ahead of us.

"Brother Andrew, give of yourself."

Andrew took the knife and made a long angled cut across his forearm. Blood gushed out and into the chalice. A flick of his arm let Andrew keep it flowing without spill or splash. When the arm became noticeably pale, he flexed again and closed the wound.

Barry took the chalice and knife to himself and to each of the others in turn. Through her haze of semi-consciousness, Rosa heard him name the others: Simon Peter and Roxana. Niccolo went last. Or rather next to last. Barry put the cup on the floor beneath Rosa's feet and sliced open one of the larger blisters, and drained out enough blood to top off the chalice.

This time she really did pass out, and the others weren't noticing at that moment. So she did not see Barry raise the chalice and say, "This is our blood, mingled in one place. In the Vinculum there is no I and Thou, there is only We. From the cup I take unity." Nor did she see each of them in turn take a long sip from it.

The next thing she was aware of was Andrew hovering in front of her, pouring the last of the ritual's blood into her. She glanced down and saw shadow legs supporting him like stilts. He watched her regain awareness dispassionately. "Do you understand what we've done?" he asked.

"I…" She paused to think. "Fuck you!"

"I'll take that as a 'yes.'"

"You've included me in your damn pack."

"Yes, we have. Now we can continue to poke at you even from a distance, and when we find your beloved heroine, you'll be there to watch us take her down. Won't that be fun?"

Wednesday, 1 March 2000, 9:00 PM
Castle of Saint Rafael the Archangel
Sicily, Italy

A single candle flickered in the midst of the darkened chapel, its smoke twining with tendrils of animated shadow before vanishing toward the blackened arches which crowned the vault. Nine man-sized columns of deeper darkness stood around it, four at the compass points and five at the points of a pentagram pointed northeast. Fresh blood glistened on obsidian inlays marking out the compass rose and pentagram.

The four chanted in a language of single syllables, strung together in accordance with a grammar that had passed out of human usage during the long war of barely sentient Homo sapiens against rival species. The words invoked darkness in all its forms: night, cave, blindness, deep water, smoke, death. The shadows flitting overhead dipped and soared in time with the chant, the shadow creatures gaining strength from the power flowing through their creators from the Abyss' ultimate darkness. As the chant entered its second hour, the shadows took on increased definition, individual wisps and strands tangling together to form totemic animals of the night.

The five chanted in a modified form of proto-Indo-European, with the pronunciation that had prevailed in the first cities of Asia Minor. Their ritual consisted almost entirely of verbs: actions of blinding, disordering, confusing, intimidating, defeating and destroying. Their unfolding chorus gained complexity with each repetition, invoking ever-greater suffering for their enemies, glorifying the Abyss for its gifts of powers. The four hundred names of the Lasombra clan's founder entered their chant, one more with each cycle of the chant. The names brought the five's chant into harmony with that of the four, the founder's names echoing the old words for darkness. The blood slowly boiled off the inlays, and darkness crept out from the obsidian, over the surrounding marble.

At the end of the second hour, a flat darkness covered the entire chapel floor. The shadows overhead orbited the chanters, four fast steps and five slow ones, marching in nine concentric rings eight feet above the darkened floor. The single candle flared more brightly as the top wick gave way to the enchanted one underneath; the carefully treated human tallow gave forth an intense red-yellow light. The shadow columns that were the transformed bodies of the participants took on greater definition, more obviously human forms, though their features remained uniformly blank.

As the second wick flared up, the five each took a step inward. During the third hour of the chant, they slowly marched counter-clockwise, a step with each cycle through their recitation. As the celebrant who stood at the pentagram's summit lined up with the celebrant at compass north, they interrupted their chant to recite a single guttural tone from before true human language appeared. It meant "come!" When the next cycle began and the pentagram celebrants stepped again, each of the pair rejoined their partners. The two chants became increasingly dissonant as the list of founder's names grew longer. At the end of the third hour, gusts of altogether odorless wind began to rise up from the blackness around the candle.

During the fourth hour, the candle occasionally guttered out. It always flared up again as the next cycle of compass point chant began. The wind from the Abyss grew steady, then stronger, until it was a vertical gale filling the space within the pentagram. The shadow creatures' pace accelerated until they were a blur of dancing darkness, and they began to give off faint cries like the tortured last cries of the animals they represented. At the end of the fourth hour, the shadow creatures shredded themselves apart back into component wisps and tendrils, which the Abyss wind smashed against the ceiling. The wind tore away the outer layers of darkness around each celebrant, whittling them down to more individualized forms.

The Abyssal wind's direction changed. It blew straight up for a few minutes, then at one angle or another, whipping around without pattern or order. One gust carried off the candle, which wedged in the intersection of two arches and hung upside down, still flaring with its enchanted glow. Where the candle had been, something now rose out of the Abyss.

The arrival was darker than any shadow the celebrants could create. It came from the realm where light never had and never could exist, where nothing like terrestrial matter or energy interacted in a way that might ever kindle illumination. The single candle necessary for its invocation pained the arrival, but it understood that when the candle ended, so did its stay in this complex realm of unfamiliar substance. The arrival twisted itself just beyond the edges of the celebrants' perceptions, moving through their minds as well as around their bodies. After probing the nine, it chose its sacrifice. For an instant all the layers of shadow the celebrant had conjured blew at once, exposing flesh, then muscle, then bone, until all matter was dust and the shadows closed again around their new master, the arrival.

A state of questioning filled the remaining eight. They understood that this was as close as the Abyss's inhabitants could come to comprehensible communication. The chief celebrant pointed upward. "Above. Prey awaits, prepared in accordance with the great rites."

The arrival continued to twist within the pentagram and compass. Suddenly it lashed out again, this time at the chief celebrant. That body too, perished in an instant. The arrival then plunged back into the Abyss, closing the gateway behind itself. The darkness over the floor receded, revealing the natural forms of the desecrated chapel once more.

The seven stopped their chanting. The wind settled, and the dust and debris in the air settled down gradually. Twisted bits of metal and glass were all that remained of old ornaments and wards worn by the vanished magicians. The youngest members of the cabal struck obsidian shards for the sparks to light ceremonial lamps, not so much for the light as for the reassurance of an environment filled with familiar things.

The assistant, now the new chief celebrant, said with a shaky voice, "We're missing something."

Wednesday, 8 March 2000, 10:20 PM
Somewhere beneath Mexico City

"Nothing?"

"Nothing."

"Dammit, Barry, there's got to be something. She can't just disappear."

"I don't think so, at least."

"I'm being rhetorical. Of course she can disappear, but only for a while. What I mean is, she's got to make contact with someone sooner or later. People like her don't move through the world without leaving any ripples."

"Right…"

"But what have we got? No sightings. No jobs. When we try to hire her, she's 'unavailable' even when we work through fresh-made slaves just for the purpose. I even tried a direct approach, and got 'unavailable' rather than 'Our primary is not interested in assignments for the Sabbat at this time.' We've got fuck all."

Andrew paced back and forth in the small monitoring chamber built to tap into main phone lines. His arms held him against one wall while shadow legs pushed off against the other, so he paced over Barry's head. From time to time Barry looked up from his portable computer with an unhappy look, but he knew better than to interrupt the bishop in one of these moods. "It's a damn Sitzkreig, Barry."

"A what?"

"Sitzkrieg. Phony war. The first moves are over and now we sit around waiting for the next step to happen."

"Oh, yeah. Well, at least it's not a total waste for the others."

"That's true." Andrew brightened up for a moment. "The pack's getting really good at combined tactics. Even Niccolo's good for something, if you pump enough Vinculum into him and beat him up once in a while. If we ever do get into a serious fight—something better than the random deserters—we'll do pretty well, I think. If."

"Yeah. If."

"Nothing more out of Rosa?"

"Sorry, no. I've tried everything I can think of, but the most we ever get are these very occasional dreaming links. They tell me that the target's still out there and moving, but nothing about where she is. And I don't get any sense that she experiences anything the other way, no matter how much we rough up Rosa for the occasion."

"Damn. Well, keep listening."

"Yes, boss."

Saturday, 11 March 2000, 9:23 PM
Jerry's Deluxe Charter
Bahía de Los Angeles, Baja California, Mexico

Jerry Staler liked to think of himself as a man of the world. His seventeen years' experience handling boats for rich clients told him that when a gorgeous woman came in well after sunset, in something of a hurry to arrange a boat, she was usually going to meet with one particular other person. This one was a little younger than the usual rendezvous-seeker: most of them were married women closing in on middle age, sneaking away from the husband's resort party to hook up with some young hunk. But Jerry had seen it go the other way, too. She could scarcely be thirty. Probably a trophy wife come down from the pedestal for a bit of fun.

The rumble on the dock just before New Year's—rival would-be drug lords, Jerry gathered—hadn't touched Jerry's own shack, but he'd still done his share of cleaning up the places that did burn or get busted. Customers didn't like coming to areas that looked like war zones. Now you couldn't even tell there'd ever been a problem, the whole pier was fresh and clean, if not really shiny.

His office was, Jerry hoped, a tribute to intelligent decoration on a budget. He traded services with local craftsmen and haunted estate sales, so that he had some really beautiful woven mats mixed in with Art Deco statues from old whorehouses. His personal office door was flanked by very good forgeries of Impressionist paintings sold to Sixties-vintage drug dealers trying to look classy. Most of the furniture had been movie props before World War II, back when the stuff that didn't need to break for stunts was actually built solidly. It took a lot of polish to keep things shiny, but it paid off in impressed clients. They wouldn't haggle over so many incidental expenses if they thought they were really getting luxury treatment.

Tonight's woman scarcely noticed. She stopped the door from swinging just before it ran into the oddly angled end table Jerry bought just after opening this office. Sharp eyes, Jerry thought. You could see the table in the mirror over in the opposite corner, but damn few customers actually did. (He started to look at the mirror, but stopped partway. She was more interesting to look at directly.) Once inside, she turned just right to avoid the one floorboard that squeaked. Had she been here before? Jerry liked to think that he wouldn't have forgotten someone like her: smooth, pale, awesomely alert.

She sat down with nary a wasted move. It was cool outside, and she had a windbreaker over a simple gray blouse and slacks. When she sat, no random creases or wrinkles disturbed her outfit's seams. Jerry wondered if, for some reason, she might actually have changed outfits just before coming in. He smelled money, and a lot of it; it took a lot for a woman to get the time to devote herself to that kind of stylistic perfection.

"Mr. Staler, I presume?"

"Yes, ma'am, Jerry Staler, owner and chief pilot."

"I need a boat big enough for two people, with fully enclosed sleeping quarters, for three days."

Jerry loved her voice, with its perfectly controlled pitch. He remembered the first time he'd gotten close to a girl who'd done the whole East Coast finishing school routine...but time for that later. This woman here looked at Jerry with almost unblinking eyes. No seduction there, he thought, or at least *he* sure wasn't going to get lucky this time. Maybe he'd read her wrong. Smuggler, perhaps?

"Certainly, ma'am. How much cargo space do you need? I've got a pair of small cruisers that'd be fine for two people and supplies, but if you want real hauling capacity, I can do that, too. Not as luxurious, I'm sorry to say, but certainly comfortable anyhow." Was he babbling? Jerry hated the sensation of losing control. This one was getting to him.

"Thank you, Mr. Staler, but I need only about three cubic feet. One of your small cruisers should serve very well. Can we take a look at them now?" She stood up as gracefully as she'd sat down. Her weight balanced perfectly and she stood absolutely still. Not a fidget anywhere. Jerry had a feeling he really didn't want to try picking a fight with her. "That is, if they're actually available now."

"Sure." Jerry locked his desk and came around to open the door for her.

The night sky was as gorgeous as ever. There were things Jerry missed about Los Angeles, but he never got tired of spending a moment under the open universe. A few clouds clustered a few miles offshore, around the hills of the island Angel de la Guarda. A few more lay further east, out across the Gulf of California. Everywhere else was crystal clear, crisp and cool. The Milky Way stretched across the sky in an almost continuous ribbon of light, with the winter constellations ranged around it like guardians. (Jerry had heard that phrase used by a visiting astronomer back in '92, and kept it around. He liked the ring of it.) Harbor lights reached far out across the bay, scarcely disturbed by the gentle waves.

The woman stood in the shadow of Jerry's office, on the concrete sidewalk, while Jerry pointed at the right pier. "This way, ma'am. We use the whole starboard side here." A private jet cruised overhead. Jerry recognized it as pushing the limits of the air lane toward the Bahía airport south of town, and muttered a brief curse. From overhead, the big C-shape of the bay was just too tempting for many pilots out to impress their passengers. It looked very artistic, going from dark land to bright town to bay full of reflections to dark land again, and never mind the noise for the poor mortals below. The woman looked up very briefly, with a motion that would have seemed hasty if it disturbed her hair or clothes, and back down just as quickly and smoothly. Jerry shrugged. "Tourists with more money than sense."

She smiled. "I understand. I was that way myself once upon a time, back home." Back to serious. "Tell me, Mr. Staler, do you get a lot of nighttime business? Most of your competitors closed up hours ago."

He started up the dock, hesitated, heard her boots on the boards behind him, and continued. "Well, I don't get much, but it's sort of a good-luck thing for me."

"Oh?"

He went past the day-trip sailboats and the big yacht, grateful that in the dark she probably couldn't see the stains and raw spots on its hull. The last group to rent it had by God run the damn thing aground while whale-watching. Most of the damage was gone now, but it'd be weeks yet before Jerry could get it in shape to warrant the good rates again. "Yeah. This was 1983. I'd been living in Baja for a couple of years, but the money I started off with ran out. Ran off, really. My girlfriend headed out one morning with my money, my dope, and even my car keys. About all I had left was the boat and some mixed junk I'd salvaged from an estate sale a few weeks earlier. Some rich guy living up the coast kicked off, and we picked out pieces that we thought might look good in an office.

"So I polished up the boat and cut a deal with a friend of mine who used to pack things up for customs handling. I'd use the office in the evenings and on weekends, and in return I'd keep it clean for him. I put up some of the best-looking antiques and lettered up a sign as neatly as I could. Nothing much happened for the first month. I ran little drug loads a couple of times, and did two one-day charters, but that was it. I thought I was going to lose it all." Jerry didn't go into the details. The goons who used to come around to shake him down were long gone now—two dead, one now in the state police and holding down a desk job in the capital.

He looked back. She was following him pace for pace, despite his being several inches taller. There was a little glint at the top of her stride each time her right foot came up. Knife in the boot? He suspected that she very deliberately wanted him to wonder. Definitely not just another trophy wife. Past the banged-up yacht now, nearly at the boats he wanted to show her. "So anyway, there I was on the brink of getting wiped out, when in came this beautiful lady. She was out for the same kind of thing you are. Told me that she had some 'regular transactions' to do and that she'd be back once a month for the next six months. I haggled a little bit, and she agreed to put some down up front. That kept me going until the big fall boom, and *that* got me into the office full-time once I could…."

They'd come to the small cruisers now. "Okay, here we are." He interrupted his own story. "This one handles better in rough weather, but it's more of a fuel pig. If you're not worried about a storm…" She shook her head once. "Then I think you'd find this one a better value." He ran his hand along the *Way Up*. "She's been in my fleet almost from the beginning, and she has yet to give a customer trouble. Will you be sailing her yourself?"

"Yes, I will. I've handled boats like this before, and I don't expect any problems."

"Good, good. Then we can draw up the paperwork." There was a sudden flash of light—someone's amateur fireworks—and the whole pier stood out in stark relief. In the little pocket of calm water between boat and pier, Jerry saw his own reflection.

And not hers.

He took two steps backward. When he looked up, she was right where she had been, with a hint of a smile. "Lady, who are you?"

This time the smile was genuine. Her features rippled and flowed. There she was, the woman from 1983. He couldn't forget that angle in her eyebrows or the somehow pale tan in her complexion. "You remember me, Jerry."

"Um. Yeah."

"I remember the *Way Up*, too. You got it after my third trip. It will serve me just fine. Let's get the paperwork taken care of."

"Um. Okay. On one extra condition."

She frowned, just for an instant. Jerry felt his blood run cold in that instant. He wondered if she could strike him dead with a look, and hoped he wouldn't find out. "What sort of condition, Jerry? I'm sure your rates have gone up, but my money's just as good now."

"No. Nothing like that. Just this. I don't want to know."

"Don't want to know what? I'd rather not make you a vegetable until I finish this job."

"I mean, I just don't want to know what you're up to. I know folks who used to mess around with the local magic, and it never worked out well, ever. So don't get me involved. I'll just pretend that you're an old customer come back and keep all the weird shit away. It's not my thing."

"All right, Jerry. I won't tell you about it. Hire me a boat, and three days from now I'll be on my way, and you can forget the rest."

Lucita didn't really need the wet suit. She wasn't breathing, wasn't bothered by the chill, and didn't think anything living in the Gulf of California could hurt her very badly. But Jerry had included it along with the other gear, and who knew, it might come in handy. It certainly offered more pockets than bare skin would. It was also good cover: someone seriously stalking her might think to check, and it'd be good for there to be routine wear on the equipment.

She'd dreamed of being a young vampire, still almost mortal, visiting this place, seeking a buried goddess of wisdom. It took her a while to remember the actual physical place, and the symbolism of reversion to childhood unsettled her.

She wished she'd thought of this cache three months ago. Ever since canceling her current contracts and instructing her secretary to spread word of her unavailability, Lucita had drifted aimlessly. She'd walked roads from her first nights as a vampire, and revisited battlefields from last year's sect war in the United States, and spent a great deal of time at sea. None of it had led her to any useful insights or even to a sense of temporary peace. She was pretty sure that the rumor mill must be saying that she had gone into the decline which ends in sunlight and ash.

A recognition that the rumors might be right, after all, grew gradually over the course of several weeks, piercing the walls of her mental edifice like a greenhouse plant allowed push first beyond its own pot and then to fill the whole space, and finally to punch through the protective layers of glass to the world outside. Her mental discipline had become appallingly lax, but she was reluctant to impose strictness for its own sake, for fear of locking herself into very definitely self-destructive patterns. This tentative openness might lead her to ruin; the alternative certainly would. So she rambled through the wreckage of her mental garden, thinking of the Renaissance notion of memory palaces and wishing for just one clear answer. Now she was pursuing it. The last of her clients of the moment were paid off or otherwise dismissed, so she was purely on her own time now. And certainly she had the resources to conduct the quest for quite a while, if need be.

She remembered diving in the Danube, in the 13th century, and in the Baltic Sea half a century after that. This modern equipment was certainly an improvement over the improvised protection she and the others had used then. Keeping up with accelerating change was seldom comfortable, just worthwhile in cases like this. So light, the material, but how much sturdier than mortal flesh and garments.

She regretted needing a faint trickle of illumination. It would have been purer to experience the deeps using only the senses other than sight.

Perhaps some night she could return to do so. This trip was purely a business matter. There were things she wanted from her stash here, and she didn't have the time to drift, listening to shifting sands and tasting the tang of mineral concentrations that would guide her to the cave she used seventeen years ago. The smallest lamp in the *Way Up*'s locker sufficed. With her eyes enhanced by a steady trickle of blood, she could see as much here as she remembered of the daylight world in mortal life.

There.

Seventeen years ago she brought several small lockers full of documents here, and buried them in one of the small openings where subterranean rivers from the Mexican mainland emptied into the bottom of the Gulf of California. A miniscule current marked the spot, bringing up salt and copper from veins beneath the gulf floor. Now she could see the crown-like cairn she built back then to mark the particular opening.

Since her last dive, sand had half-covered the entrance. That wasn't a surprise. The geology was active here, and she was prepared for more excavation than seemed likely. A few flicks of her collapsible shovel moved enough sand to let her in. The water trickling up was cooler than the sea. She drifted for a moment, bobbing in and out of the small current, before pushing herself down. Below a narrow rim—dangerously sharp for someone with vulnerable living skin—there was a nearly spherical chamber nine feet across. Angled stones marked the location of each of her lockers.

The one she wanted now was near the entrance. She drew it out in one jerk, and promptly kicked off back to the surface. She wasn't entirely sure what prolonged exposure to such depths might do to the suit and didn't feel like taking chance at the moment.

As she rose, she could feel her body's dead organs expanding and adjusting to the changing pressure. A few minutes' hard swimming brought her back to the surface. Once she dragged a man down to the bottom and back up, so that she could see the "bends" that the sailors had spoken of. It was a fascinating sight; it had taken very little empathic effort to feel the man's terminal suffering back on the surface, and his death throes were impressively agonized. In melancholy moods she almost envied him. Nothing of the sort troubled her own ascent.

She threw the locker onto the boat's deck with one hand while drawing herself up with the other. After brief consideration, she took off the wet suit, dried off, and put back on her dockside outfit. Then she turned her attention to the locker.

The documents inside wouldn't have made much sense to anyone except (what did they call it now?) a medievalist. They were written in fountain pen on legal pads, all very 20th century, with the text in the Aragonese dialect of Spanish as it was nine hundred years ago and the key nouns and verbs masked in a mnemonic code. Since she'd written them herself, recalling the associations didn't take long. In her mind there was a model of the Roman temple at the foot of the hill in Zaragoza, and each of its rooms and corridors corresponded to one of her North American contacts. The notes provided her with the counter-signs and other details she'd need to reestablish her identity.

She spread out the top folders and began mapping out possible routes.

"Jerry. No, don't get up, just listen to me for a moment.

"You were kind to me back then, and you were good this year. I didn't need it, but you mean well. So I'm going to do you a favor.

"Forget.

"Remember the woman who was your first well-paying client back then, and the woman now who let you take her for more than was strictly warranted. Normal people, whom you'll talk up in bars soon enough.

"Maybe we'll meet again. When you die, rest peacefully in your grave."

Tuesday, 14 March 2000, 11:00 PM
Route 1
Baja California

Lucita steered her new car with one hand, holding up recovered directions with the other. The car was nothing particularly special, a straightforward sedan. She chose it in Bahía de Los Angeles because some previous owner had festooned it with clips and hooks everywhere, so that she could spread out her notes and maps.

She crested the last hills and descended to drive along the Pacific shore. Reviewing the files strewn around her brought back memories, as they always did. For some reason, she felt particularly acutely the inconvenience of her inherited legacy. She would not, unlike some of her associates among vampires, ever see herself reflected in an adoring or fearful eye. No memory of a scene where her passion had run high would include a glimpse of herself in a mirror or polished silverware. It hurt to be a hole in the remembered world.

Who to contact first....

Lezinski would be good, but Lucita heard bad things about the state of Los Angeles's Cainite affairs. In particular there were stories about an influx of vampires from Asia, with exotic lineages and abilities, and even more chaos than usual in the "Anarch Free State" that had prevailed in California's night society since World War II. Lezinski was one of the archetypal deal-makers, the independent without sire or antecedent who won respect through his excellent services in procurement. If there was anything like the power struggle she'd heard about, he'd be in the middle of it, supplying resources to all sides. He'd done this before, during each of the Sabbat civil wars and in various local conflicts, and Lucita remained bemused and amused that he managed to survive all the follow-up attacks from disgruntled losers who blamed him for their failures.

Best to avoid trouble when it wasn't necessary. She made a note to gather more reliable information about the Los Angeles situation and see about contacting Lezinski later.

Ramon…what had Ramon done since the last war? The last hard intelligence she had on him implicated him in an occult scheme trying to direct the United States atomic bomb venture in accordance with some Templar vision of the apocalypse. She knew he'd survived that, and she thought he was likely still somewhere in San Francisco—most likely under a new identity—but right now she didn't care to make the extensive careful search it would require to find him. Besides, for all she knew the disorder in Los Angeles had spread north, or would while she quested.

Konstantin, then. That would do. She picked up the cell phone to make a call, when a stabbing pain descended upon her. A brief but very intense vision came to her, of a female vampire being tortured by unseen hands. In her torment, the victim cried out Lucita's name.

The vision passed. Lucita trembled as it passed. Like ghosts, omens were a part of her experience, but even rarer and less welcome than the restless dead . She wondered what this unknown vampire might be to her—or what Lucita might be to the victim—that would bridge souls this way. What did it mean? Or was it just an extension of her earlier dream of her young self? She thought not. It was altogether too much of a piece with the times. Oracles only flourish when the world is in trouble, Lucita firmly believed, and the fact that so many omens surrounded her only reinforced her fear that this time Gehenna really was coming. Who was that woman? An ally Lucita failed to recognize? What connection had been at work?

She drove north through darkness, troubled.

Wednesday, 15 March 2000, 2:00 AM
Somewhere beneath Mexico City

"We've got something!" Barry's shout echoed through the halls. Andrew and the others immediately stopped their sparring and came running.

"What's up?" Andrew demanded.

Barry pointed at Rosa, still shackled, now minus the leg they'd folded a month ago. "Listen to her."

Rosa moaned in a deeper voice than her own. As he listened, Andrew realized that she was speaking out something one syllable at a time. "San - Quin - tin - 1 - 5 - k - m - San - Vin - cen - te - 1 - 4 - 5 - k - m…"

Andrew looked over at Barry. "Is that what I think it is?"

"If you think it's highway directions, yes, boss, it is. Those are towns on Highway 1 in Baja California, headed north toward the US."

"So Rosa actually had a clue about her coming to Bahía de Los Angeles, she was just early."

"Looks that way to me."

Andrew smiled. By this time the others were all crowded around listening to Rosa recite traffic signs. Somewhere to the west, Lucita was glancing at those signs, and the images formed in Rosa's nearly broken mind. "Okay, gang," Andrew said. "I think it's time we hit the road."

Tuesday, 21 March 2000, 3:58 AM
Somewhere in the Nelson Range
Death Valley National Park, California

Lucita remembered when she first heard about Joshua trees. It was New Year's Eve, 1500, and she sat with her mentor, Anatole, in a corner chamber of the Spanish palace. In the main hall a floor below, the Italian mariner, Columbus, was once again preaching the glories waiting for Spain to scoop up. Lucita and Anatole had been listening quietly until one of Anatole's fits came upon him; she'd escorted him to a quiet space and waited for it to pass. As he recovered, he spoke of peculiar plants and animals. Two and a half centuries later, as she walked through the California desert for the first time, she realized that he'd seen these barren mountains and canyon oases and tried to tell her about them.

Even now the trees seemed more visionary than altogether real to her. They rose like dead things, suddenly crowned with sharp green leaves, as though God had taken to making plants for the New World while deranged or forgetting just what it was He was doing at the moment. Around their bases grew bushes with leaves almost as hard as bone, and tiny little flowers that remained open through the night to harvest moisture from passing breezes. The whole landscape leeched vitality.

Tonight she moved through the canyons at a comfortable stride, following her host, the loner vampire Konstantin. Like him, she carried a mortal slung over one shoulder—unconscious and securely bound. She had plenty of time to watch the scenery as they walked toward Konstantin's cabin. High clouds framed distant mountains. Close at hand, countless small creatures both warm- and cold-blooded scurried over the rocks and stunted plant life, all seeking their food before the sun struck them all down. (In this high desert, almost everything could suffer as if under the curse of Caine.) Konstantin led her along a secret trail defined by subtle mounds of rocks here, apparently flood-carved steps there, nothing any searcher would likely notice. Lucita enjoyed the feel of basalt slabs shifting beneath her feet as she and her host made gentle leaps, no more than five to ten feet each, along the rim of a seasonal stream's gorge. Her meal stirred occasionally but never slipped off its perch.

Her car lay an hour behind her, buried under artfully arranged sand and stone. Since then she'd been content to travel in silence, but the need for information rose in her like a dry well returning to life. "Konstantin?"

"Yes." His voice was flat, free of affect and emotion. It was what remained after all mortal concerns drained away.

"Who are these people?"

"That depends on who you ask."

"I'm asking you, since you're here and you asked me to pick them up on the way through Barstow."

Konstantin paced on for almost a full minute before continuing. "They're ghouls belonging to some would-be prince on the east end of the LA urban sprawl. The Sabbat packs on the scene got their asses handed to them in an abortion of a war two years ago. Now they're trying to be cunning. This is part of some scheme to destabilize the prince so that she'll be easier to push over."

"Since when do you hire out to the local Sabbat?"

Konstantin spun in place and walked backward, never missing a step. "Since half my assets in LA went under in the midst of some battle between the head honcho anarchs and a bunch of would-be princes from China. I've got expenses. This job paid me in verifiable funds. When I'm stable again, then I'll tell them all to go to hell, move my stake, and settle down again. Since when do you *care* who I hire out to?" He faced front again and continued walking.

Now it was Lucita's turn to consider her words. They walked up over the gully ridge and into a series of steep hills, gradually rising into real mountains. The basalt slabs gave way to granite outcroppings dusted with thousand-year-old grit from the extinct cinder-cone volcanoes on the far side of this ridge. "Self-examination, I suppose. I wonder what the end result of our kind of work is. Are we just keeping the pot stirred?"

"God knows. Let him have his opinion. I care about my hide."

"Heading for a Gehenna cult?" She meant it as a jest, then realized with a horrible, vital sinking sensation that he just might.

"Not me. If the end times are coming, my praying isn't going to make it any better. I want my place safe, and that's all I care about. If you want to go chase the big guys, do it somewhere I'm not."

"No, thanks. Anyway, I just wondering. Do you think that getting rid of this pair is actually going to help your clients any?"

"No. They're doomed the moment some competent archon arrives on the scene." Konstantin crossed the last of the parallel ridges and half-slid down into a narrow valley. The dark front wall of his home lay almost flush against the far wall. "Or some competent templar. The whole operation's a classic newbie sort of ploy. Does that make it better or worse for you?"

"I'm not sure." Lucita pondered the matter as they reached Konstantin's home. The approach included two ten-foot vertical jumps and two one-handed swings across deep crevasses—scarcely a problem for anyone Konstantin would actually want as a guest. The front wall was clearly artificial, but thoroughly weathered. (Lucita remembered helping Konstantin with that when he'd finished the home's framework. They'd thrown fistful after fistful of gravel at the wall with blood-enhanced strength to produce that effect.) It looked like a played-out mine or military dump, with nothing of interest to treasure seekers or anyone else.

The door supported the image. It was a massive rusted steel block fifteen feet tall. Konstantin shoved it near the bottom, pivoting it vertically around an axle running through the middle of the frame. Once he and Lucita were both inside, he shoved the door back into place and draped a black plastic tarpaulin around its edges.

The illusion of abandonment ended at the tarpaulin. The chamber just inside was furnished very comfortably, with bookshelves and couches Konstantin had scavenged in Prohibition-era raids. The lamps were World War II Navy lamps, taken from a ship being disassembled on a beach in

India at a time when Konstantin was burying bodies up the coast a bit. Steel doors covered smooth-walled corridors, the other chambers embedded further from the surface. A massive fireplace in one wall vented into an elaborate system of filters and concealed outlets. Opposite hung Konstantin's collection of favored weapons, from knives as small as one of his fingernails up to machine guns no human could carry.

Konstantin hung the prisoners on hooks flanking the fireplace. "Time to rest. We'll talk after sleep." Lucita stretched out on the couch, trusting her reflexes to alert her to any trouble.

Lucita was up well before Konstantin, so she looked in on the two prisoners, meals-to-be. They were still unconscious. Stepping close, she could see that they'd been bludgeoned repeatedly by someone who knew human physiology quite well. Their skulls were slightly crushed in very specific locations. Even if they did regain consciousness, which they wouldn't, they'd lose some significant portion of their minds.

In the flickering light of the main room's fireplace, Lucita sat cross-legged on the floor and watched the prisoners' auras. Mortal auras were so much more alive than vampires'. The Beast makes us simple, she thought. We don't have the time to dabble on our way to our obsessions. These people still have options, they could be almost anyone if they weren't sucked into our war. Her tired thoughts rambled on. She'd been told as a girl that God gave the especially holy insights into the human heart. Certainly she was not holy…not unless absolutely everything she'd learned then was a lie, and she wasn't at all ready to make that leap.

Lucita had met vampires who claimed that they were God's chosen. Some of them even acted like it. Dear, lost Anatole had done his best to administer God's mercy and justice to the night society. Others claimed that their chosenness went with an exception from the moral duties so important to Anatole, that the frenzy and the power were themselves the point. Was she an angel or saint unawares? The notion seemed laughable…except that the whole thing was ridiculous in some ways, wasn't it?

Konstantin emerged from the doorway across the room. Lucita remembered how his full mane of untamed hair would brush against the low lintels. Now he shaved bald upon awaking, and cleared the doorframe with inches to spare. "Waiting for an invitation?" he made a dry cough in an effort to suggest a laugh. "Dig in."

He snagged the ghoul nearest him with one hand and held the man up for close examination. Mid-40s, beady eyes, air of desperation. Just the sort of fool willing to drink dead blood in exchange for petty favors. Konstantin snapped the man's neck with a precise flick of his wrist, used two fingers to pry open the skin around the jugular vein, and positioned his mouth over the resulting spurt. With each dying heartbeat the blood pumped a little lower. When it ceased altogether, Konstantin held the man upside down to suck out however much secondary flow gravity would produce. He set the man down dry.

Lucita preferred not to play with her food on business occasions like this. She left her man alive and simply drained him where he lay, lifting him just enough that she didn't have to actually crouch over him. The blood had that distinctive reek of ghouling, and she knew that if she ran into the man's mistress, she'd recognize the princeling immediately.

Sated, Konstantin sat beside her. "So tell me. What brings you into the desert?"

"I don't expect you'd believe me if I said that I just wanted to see you again."

"No. I'd want to know *why.*"

Lucita shrugged. "Did you hear about what happened in Madrid? To the cardinal?" She didn't have to say which. For there was only ever one cardinal that mattered.

"Yes."

"I've been on the move ever since. Went home to Zaragoza for a brief visit—"

"Like a damn fool," Konstantin interrupted. "You taught me yourself: that life is through, leave it behind, if you try to dig it up you'll just push yourself that much closer to the end."

"Generalizations have exceptions. I taught you that, too."

Lucita remembered Konstantin as a young vampire, still making his way through the streets of Vladivostok, youngest childe of a Lasombra *antitribu* who held sway over the port and trains, struggling to make sense of it all. She remembered finding him unexpectedly on the streets of Los Angeles, forty years later, and extracting the story of his diablerie and flight. Clearly he'd expected her to destroy him on the spot, but she'd merely shrugged and told him that he was the one who had to survive with the memory of what he'd done. Twenty years after that he was an enthusiastic member of the Sabbat, and twenty years after *that* he'd gone independent. When he told her that story (voluntarily this time), she nodded and told him once again that he'd have to cope with the memories.

They didn't see each other very often—every twenty or thirty years—but they found that when they met up, they could talk. He felt confident criticizing her in ways that few elders would tolerate, and in turn she dropped him occasional hints that she hoped would enhance his survival. He changed identities and contact points every few years; by now his old packmates were all long gone, freeing him from Vinculum-created obligations. Carefully constructed rumors led curious California Sabbat to regard Konstantin as an observer for some Old World Lasombra elder…which, Lucita supposed, wasn't all that far from the truth, after all.

This time around he'd asked her to stop and pick up the two captives on his behalf, saving him a trip out of the desert. She wondered how much of his skeptical hostility was simply channeled away from himself and his own guilt.

"You did. But you ain't one of them this time around. You damn fool. Why not just stake yourself out for the sunlight and have done?"

She thought of the scene in her hotel room. "Something like that. Then I took a boring case and dropped it. Then I realized that someone was going to convene a Court of Blood and come looking for me. So I'm making the rounds of old havens and allies, just to see if anyone's had trouble."

"Not me. Just some good eating like this."

"Good. Glad to hear it."

He stood. "Let's go outside."

Tonight there were no clouds. The land lay pitch black in night shadow, and the stars blazed overhead. Konstantin looked at Lucita, then up, then back to her, again and again. "Are you getting set to really die?"

"I don't think so."

"You don't *think* so. What the hell kind of answer is that?"

"An honest one."

"'An honest one,'" he said in a frighteningly accurate imitation of her voice. "It's a shitty answer. If you're not preparing to survive, then you're letting someone set up your death. Guilt got you?"

She flinched.

"Uh-huh, thought so," Konstantin continued. "Look, the bastard had it coming. You know it. I know it. Everyone knows it. His old lackeys are probably fighting over whatever's left of his furniture right now, and the big boys must be glad to have one less Christoid nut case around. So who cares?"

"Every single elder who thinks that threats to the nobility need to go punished, for starters. Every single neonate out to earn her spurs by taking out the big bad *antitribu*. Everyone in between, too."

"That's shit talk. That's not *news*. You've been doing this for longer than any dozen neonates have been around. You've taken down some of the best there. This is about your damn attitude."

"Maybe so."

"Definitely so. Listen to me. If you ever took your clan seriously, you can't give up now. I don't think this is Gehenna coming, but I see enough to know that there's a whole lot of shaking up going on. You used to talk about sabotaging the old bastard's schemes partly by replacing them with better ones. Now you've got your chance, if you'd just take it. Don't you dare go getting scared now."

"Scared?"

"Scared." With that, Konstantin lapsed back into silence.

Tuesday, 28 March 2000, 11:00 PM
Castle of Saint Rafael the Archangel
Sicily, Italy

Once again, a single candle illuminated the vault. Seven shadows without sources leaned against the walls: four along the north wall, one in the middle of each of the other walls. Only the boundaries of their heads moved as they whispered softly to one another.

Two women and one man stood at the points of a triangle six feet across, inscribed in their blood, the candle resting on an ebony stand in the middle of the triangle. Their eyes were glazed, their motions sluggish though precise. Their arms and legs bore countless scabbed-over cuts; the magicians who'd stolen their wills didn't intend them to survive the night anyway and didn't care to waste blood or time on fixing damage unless it were severe enough to endanger the ritual.

The man was mortal. He began his chant in the single-syllable ritual language and punctuated each cycle by stabbing himself with an iron needle. Gradually he built up layered runes, the individual wounds leaking blood that flowed in unnaturally straight lines to cover the gaps. His voice trembled as the hours unwound. The shadows along the wall whispered to each other, carefully gauging the chances that he might just die prematurely. So far, though, he endured enough for this test.

The women were zombies, of a sort: dead bodies into which the celebrants had installed the souls of mortal magicians tortured to death in the chapel two stories overhead. They sang the proto-Indo-European chant in perfect harmony, as they'd performed rituals together in their two hundred years of life. They also stabbed themselves with needles at the end of each cycle, but no blood flowed. Sometime in the second hour, a gray-white liquid oozed out of the tissues around each hole, slowly drifting from irregular blobs into smooth lines and curves to match those on the man.

The shadows continued whispering to each other.

Tonight's summoning was deliberately abbreviated. It couldn't draw a great power out of the Abyss or keep it in the material once summoned. This was the time to test each step of the way....

There. Darkness erupted like the shadow of a fountain, tumbling out of the candle's smoke and pouring over the celebrants and their surroundings. Within seconds it was all a homogeneous pure blackness, and the wind began to blow from the Abyss. A single massive black cylinder rose up. The wind shifted to lead into it, and the engulfed celebrants all tumbled in. The cylinder sank, the shadows withdrew, and the candle continued to glow.

The observers nodded. That was one step passed. Now to try again with the next.

part two: interrogations

Saturday, 1 April 2000, 3:23 AM
Brentwood
Los Angeles, California

"He threw his *head* at you? How the hell can he throw his *head* at you?" Andrew didn't think Simon Peter could get totally stoned in three minutes, but he was beginning to wonder.

"*I* don't know! I just know that he got one good look at me, and fucking ripped his head off and threw it at me! Damn thing kept biting all the way out, till I could put on some decent speed." Simon Peter pulled down his coat collar, and Andrew had to admit that there were very plausible fang marks all over the magician's neck and shoulders.

This was all starting to look fairly seriously screwed, and in mysterious ways to boot. Andrew didn't like mysteries in the middle of combat situations. "Okay. Go grab someone and get yourself healed up. I'm going to check things out myself." He paused. "Where's Roxana?"

"I don't know, that damn head started at me and I just split."

Andrew fought back the urge to make some nasty retort. It wouldn't help. This now looked *very* screwed. "Okay. Barry, Niccolo, go with Simon Peter. Wait. Better yet, one of you go grab someone and bring them back here for Simon Peter. I'll go check it out." Barry nodded, waved a "keep low" signal at Niccolo, and trotted down to the main street. Andrew wrapped shadows around himself and moved as quickly as he could up to the house.

Two weeks of detective work had brought them here. According to the last information they had, from about four years ago, this particular estate belonged to a retired jewelry broker named Tadeuszco. That was a cover identity for one Wijkold Lezinski, a nearly anarch Lasombra who dealt in arms and other contraband. He'd spent the whole 20th century in Los Angeles under one alias or another, and he was a known associate of Lucita.

shards

Title search confirmed that Lezinski, or rather Tadeuszco, was still the owner of record and still kept the bills paid. But Lezinski had never been known to go throwing his head around. So it was time for Andrew to go demonstrate a little leadership. He checked that his portable radio was on and ready to go.

The estate lay up a small but twisty driveway hemmed in by ten-foot hedges. On the other side, according to official records, lay a sweeping expanse of front lawn, with gardens and fish ponds around back. There was one car—the Ferrari listed in Lezinski's name—in the driveway. There were also the footprints Simon Peter had made in his hasty retreat, along with a few smudges that he or Roxana probably made in their approach.

The original plan called for the two to simply ring the door and present credentials taken from the Sabbat refugees the pack found and destroyed in San Diego last week. Lezinski was expecting someone with the right letters to show up and claim a shipment of stolen military hardware for use in a dispute over domain down south. They'd do their business, get a good look at the place, and leave, then prepare for a follow-up assault once Andrew assimilated their information. Now it was going to have to be something else.

Andrew came around the last bend and got a good look at the house. It was familiar, in that way that a lot of Brentwood homes were—he felt pretty sure he'd seen it in movies or TV shows before his Embrace. It was dark except for a single light on the front porch and security lights on the corner. Nothing inside moved, as nearly as he could tell. Assuming that the one who'd thrown his head (*thrown his head?*) at Simon Peter was still there, this next bit would call for fast action. Andrew paused to be glad that he'd had them all hunt right after sundown, so that he still had just about much blood as his body could carry.

He started his dead heart pumping, forcing its power out through his pores in the form of writhing shadows. They wrapped around his legs, turning his usual shadow legs into massive pillars, capable of kicking with all the strength his will would allow. And he trembled on the edge of the Black Metamorphosis, feeling shadow-self ready to erupt at a moment's notice and turn him into a blackened demon. He extended one shadow tentacle to punch the doorbell while he stood half a dozen paces back.

After a moment of silence, the door swung open. Standing on the other side was…a demon. It looked like something out of a monster movie: nine feet tall, covered in silver armor that moved without more than a whisper, and carrying a two-handed ax which glowed with an inner fire. The thing stepped out onto the porch and quickly scanned the grounds. When it got to Andrew, its head stopped and it drew the axe up for a charge.

Shit! It could see through his obfuscation! This was going to be trouble. "Get up here!" he called, both physically and through the Vinculum, as he unleashed the metamorphosis within himself. By the time the thing was on him, he was ready to meet it on something like equal terms. Shadow tentacles erupted in a writhing mass from his chest, and black lightning ran along his arms. He thrust both arms and all the tentacles up, and deflected the first blow. His counter-strike, unfortunately, didn't do any good; his kick hit the armor just wrong and slid off.

What the hell was this thing? Andrew tried to puzzle it out as best he could in the thick of things. Footsteps pounded up the driveway, but they couldn't get here right away. Andrew leapt back and up, extending his tentacles to grab at the ax and tug it out of the thing's hands. He got a good grip, but it had a better one, and the ax stayed where it was. Now there was sound: the fire within the axe crackled and sent a chill arcing up through the tentacles back into Andrew's chest. The demon spun around and wrenched the ax altogether loose, tearing off two tentacles in the process. (In the twinkling of an eye, Andrew had closed the wounds with quick thrusts of blood, but the stumps still hurt.) Then it was back into the overhand stance and ready for another charge.

"Coming!" That was Barry. Good man, Barry, but if he felt the urge to say that, that meant he wasn't here yet. Time to change the field a bit. Andrew lengthened the cords around his legs and took a huge stride around one side of the demon. Now it was between him and the others. It apparently didn't quite realize what it was setting itself up for…though maybe it

shards

didn't care. It dropped the axe and…Andrew didn't quite believe what he was seeing. It flapped its arms, and they came off, flapping through the air to strangle him. They couldn't get a good purchase on the slippery nightmare essence that coated his neck and shoulders, but it wasn't for want of trying. He was forced to concentrate on holding them at bay while the demon stalked up close. Its armored helm slid up to reveal a mouthful of fangs unnaturally large even by vampiric standards.

There was no time for subtlety, and apparently Barry, Simon Peter and even Niccolo all realized it. The priest leaped up to grab at the demon's helm while Simon Peter and Niccolo dove low to pull its legs loose. The triple attack succeeded, mostly. The demon did fall backward, but the helm stayed on, though Barry did manage to slam it closed over those hideous teeth. Andrew managed to wrap his remaining tentacles around the arms and force them down into the driveway.

The three pack members simply bludgeoned the demon until it stopped moving. When the main body passed out, the arms fell limp, too. Andrew wrenched loose a pair of unlit driveway lamps and impaled each arm on a short spike. It wouldn't hold them, but it would slow them down. He looked back to see the demon's armor shriveling up. Its body also shriveled, Andrew realized in a moment. The whole thing must be some equivalent to the Black Metamorphosis. What was left behind, a few eyeblinks later, was a middle-aged Chinese man in an immaculate white suit stained with blood that smelled of Roxana. The detached arms were normal-seeming human arms, too, but somehow Andrew felt no desire to try the reunion just yet.

"What the fuck is that?" Barry asked.

"I don't have a damn clue," Andrew answered. "I've heard the old-timers talk about 'Cathayans,' but they always sound like a bunch of Tremere wannabes or something. I never heard about anything like this from anyone who wasn't obviously deranged. Look, you guys make sure it doesn't go anywhere while I go check for Roxana." The three nodded, and kept the body under very close watch indeed. One of them gave it a fresh thwack every so often. Just making sure, no doubt.

Andrew turned on the lights as he made his way through the house. It wasn't strictly necessary, but it was a little touch of defiance—one more mark that this was now an environment controlled by the Lasombra rather than by little men who turned into big demons. Roxana lay on the floor of the second room he checked. She'd been bound up in drapes obviously pulled down for the purpose. She was unconscious, but it didn't take long to revive her, and just a few drops of blood sufficed. Not enough to risk a blood bond; Andrew was careful about that. Once he saw that she was coming to, he resumed his search.

There was no actual body of Lezinski anywhere in the home, but the ashes and coffin in one corner of the basement were pretty suggestive. It looked to Andrew like someone had staked Lezinski and pushed the coffin over to catch the morning rays. Was that the east side? Yes, it was. Right.

The office on the second floor was stuffed full of papers. Andrew had Barry bring their sedan around and put all the most interesting-looking documents in the trunk. They'd have to study things later, once they had a proper working haven again.

"What about him?" Niccolo asked as Andrew went by with a final armful of bills and purchase orders, gesturing at the ex-demon.

Andrew pondered. "We don't really have a place to put him, do we? I think we should destroy him. See just how much abuse he can take before he falls apart."

The answer proved to be "quite a lot." But in the end, he let go just like any Western vampire, his corpse crumbling into dust and drifting away. The pack drove away, with the first of the fires Niccolo set on their way out just beginning to shine through the upstairs windows. Time to shelter for the day.

Saturday, 1 April 2000, 4:12 PM
Motel 6
Gunnison, Colorado

She is sixteen. It's a summer evening, and the stars overhead shine dimly through the smoke of countless chimneys. The city below reeks, but her father sees that the palace is swept and cleaned and garnished with incense. In the courtyard, grooms tend to the horses after the last messengers of the day have arrived, and the cooks and scullery boys start to gather the ingredients of tomorrow's meals for slow cooking.

She walks along an upper hallway to the family chapel, where the archbishop waits for her and her confession. She does not like Archbishop Monçada, and never has. From the moment she began to form impressions of people, she thought of him as a hole where a soul should be. His march to power has not changed that. As she studied rhetoric and poetry, she learned of mystics who regard themselves as vessels through which divine light pours. Monçada is like that, except that within him there is no light. He sees himself as nothing, but he also sees the world as nothing but himself. She suspects that his vision of heaven is himself, endlessly repeated.

Though most ignore it, the archbishop is more secretive than any other clergyman. He will not come out during the day, and quotes strange mixtures of passages from the Old Testament about evil under the sun. He meets with others only at night, and almost always in darkness. Lucita has tried to warn her father that their confessor is up to no good, but her father remains awestruck by having such an important cleric pay attention to him. Perhaps there is something more sinister at work, too; she suspects many things but cannot yet prove them.

She enters the chapel. The decorations have changed. The altar cloth is now pure black. The stained glass windows are purely red, and they seem to be wet, as if some force held liquid in place. The walls shine with reflections of scenes Lucita does not recognize, though her older self knows that they are moments of faith and doubt from later years. The Archbishop does not wait in the confessional booth. Instead he stands as if for a sermon. When she enters, he motions to her to shut the door.

"Child," he says in that grating tone, "what are the great commandments?"

"To love the Lord, my God, with all my heart, and to love my neighbor as myself." She speaks with reverence toward the commandments, even though she despises the Archbishop's use of "child." She is not a child, and she will show him a woman's understanding.

The candles begin to flicker out as he lectures her. "What is the duty of the child to her parents?"

"To honor them, that her days may be long in the land that the Lord has given her."

A red glow kindles somewhere near the ceiling. She can see that the redness in the windows is in fact flowing, steaming off as it leaves the frames. Monçada drones on. "And what is the duty of the bride?"

"To forsake her home and cleave to her bridegroom, to become one flesh."

"That is correct." The red glow is now clearly coming from a hole in the ceiling, a single light in the darkness. The chapel smells of musty upturned earth. The Archbishop seems to loom larger in front of her. "You have forsaken your parents. I have drawn you out of that world. I am your father, and yet you do not cleave to me, nor do you respect me. What are the wages of sin?"

She is lying in a coffin. Things scrabble all around her. She feels her flesh crackle, and smells corruption within her. "Death."

"That is correct. The wages of sin are death. You are in disobedience of God's holy plan."

She only barely manages to draw breath and whisper, "How do I know?"

"You have never seen God, and you never will. You see His chosen ministers on Earth, of whom I am one. I tell you what God's will is, and you obey. If I were to stray from the path, God would judge me and you would know. But as you see, he has crowned my work with success." The coffin opens, and she finds herself standing in the basement of the great cathedral in Madrid. The moon passes by an open window...and again...and again, faster and faster. Trophies accumulate. Defeated enemies come in to prostrate themselves at the Archbishop's feet. He grows fatter and meaner. "God rewards my payment of the ultimate price."

She struggles to answer, but cannot now find air.

"You see? Your own body knows your sin. Come, let me show you what should have been." Again she steps from the coffin. But now she steps to his side. The tribute comes for her as well as him. She feels the power of enemies chosen for destruction coursing in her veins, providing her fresh power. As her sire's power grows, she grows with it. In time she strides across the New World as its dark queen, reaping an endless harvest of blood and sorrow as she serves her sire in his quest to punish all sin and create the New Jerusalem on Earth.

She feels herself within that other self, but it is a lie. She tries to tear off the mask, but cannot. Gradually she forces herself out through the lie's pores, one drop at a time. In the end, after countless years of effort, she draws herself up out of a black puddle and watches the lie's barren husk collapse. "I reject you."

Everything—people and building alike—ooze and crumble as did her lie. Soon she and her sire stand on a featureless plain, ankle-deep in dust. "Do you? Tell me, daughter of my blood, what is it you reject?"

"You. Your schemes. Everything about you. Whatever you are, I am not. Whatever you do, I will stop you." She is so young, she knows in the dream, and has no idea what she's promising. But she knows, in the dream, that she will spend nine hundred years trying to live up to those words.

"Tell me of these schemes."

"I…you…the throne…the ships…the colony…" Her thoughts mash together. None achieves complete expression. She stammers in frustration and anger.

"You see? You rebel not against me, but against your image of me. You do not see that you are my child in truth, the image of my soul. You do my will as I do God's will. You are just like me." He smiles at her. "Everything you have ever done serves me. Everything you are serves me. When the great trial comes, you will stand confirmed as my worthy heir." In violation of the great curse, Monçada suddenly appears reflected in all the mirrors that had sprung up unnoticed. The source of the reflections reaches out to touch her, his hands tracing the lines of her horrified face. In the mirrors, his hands leave behind a faint impression, which takes on clarity and definition: it is his own image.

Lucita woke with a scream. The words "child in truth" echoed out from under the bed. She jumped up and ran into the bathroom, pressing blood-sweaty hands against the mirror, which, of course, showed nothing. Blood dripped down into the sink, forming letter after letter as it swirled it away. "Child in truth." Gradually she emerged more fully into wakefulness, and the manifestations settled down. The Beast, she realized, had been goading itself into activity, and she took calm slow measures to subdue it again.

She could feel the press of daylight outside. Fearful of attack, she calmed herself and conducted a lengthy probe of her psyche. In the end she found no trace of manipulation. But though she lay almost stupefied with the agony of daytime wakefulness, she could sleep not again that day.

Lucita sat in a pickup in the motel parking lot. The pickup's owner was still in the driver's seat, frozen into immobility with a few well-chosen words. Lucita was hungry, but felt a warning intuition that someone was on her trail and so she didn't want to risk leaving any permanent evidence. While the driver sat, she used a cell phone taken from the room next to hers to place a series of calls: to a voice mail box in Chicago to retrieve an access code to a relay number in Boise which, given the access code, switched her two private networks to another voice mail box in Bermuda to retrieve a second code, and then finally to a second relay number in Los Angeles which, given the same access code, transferred her to a voice mailbox in Berlin.

"Miss Gebenstaler, this is Madame De Spain. Reserve Fund B remains active. However, please issue authorization for a Class 2 package, destination London, transfer as soon as is practical within the usual constraints. One item only. Place confirmation in the Papal slot. There will be no direct contact at this time. Thank you for your attention."

Time to move.

She got out of the truck and told the driver, "Wake in 200 heartbeats." His lips began moving with the count. She placed the luggage she'd brought from California into the dumpster, beneath a layer of newspapers. It only took a moment in the motel office to complete her business: she signed out, and instructed the clerk not to notice it until midnight. Then she was off, walking at twice human speed along the side of the highway, wrapped in shadows no headlights would pierce. By the time the clerk completed her checkout, she'd be well on her way.

As she walked, she tried to explain her actions to herself. She'd twice had visions of the female Lasombra being tortured and calling out to her. That wasn't enough to explain her unease. After all, she was *the* preeminent symbol of rebellion within her clan. Inevitably there were would-be followers come to seek her (imagined) wisdom and would-be avengers come to punish her (also imagined) sins. It happened several times a century, and while she regretted the ends to which her pursuers almost always came, it didn't usually gnaw at her this way.

There was something darker at work. Nor was that itself unprecedented. While Monçada had forbidden efforts to destroy her without his sanction, no single voice dictated to the rest of the clan. (The Great Diablerist, Gratiano, could have, if he chose. But he didn't, and nobody else had the standing.) Courts of Blood periodically pronounced sentence on her and sent out killers, sometimes very formidable ones. She had come very, very close to destruction in the chaos of 1848, and again after World War I. Lesser encounters had driven her out of havens, cost her comrades, and shattered her rare efforts at systematic influence-building in mortal society. She felt there was a hunter after her again, but there was something else. It nagged at her.

The dream also haunted her, and more forcibly. She couldn't shake that last image, of her sire creating himself out of her. She wanted to say to herself, "Of course that's not true. You are not his image. You are…" But there words failed her. What was she?

She was his childe, of course. Nothing could change that. His blood was in her veins; when she woke from slumber, she could sometimes taste it in her mouth, as in that very first moment when he'd opened a vein to drip twelve drops into her unresisting throat. It had been a very long time since she believed that the blood was the life in the sense the Old Testament meant it. Whatever the soul might be, it didn't reside purely in drops of blood, and her soul remained her own, even tainted as it was by a millennium in darkness.

Except of course that it didn't.

She remembered with agonizing clarity how he had commanded her, that terminal time in Madrid. He brushed past all her defenses as if they were nothing, and compelled her obedience. She knew she didn't have complete recall of that last week, either. The trauma of battle and flight accounted for most of it. But could she be so very certain that he hadn't left behind orders to make her into his tool even after the wind carried his ashes away? For that matter, could she be sure that she *didn't* have his soul inside her? She hadn't learned everything he had to teach at the outset, and he'd scarcely stopped his magical research in later centuries.

He was gone. Apart from whatever legacy he might have hidden inside her. The great task of her unlife, the frustration and ruin of all his schemes, was now done, for good or ill. Oh, there'd be investigation and mopping up to do for decades yet, maybe for centuries. But everything now unfolded without his hand to steer it. There'd be nothing new from him, and none of his flunkies began to approach his daring or innovation. She could outthink them, outmaneuver them, and if necessary outfight nearly all of them face to face.

What, then? What to do with herself?

The thought had come to her, as she lay quivering on the bed with daylight mere inches away behind thick draperies. *Know your kind.* She knew who and what she was, of course, so at first it seemed nonsensical. Then she realized that she knew very little about how most of her fellow Lasombra conducted themselves. Beyond the massed ranks of the Sabbat, there were half a dozen varieties of independents, plus the lone individuals, and most of them were nothing more than occasional clients or targets to her.

After the Great Fire in the 17th century, Lucita had noticed that London had a larger and more diverse Cainite population than most cities its size. She decided back then that if she ever needed to try posing as a loyal member of the Camarilla, it would be a good choice, since the court was more used to unusual members. An hour of tallying her options now, in 2000, suggested to her that it remained a good place to go to see what it was like to be Lasombra and Camarilla. How did it feel to have commitments of that sort? She didn't truly know, and chose it as her first step.

The Class 2 package she'd requested from her German assistant would get her from any American airport to New York and from there to London in sealed boxes with multiple layers of fronting, to avoid trace smells and chemical residues of any kinds. The containers had passed field-test inspections laden with drugs and various strong scents, and none of them alerted dogs, sniffing sensors, or other inspection. She had the option of transporting up to half a dozen fellow vampires, though this time she'd go alone.

The Papal account was a voice mail box in Avignon, France, ostensibly owned by a struggling small vineyard whose field agents used not-terribly-sophisticated word codes to report on their pending deals. Most of the messages were randomly generated by ghouls trained for the task. (In Miss Gebenstaler's experience, few things were as reliable for drudge work as mortals who'd become addicted to vampiric blood. They would go to charming lengths to debase themselves for the sake of another sip, and could be counted upon to keep up boring chores for years on end if tended properly.) She could insert a few messages of her own without attracting any attention. Within the week, Lucita would have the information necessary to arrange her local charter and connect to the transatlantic carrier. A touch of cleverness in using appropriated phones and Lucita should be safe from surveillance. If only she didn't have that nagging sense of some other unseen watcher.

Sunday, 17 May 1198, just past midnight
On the Salzburg Road
Duchy of Austria

Lucita knew perfectly well, on an intellectual level, that no normal temperature could actually chill her. Her sire the bishop explained—and demonstrated—very early on how the subtle essence of vitae infuses the organs of the body, rendering them insensible to outside forces except in extreme cases. (He also demonstrated how the elemental force of fire draws forth a peculiarly intensified reaction from the vitae.) Nonetheless, this damp forest felt cold to her. She drew her cloak around her and wished once again for a carriage to replace the one they'd lost after its axle broke, four nights back.

Her companion didn't seem bothered. He rode with the natural confidence of a prophet, his long blond hair briefly glinting when moonlight stabbed through the shadows. In darkness, his eyes glowed faintly, with a red less reminiscent of blood than of altar candle flames. His tattered woolen tunic and trousers didn't conceal the taut movements of the body beneath. Even the random movements seemed purposeful, the controlling mind responding to realities beyond Lucita's perception. His speech continued in a calm but vigorous stream, sliding apparently without decision from French to Latin to tongues Lucita knew only by reputation.

"You see," he told her, "it is the height of pride to presume that one is ever beyond God's reach or grace. Consider…."

"But, Anatole," she interrupted. "The Church tells us clearly what are the cardinal sins. This isn't guesswork. This is knowledge. It is a fact that some actions, some conditions, put us beyond grace."

He smiled. "Is murder a mortal sin? It is. Is treachery? It is. And yet look: God chose Peter, who betrayed our Savior incarnate by his triple denial, to be the first Pope. Show me any sin, any sin at all, and I will show you a man or woman for whom that sin itself became an instrument of grace."

She pondered. "Monçada says that he is damned, and clearly he is wise in the faith."

"But he is just one man. Does God speak only to him?"

Lucita shook her head. As nearly as she knew, her sire had never claimed a direct word from God. He came to his understanding through the reasoned analysis of general revelation.

"There, you see? No one of us ever gets the last word. God is the Omega as well as the Alpha. God doesn't tell me some things He tells others. But then He doesn't tell others some things He tells me. And I tell you that none of us are beyond Him."

Lucita shook her head again. "That's easy to say. Yes, you can point at Peter. And I can point at David, God's favorite servant despite murder and all the rest. We can multiply examples. But…nowhere in Scripture or tradition can I find pardon for anyone whose very existence depends on murder, again and again." She had been undead for eight years, and the weight of conscience pressed very heavily on her.

Anatole laughed, a rich laugh that shook out through the matted strands of his blond hair. It was like, Lucita thought, sunrise above a stormy sea. At least she remembered the sun rising that way. "Do you remember what God showed Peter?"

Lucita didn't.

"Peter had a vision, while he lived in Joppa. God unfurled a great scroll, and on it were written the names of every kind of animal, fish, and bird, clean or unclean. God told him, 'Rise, Peter, kill and eat.' Peter protested that he'd never eaten anything unclean. God answered, 'What God has declared clean, do you not call unclean.'"

"But, Anatole, neither of us is trying to exist by the kashrut of the Jews anyway. What's the point?"

"Don't you see? The Holy Fathers tell us that the list included *every* kind of animal. No exceptions. So why do you assume that God didn't include the human animal? Do you not think that if He requires something of you, he will not make it lawful for you to do what He assigns you to do?"

shards

"But…don't we honor the martyrs who chose death over what they would have been compelled to do? Isn't it true that the courage unto death is one of the most precious gifts of all?"

"Do you feel God calling you to death?"

"Well, no."

"No, of course not. You feel the pang of condemnation, and that is the Adversary's voice. God calls us to repentance and good deeds, not to despair. Suicide is, remember, a mortal sin, because there is no repentance once it's done. If your heart troubles you, renew it in right acts. We, those who carry the curse of Caine, do not have the luxury of self-indulgence. The sins of the world are many, and we are few, and there is much work appointed for us."

Lucita rode on in silence.

Monday, 3 April 2000, 3:15 PM
Gunnison County Airport
Gunnison, Colorado

The call came while Angelica Tranh had her head and shoulders deep inside the Cessna's engine compartment. She ignored the cell phone at first, thinking to check the message later. She let the phone take the second one, too, a minute later. But when it rang a third time, less than two minutes after that, curiosity and irritation combined to make her answer.

Caller ID showed a Denver number and Cardinal Networks as the name. Oh, yes. Charter work. They'd sent around a creepy-looking lawyer back in February, who trolled all the available pilots for people willing to take sealed containers on short notice. Depending on the details, this might get a little awkward. But then the money was good, and they *had* offered a very comprehensive indemnity against hassles from transporting any restricted substances. "Tranh."

A woman with a German accent was on the other end. "Miss Tranh, this is Cardinal Networks calling. Are you available for discussion at this time?"

Angelica rankled. "Ms. And yes."

"Ms." The woman leaned on the "s" in a slow hiss. "We have a client who seeks transportation for objects of personal interest from your airport to London, via Logan International Airport. Do you retain an active certification for jet aeroplane operation?"

Where had this woman learned English? "Yes. What sort of schedule are you looking at?"

"The goods will be ready for shipment 40 to 48 hours from now. We would prefer a single pilot handle all aspects of the transportation, from receipt at your airport to delivery into the custody of our London agents. However, if circumstances prohibit you from making a transoceanic travel at this time, we can arrange for you to transfer the goods to a second pilot in Logan International Airport. There will be the customary percentage reduction in fee for the costs of securing secondary service."

Angelica thought about the contract provisions, and her schedule. She'd lose two tourist trips if she did it all. But one of those was a sexist pig of a self-styled skiing ace, and she wouldn't miss him trying to grope her again, and the other was a nice couple who'd have no trouble finding a replacement. Angelica could steer them towards friends of hers. "I'm available. But I don't have a jet, which is what you need for Boston to London, and...."

The woman broke in. "Cardinal Networks customarily arranges a Bombardier Challenger 604SP. We are not hiring you as an aircraft broker but as a pilot, and do not expect you to negotiate this matter. Is the Challenger an acceptable aircraft that you are competent to operate?"

Whoa. Angelica knew the plane; she'd hung out with and not quite dated a guy who flew one of the early units out of LA and Denver. It was classy. "It's acceptable, yes," she said in what she hoped was a controlled tone. So I'll fly to..."

"If you wish the use of our aeroplane as in accordance with the provisions of our piloting hiring of you, we will have a handler deliver it to you simultaneously with or before the delivery of the goods to be shipped."

"That's very acceptable."

"Good. You sound enthusiastic."

"Um, I am. This is a great opportunity for me."

"Good. That is our wish for all Cardinal Networks clients and associates." There was a brief silence, and a series of three beeps. "Do you have a preferred number at which to receive facsimile documents?"

"Um...."

"If you do not have personal access at this time to a facsimile machine, we can transmit the necessary information in other media."

"Yes, please. Plain-text e-mail to—" Angelica gave a business account "—will work just fine. That gets relayed to my phone and I can retrieve it here."

"Very good. Transmitting contact information. Do you have any questions at this time?"

"Er, yes." Angelica was trying to keep thinking as fast as the woman was moving, and it was hard.

"What information do you desire at this time?"

"What *am* I going to be carrying?"

The woman typed briefly. "Physically, you will be carrying one container, 2.8 meters long, 1.2 meters high, 1.2 meters wide. It weighs approximately 275 kilograms; appropriate loading and unloading charges are included in your fees. It bears security tags...."

Angelica cut in. "But what *is* it?"

No hesitation on the other end. "You do not need to know that, and your contract does not include a provision to require that information. You are indemnified against any and all charges that might arise for violation of law, regulation, or procedure at any destination or transit step of your contract. You are also, though this is not a provision of your contract, assured that you carry nothing illegal or restricted in international commerce. Is this a satisfactory answer?"

"I've heard better. But if you're serious about the indemnity..."

"We are."

"Then it'll do."

"Very good. Thank you for your service, Ms. Tranh. Review the transmitted information for further details." Then there was only the dial tone.

shards

Monday, 3 April 2000, 11:30 PM
(3:30 PM Gunnison time)
Museum der Arbeit
Hamburg, Germany

Willa Gebenstaler hung up the phone with a weary, languid gesture. She didn't like talking to mortals very much under any circumstances. She never liked talking to Americans. Least of all did she like trying to talk business with American mortals. Their thoughts were not orderly or systematic, their priorities seldom coherent.

The communications system had done its usual impeccable job. Spot checks before the actual call to Miss Tranh showed it processing a faked identity correctly, and Miss Tranh hadn't remarked directly or indirectly on anything unusual. Willa did enjoy throwing linguistic misdirection into her speech, like the mix of anachronisms and slightly wrong constructions she'd given the pilot girl just now.

Almost certainly the girl would have to go away after finishing this assignment. Not right away, that would be an invitation to trouble. Willa had done this sort of work before: set up at least two plausible sources of distraction in her life, raise the tension notch by notch over six to twelve months, and then do the removal. Nothing would connect the disappearance to Cardinal Networks; it would be one more statistic about millennial restlessness, irresponsible immigrants and the like. A little careful rumor-spreading would make Miss Tranh's disappearance seem something of a relief, and the rest was straightforward manipulation of law-enforcement data.

Madame! Madame was out there, and wanted Willa's help! *That* was the important thing. Willa could still scarcely believe it. The contact checked out. It was Willa's beloved mentor. What on Earth could she be up to in such a remote part of the world? Even for America, rural Colorado was unusually, well, rural. Not urban. Removed from Madame's favored mode of existence. Unsafe, even; Willa had heard that the were-beasts ran more freely in the New World, thanks to the lack of a proper organized effort to wipe them out.

Willa decided to take a small risk. There would be no overt communication back to Madame, but that case would bear a small note from Willa. Surely there could be no harm in that. Now, time to arrange the jet....

The pack didn't often bother with actually arranging accommodations from humans, but this time they needed space to spread out their haul from Lezinski's office. It was no particular trouble to get some money and rent a nice set of suites in a hotel catering to business travelers, many of them in the international trade and therefore on all sorts of hours. Boxes of bills, correspondence, and documentation of all sorts now lay strewn across the tables and beds in three adjoining suites. Each member of the pack started with subjects they knew something about, and gradually they converged on their mutual ignorance.

When the mantel clock in his suite chimed two, Andrew stood up and stretched. "Okay, time for a tally." The others looked up.

"First. What's the last document we've got that definitely did originate with Lezinski?" They rummaged for a few minutes. Niccolo produced a receipt for a crate delivered from Long Beach on February 26th. Everything after that date had initials or scrawls that could have come from anyone.

"Okay. Now, do we actually have a name for this other guy?" More rummaging. There were several letters in Chinese, which nobody in the pack spoke. "Great. So we've got to farm these out to someone else. Right. So, someone take a guess at a reconstruction."

Simon Peter spoke up. "It looks to me like two or more Cathayans have decided to set up shop in Los Angeles. They went for Lezinski because of his network of connections and resources."

"Good. Why 'two or more'?"

"Because our guy was writing to someone, and getting mail in Chinese from at least two origin points."

"Right." Andrew knew that Simon Peter saw himself at times like this as a master detective, something like the "blond

Satan" of Hammett's Sam Spade stories. (The prose stories, that is, not the Humphrey Bogart film version.) But if it helped the magician perform genuinely useful tactical analysis, Andrew was willing to indulge it. "Now, since we're not equipped to handle this, what do you suggest?"

"Well, we've got two options. First..." Simon Peter held up a clenched fist and used his other hand to pull out an extended index finger. Andrew wondered where on earth the magician had gotten that mannerism. "First, we bundle up all this and ship it to our loyal brethren someplace where they're equipped to translate Chinese and analyze the business stuff. Portland or Seattle, probably. We get on with our mission and let someone else reap the rewards that'll come from cleaning up after the Cathayans.

"Second..." Simon Peter paused immediately after pulling the clenched thumb upright. "Um..." He took a more formal stance. "Ductus, I propose to discuss matters pertaining to the well-being of our pack. I stand as a loyal and confirmed member of the Sword of Caine, whom you know through the blood to be devout and dedicated to the struggle."

"You're about to suggest something disrespectable, aren't you?" Andrew couldn't repress his amusement.

"I am, and I'd prefer not to be punished for bringing it up."

"Brother Simon Peter," Andrew said in his best formal voice, "I acknowledge you as a true and worthy comrade in the struggle, and I will listen to your words, so that you may speak honestly and without fear of reprisal. Now, proceed."

"We could send this stuff to a mortal translation agency," Simon Peter explained. "We'd probably have to kill them afterward, but that's the breaks for them. We could find out what's going on our selves and then clean up once our hunt for Lucita ends, one way or another."

Andrew saw the others nodding in agreement, and decided that one of two things would likely prove true. It might work, in which case they'd all reap the reward of independent initiative. Or it might not work, in which case he could stand back and let the others learn a potent object lesson. Either way, he was unlikely to suffer himself if he covered his ass with a bit of correspondence on the side. "I like the way you think," he said, and the magician beamed broadly. "Find me someone to send the load to, and we'll take care of it.

"Now, our other business. Anyone got any thoughts about the hunt, which is after all our real business at the moment?"

Niccolo held up a notepad that Lezinski had clearly added to over the course of months or even years, his handwriting varying from rigorous and precise to outright illegible. "Um, yes." He paused.

"Go ahead," Andrew said as patiently as he could.

"This is a list of shipments—a mix of guns and camping supplies—to 'K.' at a Death Valley post office box. And wasn't 'Konstantin' on that list of contacts we got?"

"It was." For once Andrew felt genuine approval for Niccolo, and let it show. "Good work. I actually went through that stack myself an hour ago and missed it. Looks like we're off to the desert."

Wednesday, 5 April 2000, 9:00 PM
Gunnison County Airport
Gunnison, Colorado

Angelica paced around the jet, admiring it from all sides. It was a marvel. A bit under 70 feet long, painted a smooth black with "Cardinal Networks" picked out in red with an unusual embossed effect, the plane seemed a creature from a world wholly other than Gunnison. It looked, frankly, like a movie prop.

Her colleagues were wildly jealous of the whole thing, and Angelica was loving it. She carefully refrained from outright denying any of their guesses, from Triad drug dealers to Silicon Valley sexual fetishists. Ben, the borderline schizophrenic, happily riffed on "Cardinal" with a tale of returning occult books to the Vatican so that the cardinals could perform the rites necessary to choose the next Pope correctly. Angelica very nearly managed to keep a straight face even for that one.

The guy who flew it in that afternoon, now, he was part of the scene: a burly, bearded African-American, maybe fifty years old, with tattoos for service in two wars and (if Angelica was reading the symbols correctly) at least two volunteer efforts in other people's wars. If he were to change out of that spiffy flight suit and into jeans or overalls, he could vanish into the crowd at the closest bar and nobody would ever find him again. Apart from his height, maybe. Angelica was used to pilots being taller than she—at five foot two she was usually at the bottom of any conversation. But this guy was *big*, well over a foot above her. She wondered if he'd been a basketball player.

Pity he was so very close-mouthed. Had he been to Gunnison before? "Yeah." Did he like the field, the town? "'S okay." Had he flown much for Cardinal Networks? "Some." What were they like, how did they treat pilots? "Okay." The usual crowd of locals gave it up as hopeless within fifteen minutes; Angelica gave it almost an hour more before admitting defeat and heading off to the weather room. He continued puttering around the jet, making minor adjustments, while she gathered up charts and looked over reports.

The flight times took a bit of getting used to. Gunnison to Boston in her usual plane would be something like fourteen hours in the air, plus three refueling stops. London wouldn't have been accessible at all. Everything changed with the Challenger. Three and a half hours to Boston, given a slight tail wind; no more than an hour at Logan for refueling and provisioning, the Cardinal contract explicitly authorizing the extra fees for expedited service; seven hours and fifty minutes to London and Heathrow.

A commercial airline wouldn't let a pilot do that long a continuous haul. But it wasn't actually unsafe with rest and preparation. Angelica had been getting her rest, and would take in a good meal while in Boston.

Once she had her charts in hand, Angelica made her second trip through the plane. The first had been a fairly hurried awe-struck loop. This time she took her time. The passenger cabin included nine seats and two couches. The cargo space was accessible through an elegant oak door at the back of the cabin. That was a little unusual in Angelica's experience, and made her freshly appreciative for the indemnity clause. (People who needed or wanted to spend a lot of time with the cargo in flight were probably not up to anything all that good.) The carpet and upholstery were rich black velvet, the trim redwood. There wasn't any visible synthetic material: the switches and knobs on controls were all polished brass and nickel, with redwood plates covering rubber fittings.

Suddenly a thought struck Angelica. The anonymous German woman said they *leased* the Challenger. Surely they couldn't have done a full customization like this in two days flat, less procuring time. It must be part of Cardinal's permanent fleet. She made a note to herself, to watch for other deception.

The cockpit wasn't as luxuriously appointed as the cabin, but just as expensive in its own way. The Challenger 604 normally takes two pilots. The SR series were adapted to single-pilot operation, but this cockpit took it all much further. The chair was a peculiar ergonomic design Angelica had seen reviewed in a pilots' magazine last year, with weird six-inch-long panels that were supposed to distribute back and leg stresses more efficiently. The controls were on a series of extensible panels so that she could arrange the whole instrument bank within arm's reach; with a moment's search she found knobs on the chair's arms to move the panels. There were six parallel grooves on the inside of the windows, and a little more experimentation found the knobs to raise and lower six almost invisibly thin tinted panels, each polarized in a different direction. With all six lowered, glare was almost completely removed at very little cost to overall visibility.

It went on like that. Someone put as much money as thought into this setup. They were trusting a lot to Angelica. Well, she thought while remembering the deception, they were putting a lot in her temporary control. Not exactly trusting her.

By the time she was done with checkout, it was just about sunset, and still no sign of the cargo. Her manifest said that delivery was guaranteed by midnight, but she hoped it wouldn't take that long. She really didn't want to be flying all night. For dinner she loaded up on salad and sandwiches in the Airport Diner, cheerfully fending off more envious speculation from the other pilots. No, she wouldn't let them tour the plane, her insurance didn't cover that. Yes, of course this meant she was hiding all the good stuff from them. Why, dear old Mr. Hoffa…but she'd said too much already. (That got a few laughs.) Only her closest confidants got to hear any of her uncertainty.

The big guy who flew the plane in came in for coffee, and then went back out to tinker with something around the wheel housings. He didn't speak to anyone.

Finally, at 9 p.m., a U-Haul drove up. Two young guys, both with the distinctive glazed look of men who really wanted to be back with their reefers rather than doing the job that would buy the next dime bag, got out of the cab and went around back to unload their cargo. It was a single case as described to Angelica on the phone. It was made of black impact-resistant plastic, secured with half a dozen steel bands, each secured with a pressure-pad lock. Angelica was reminded of musicians' instrument and amplifier cases—the thing looked very practical.

They tilted it up to put it on a dolly. Once it was ready to roll, the black guy stepped in with a nod and pushed it over to a small hoist at the back of the jet. A chain drive pulled him, dolly, and container up inside. A moment later he and the dolly came back. He handed the two young guys a handful of bills and watched them drive off.

"Call me a cab," he told Angelica.

"Huh?"

"Call me a cab. Package is ready to go. Plane's ready. You're ready. I gotta go."

"Oh, um, sure." Angelica called the first cab number she could remember and placed the order. "Fifteen minutes, they say."

"You go."

"Should I wait to see that you get picked up?"

"Nope. I'm fine."

"Okay, then. Er, see you sometime." He didn't answer, so Angelica climbed back up into the cabin and began her preflight checklist. Ten minutes later, she took off smoothly. The last sight she saw on the runway was that guy, watching her as she went.

Thursday, 6 April 2000, 12:45 AM
Over Pennsylvania

Lucita lay in her "traveling coffin," as she sometimes liked to call it, and listened to her pilot's thoughts. A slight tinge of hunger tainted Lucita's poise, but she'd fed generously before ordering those two boys to pack her up and she knew that she wouldn't really need to feed for several nights after her arrival in London.

Dependable Willa, as efficient as ever. This Angelica was an excellent choice, with enough intelligence and curiosity to find the temptations appealing, but not filled with the pride or destructive passions that would make her likely to turn on her employers. As long as Lucita and her agents treated her well, Angelica would continue to serve. No doubt Willa would want to dispose of the girl once this assignment was done, but Lucita had the nagging feeling that she'd have more travel ahead and would order Willa to refrain from termination plans.

Angelica's pleasure in flying the plane echoed comfortably in Lucita's mind. Lucita enjoyed this experience of mortal happiness, so bound up in being a soul in living flesh. Angelica wouldn't think of it, but Lucita could see how much basic sensual data, like pulse and sweat and skin temperature, all contributed to the intellectual and emotional satisfaction of flight. The cockpit's climate system and its constant adjustment produced changes in Angelica that she didn't consciously realize. Even the imperfections had their charm: Lucita could never be as occasionally clumsy as Angelica, for whom hormones and digestive processes could still disrupt a chain of nervous and muscular reactions. Being alive was such a *complex* thing.

Two taps on the computer screen mounted flush into the lid of her case let Lucita view the flight plans. She didn't like the thought of landing in London during the day, and considered arranging delays to keep Angelica from taking off until an hour that would guarantee night-time arrival…but no. That would require more complications than Lucita wanted to risk. She was using up a favor as it was with an old acquaintance in Boston, who maintained an interest in the transportation field. He'd see to it that the customs inspection was as quick as possible, and would provide cover just in case some local vampire somehow detected Lucita's presence. (Neither she nor he expected any such problem—vampires have better things to do with their time than scrutinize each of thousands of cargo containers every night—but it never hurt to prepare for bad luck.) He'd be willing, as part of the favor, to do things to keep Angelica on the ground for six to eight hours. But each added delay increased the risk that some outside party would notice and suspect something unusual.

Daylight landing was safer than that, all things considered.

That decision reviewed, Lucita gathered her thoughts for the London challenges. They wouldn't be easy, though she had confidence in them. London was a city unto itself in the night society as well as in the realm mortals knew. Its vampiric politics were convoluted and bizarre. If it hadn't been for one key fact, Lucita would gladly have gone elsewhere, but in the midst of all its infighting, the London court was unusually welcoming to or at least tolerant of vampires approaching the Camarilla from independent existences. It had established members willing to instruct the newcomers, guiding them in the paths of sect wisdom and guarding them from the threats facing vampires dwelling alone. It was easier to pass herself as such a newcomer there than anyplace else she knew of— certainly easier than in any other comparably sized city, and she wanted to see the Camarilla on its cosmopolitan home ground rather than its manifestation as a ragged band of inconsequential juveniles hiding in some backwoods town.

Thursday, 6 April 2000, 10:05 PM
Grand Court Hotel
Earls Court, London

At last it was time to come out. Lucita listened to the clasps coming undone one by one, and was aware that the case stood on end. The lid swung open smoothly, and she stepped out into her London quarters. As she'd hoped, her old comrade Stephen was the one waiting for her. Naturally, his features hadn't changed in the centuries since their last encounter, though he now concealed his heavily scarred head beneath a wig in a fashionable wave. As always, he was in the height of fashion, with a white suit highlighted in silver thread. He smiled a tight, closed-mouth smile as she recognized him.

"Hello, dear. Travel still suiting you?"

"As ever, Stephen. 'The greatest haven is motion,' as I believe you once told me."

He nodded his head briefly. "So I did."

"And yet here you are, looking distinctly stationary."

"Ah, but my *mind* is active, roaming the world on my behalf."

She laughed. "Very well. Tell me, now, how the arrangements went."

"Oh, not a problem." He withdrew a pocket computer and consulted it. "Unloading was no problem. Living History Productions took possession of one case's worth of video equipment from Cardinal Networks, and there's a customs officer who's quite sure she gave it a thorough going-over. I went to a trade show just two nights ago to refresh my memories, so it's all vivid and clear for her. Your pilot is in the next room, asleep. She thinks she had a good night out on the town and then chose this hotel because it was where she was when exhaustion and jet lag kicked in. She'll wait there for the time being, developing a slight but annoying stomach upset if she rouses before we decide what to do with her."

Lucita smiled again. "That sounds just right. I'll think about the pilot later. She did a good job, and I like the rhythm of her mind. I'd prefer to keep her around if it's not too much trouble."

Stephen made a note on a cream-white notecard. "Very good. Now, let's talk about the court. How much do you know about the current state of affairs?"

She paused. "Mithras has been prince every time I've been in London. You wouldn't ask that way if he still was. Who's taken his place?"

"Anne."

"Little Anne Bowesley? The little social climber with the Restoration obsession?"

"Yes."

"That's a surprise. What happened to Mithras?"

"That's…not entirely clear, actually."

"Since when is it 'not entirely clear' what happened to one of the oldest surviving princes?"

"We last saw him in 1941, during the Blitz. There were conflicting stories. Everyone who reported seeing his remains was one of Anne's toadies, so the question remained open. She took power, and mustered just enough support to hold onto it. Just a couple of years ago, the story got out with some hard confirming evidence that Mithras had been imprisoned, got out, and was destroyed while weakened by yet another enemy. This time we had confirmation from people who aren't Anne's. There were some power games after that, which ended with Anne in much more secure position and her most serious challengers in disgrace."

"So Anne is prince at last."

"Queen."

Lucita blinked, a deliberate signal of ignorance. "Queen Anne?"

"It's what she prefers," Stephen said dryly.

"I see. So what does Queen Anne think of Stephen the Lasombra?"

Stephen straightened and smoothed his suit. "Madam, I am one of Queen Anne's most devoted supporters. I am an unliving testament to the truth of the Camarilla's claim to represent all Kindred. My clan may be regrettably unfaithful, but I as an individual am beyond reproach. I am renowned throughout British

Kindred society for my intelligent service in matters regarding commerce and the arts. Though the public never sees me, I exert a constant, dignified pressure to direct mortal eyes away from Kindred affairs, through my various supporters and allies. I am the very model of an honorable *antitribu*."

Lucita laughed.

Stephen remained somber in expression. "You wound me, dear. It's all true, after all. The essence of the Camarilla is that all vampires trade a measure of self-determination and submission to the Traditions as formulated by our exalted founders in exchange for protection and community. I demonstrate in my person that although six clans provide *most* of the Camarilla's members, all lineages are welcome and that individual choice rises supreme over a legacy of unfortunate actions by one's predecessors."

"Oh, certainly, certainly. And I won't even bring up your not-so-honorable allies."

"Come now. I actually do help most of them. You've sent, what, six…"

"Seven."

"…seven little Lasombra my way over the centuries, and I've helped each one find some suitable shelter. Two are here in London as my adoptive childer, three are residing in other Camarilla cities, and two settled on hermit existences, and I supply them with books and supplies. You're not the only referrer I deal with, either. I was quite busy in the aftermath of that sordid affair on the American Atlantic coast, all those sieges and counter-attacks gone horribly awry. Do you think the Sabbat's leaders have any idea just how many of their rank and file made quiet departures in favor of sanctuary with the Camarilla? I presume not, or they'd be acting much more vigorously than they are. In any event, as I was saying, I spent half a year badly neglecting my own affairs, so great was the tide of new members to our happy band."

"And if you happen to shelter an occasional spy, who's to complain, really?"

"Dear," he said with real rather than playful seriousness, "surely you wouldn't want me to end my secret affairs just right now. It would, after all, be worth something to me to be known as the one who lured the infamous assassin into a trap and delivered her to Camarilla justice."

"Do you plan on doing that?" She thought she saw a spark of real madness in his eyes, and wondered if perhaps the cumulative strain of so many deceptions might be shattering his personality like a delicate vase in an earthquake. It would be sad to have to destroy an old associate to preserve herself, though she'd done it before and knew that she could do it again if necessary.

"Read and see." He stood with his eyes closed now, all psychic defenses down. Lucita closed her own eyes and swam through the turbulent ocean of Stephen's endless schemes. There were matters walled off from her, but they seemed to all deal with the identities of his other contacts and the occupations of his protégés. There was no hint of treachery toward her, and she didn't think he was good enough to hide it all.

"Thank you."

"Please don't question my integrity too often. Some century I might decide to take you seriously."

"I'm sorry, Stephen. It's a difficult time."

"Yes, well. Let's talk about you for a change." He laid out a passport and an assortment of other papers, and expensive accessories so gaudy that they looked like cheap knockoffs of themselves. Lucita handled them with a detachment that only an old acquaintance like Stephen could have recognized as disdain.

"So who am I to be?" Lucita slid into her professional attitude. This was a job; it's just that this time the client was one Lucita of Aragon, seeking information on the condition of Camarilla Lasombra in the example case of London. Like her predecessor, Anne might be (was) a paranoid maniac, but the London court remained relatively willing to accept individuals not avowedly part of the seven (six now, she reminded herself) usual Camarilla clans. Lucita would be a young American vampire, tragically dragged into the Sabbat but courageous enough to flee once she heard of the welcome that might await her in London if only she could make it there.

She paused for a moment to direct her mental "ears" at the next room. Angelica's thoughts soon came into focus:

Drifting. A pleasant party, and the tall man, Stephen, with the bright eyes. Flying high, above the atmosphere, no pressure, into the endless void of night, free forever from the bonds of the world. Rest. A busy night. A pleasant party. Drifting. The package safe. The return soon. Drifting. Into the void.

Nothing amiss there, Lucita thought; Angelica would be safe for the time being. She set the pilot out of her thoughts and began building up the role for herself.

A young American life, opportunity wasted frivolously. Merchants living in ways kings never dreamed of, their progeny trained to expect perfection. Filled with rage at any limitation. Lured by the image of perfection, that artful artless innate untouchability. The horror of the truth discovered too late, perfection now farther away than ever. Four…no, eight years in the bowels of the Sabbat just barely avoiding destruction again and again. Watching maybe-friends burn in failed flight, the fear night after night after night, the rumor of sanctuary. The growing knowledge of self leaking out into others through the Vinculum. Time running out. Stowing away on a second-rate cruise ship, struggling not to lose control. Then…

Now sunk into the role, Lucita buried, the young vampire persona asked Stephen, "How did I meet you?"

"Just around the corner from here, as it happens. You were wandering, trailing shadows out in public. Your mental defenses crumbled and I read the whole story. Three nights ago, that was. I put you up here and taught you rudimentary manners. Now it's time to present you…what was your name again?"

"El. Mom and Dad named me Elspeth, which I never liked, but the first part sounds cool."

"'Cool.'" Stephen was icily amused.

"Yeah, you know, cool."

"How very American."

The real Lucita surfaced then, El's broad flat vowels subsumed into archaic Spanish tones. "Thank you, Stephen. Is there anything else you need to tell me?" As she finished asking, El's confused expression and frightened jitters returned to the surface.

"Rather a lot, of course." Stephen turned to a previous page in his notebook.

shards

El looked up doubtfully at the Exhibition Centre. Its brazenly modern front clashed badly with the surroundings. She'd seen the same pattern before: Earls Court had been a fashionable neighborhood once, then gone down downhill and become the haven for successive waves of immigrants. Many of the white people around them had Australian accents, and something like half the people on the streets (at least late at night) seemed to be Middle Easterners of some sort. El didn't know much about such things (Lucita did, but that larger awareness lay at a distance from the senses), so she didn't quite know where they were from. But native British people looked pretty scarce.

There wasn't much night life around here. Pubs clustered around the Underground station and a few favored intersections; darkness held sway between them. The people moved with varying mixtures of anxiety, confusion, and despair. Nobody, as nearly as El could tell, went bopping through Earls Court after midnight in the midst of a good time. She overheard fragments of conversation about lost jobs, struggling to keep not-very-good jobs, the hunt for new jobs, the treachery of a friend or lover, the turmoil back home.

The Centre was lit up on all three floors. The windows were lightly frosted (or something; El didn't know the term, and the technique was one Lucita knew only in terms of its results), so no details showed, but El could see figures moving around inside. Two burly Arab guys guarded the doors, and their immaculate white suit coats didn't quite conceal shoulder holsters for big handguns. (Lucita made a note of that for later examination. As a suburban Midwesterner, El wouldn't think about a really thorough gun control regimen, but there might be hooks there in case Lucita or her allies needed future leverage.) El felt uncomfortable in this burgundy dress Stephen had recommended she buy, and would undoubtedly have fled if it weren't for Stephen's presence beside her. He moved with the quiet confidence of the man who owned all this, or could if he wanted to.

No hesitation marred his gait as he greeted the bouncers. "Good evening, Hakim. Good evening, Aloun. Is the Queen in tonight?"

They didn't open the door for him. "Sir, you know that we need to verify your identity. Your invitation, please."

Stephen smiled and held up a little gilt-edged card. It was red, in precisely the hue of blood.

"Thank you, sir. And your guest?"

"The lady is new to this fair domain, and comes under my protection."

The right-hand guy, Hakim if El had gotten the name right, bent his knees to look her straight in the eye. "You've got a clean aura, miss. Are you with the gentleman?"

"Um, yeah," El answered. "I mean, yes, Stephen said he'd take me to meet the court and stuff."

Hakim chuckled, a surprisingly high-pitched tenor sound that contrasted sharply with his baritone speaking voice. "'And stuff.' I'll just bet he did. And did he explain the rules to you?"

"Yes, sir. He told me to stay with him, to take directions from him, to not bother people, and to take directions from anyone he tells me is okay to give me orders. He said that if I behave and do what I'm told, I'll be okay."

Hakim nodded. "A little informal, but I think you've got it." He straightened up to address Stephen. "You and your guest are fine, sir. Please don't make any trouble for us, and enjoy your evening. We'll be formally closing at four, and anyone staying after then must have the Queen's authorization."

"Thank you, Hakim." Stephen waited. The bouncers swung open the doors, and Stephen stepped in, then turned to extend a hand to El. "Enter freely and of your own will." She didn't get the joke; he shrugged minutely.

The lobby was deserted apart from Stephen and El. Escalators ran up to the second floor, and the sounds of people visiting and a faint whiff of blood carried down. Stephen stopped at the foot of the nearest escalator up. He didn't look at El as he said, "Keep it clear and honest." She muttered something and followed him on up.

Half of the second floor was one big open space. It was full of people...vampires, El quickly realized, not one of them breathing. Even the servants were vampires, rather than ghouls or anything. There were at least two dozen vampires in the room. El tallied four men and one woman in servant's garb, black suits with bright brass buttons and scarlet shirts. In apparent age, the people present ranged from even younger than El herself to so decrepit she wondered how they could move, with most in sort of an indeterminate adulthood. Fashions covered the timeline from this year's hits as seen on the covers of the really expensive fashion magazines to outfits that El vaguely thought of as medieval, or at least really old. They seemed about evenly divided among men and women, with a few of vague or just plain weird gender; almost all were white, though she saw a couple of black people and one or two Asians.

The room had pastel blue carpets and vividly white walls and ceilings. Someone had hung fabric over the fluorescent lights: lengths of some woven material with heraldic patterns, so that there was pure white light between images and an effect almost like stained glass elsewhere. Dark wooden tables ran down the center of the room, with a narrow aisle between them. A raised platform opposite the escalators held four elaborately carved chairs, none of them occupied at the moment. Racks on each side of the escalators held coats and jackets, most of them very expensive. Neither El nor the quiet mind inside her knew many of the details of the hanging garb, but both knew enough to recognize individualized tailoring in designs that would be popular once the trend setters had their say.

The first person to speak with them was a man who seemed cut from the same mold as Stephen: completely dignified, a little taller than average, dressed in a suit that would fit into any decade after the general passing of tails on men's coats. He glanced at El with something far worse than hostility: a simple disregard, as though she had no more significance than the coats. El preferred destructive rage, where at least she seemed to matter to her attacker. The man gave her one look and then confined his attention to Stephen. "Good evening, Mr. Lenoir. How are things in the salvage trade?" His accent struck El as something that belonged in a BBC documentary, all the differences from American English carefully exaggerated.

"Thank you, Lawrence, I'm fine," Stephen answered. His always cool voice came out icy. "My enterprises flourish, and I've brought an outcast for presentation. Is the Queen in tonight?"

Lawrence didn't do anything so overt as sneer. "Regrettably, no, Mr. Lenoir. The Queen was in attendance earlier, so as to open the gathering appropriately, but had to leave more than an hour ago on another matter. In her absence, Sir Harold and I are attending to presentations."

"Very good. I'll speak with Sir Harold, then. I'm sure you have important matters to attend to among the drains." Stephen didn't sneer, either. El couldn't see either of them move at all, but sensed big tensions around them. In the Sabbat, a challenge to monomacy, the ritualized dueling, could happen at any point. Apparently they did things a little differently in the Camarilla, though the underlying dynamic was, as nearly as she could tell, just the same. Lawrence, whoever he was, stood stock still for what would have been two long mortal breaths, then paced off.

Stephen turned smoothly to El. "I imagine you found that entertaining. Putting my inferiors in their place is amusing in its way. But his threat is very real. Lawrence Dickell handles many of the Queen's contacts in mortal society, and with a few choice words he could ruin most of my network, perhaps even have me destroyed on some trumped-up charge. I balance between submitting to his whim and risking his expressed anger. Please restrain any impulses you may have toward wit until you understand the social dynamics at work. That should take anywhere from five years to a century or so." El just nodded.

At first El thought that the crowd was one big tangled mass, but as Stephen led her around the edges of the room, she could pick out patterns. Those four women, all in dark wool dresses, sometimes spoke with others, but always as a group. Those three, two men and a woman (as nearly as El could tell) in white fashions, carefully did *not* ever end up in the same little knot of conversation at the same time. Every few minutes they all gave a single nod in synchronization without looking at each other; El recognized mental powers at work. There was a set of four men and two women whose dress and appearance had nothing in common with each other, but they all wore the same pendant, a square in a circle with a triangle extending off to one side. (A clan marking, El supposed. She'd heard that the Camarilla fussed a lot more over clan than the Sabbat did, since the Camarilla didn't have the Vinculum to tie vampires together and needed artificial social structures to take its place.) She realized that Stephen was being very generous indeed with his five-years' estimate.

One of the few really old people present was apparently Sir Harold. Stephen raised a hand briefly, and the man nodded back. He must have been Embraced in his seventies, much later than the vampires El was used to. To El's untrained eye, he also had the look of someone who'd walked out of a BBC drama, with an old-fashioned suit and a silver-plated walking stick topped by a twisted mass that might once have been a coat of arms. His face reminded El unpleasantly of some of the nastier teachers she'd had, the wrinkles deep enough to end in dark shadows that could conceal any mixture of arrogance, perversity and outright rage. She found him interesting precisely because he was so forthrightly passionate, in contrast to the polished manners and affected calm all around him.

"Mr. Lenoir," the man said. "I see you've got another stray for us. As I gather Lawrence told you, Anne has left the scene, so I can handle the formalities, if that's acceptable to you."

"Very much so, Sir Harold."

"Then let's step to someplace private." Sir Harold turned to El with a coldly appraising eye. "We'll see if you know your manners. You don't look like the worst Mr. Lenoir has dragged in, at least."

The next few minutes only confirmed El's impression of a schoolmaster nature. In one of the small offices off the main room, Sir Harold grilled her about the "Traditions" as Stephen had explained them to her: somewhere between law and custom, much more like the folkways she'd grown up with in post-Rust Belt suburbia than the overt religious fervor of the

Sabbat. She passed his tests, apparently. Without warning, he said, "Very good, you are discharged into the authority of Stephen Lenoir, subject to review at the next solstice," and strode vigorously back into the main room.

Stephen smiled at her. "Yes, dear, that was success."

Friday, 7 April 2000, 4:42 AM
Earls Court Exhibition Centre
Earls Court, London

Dawn was still far off, but both Stephen and El felt the compulsion to sleep growing stronger in them. They stood on the street half a block down from the main entrance, watching the bouncers bid farewell to each departing guest.

"So," Stephen said. "What did you learn tonight?"

"I'm not quite sure," El answered. "It's really not what I thought was going to happen…"

"Yes? And how is that?" El jumped (slightly, but she really did jump) at the unexpected voice from not far behind her. She whipped around to find Sir Harold standing right on the edge of the streetlight's cone of light, smiling tightly.

"How'd you do that?" she demanded. "Stephen's all old and experienced, and I learned a bunch of things about ambushes in my time."

Sir Harold chuckled, a dry grating sound. "How old were you when the Sabbat found you? Twenty? Twenty-five? No more than that, certainly."

"Something like that, yeah."

"Well, child, I was more than seventy, and I'd given my entire life to deception in various forms. I learned how to conceal secrets from my closest associates for twice your mortal lifespan, how to move people and goods across the tightest borders mortals could construct…'tradecraft' as we called it. My colleagues and I were the people whose exploits were toned down for the sorts of spy thrillers you, or perhaps your parents, read."

"Um, okay. So being James Bond in real life makes you Super Vampire or something?"

"Something, yes." Out of the corner of her eye, El could see Stephen smile at that remark of Sir Harold's. She shrugged and wondered if it were just a guy thing. "In any event, Miss Elspeth, I am innately curious about social matters. What did you expect, and how did the reality differ?"

El felt a brief whisper in her mind, Stephen sending reassurance and permission. So she gathered her thoughts. "Sir Harold, you ever been to a Sabbat rite? One of the big ones, I mean?"

"I have indeed. It was in Moscow…just about the time you were Embraced, I suppose. I owe my continued existence in large measure to a few well-aimed blows against my assailants; I keep this commemorative cane as it is, twisted and all, as a reminder to myself. Mortal honors such as it represented mean nothing if one perishes for fear of damaging them."

"That's a 'yes'?"

"It is."

"Okay. So, you know, it's *intense*. Everybody's really into it, or they're supposed to be, and the Vaulderie makes it really hard not to be. You know?" Sir Harold nodded, so she continued. "We used to hear different stories about the Camarilla. Some said it was all stuck up, and some said it was like a religion or something, and some said other stuff. From what Stephen said, I was expecting it be calm. But it wasn't."

Sir Harold and Stephen both looked slightly surprised. El explained, "I mean, yeah, it wasn't a bunch of fights or anything. If there was any dueling going on, I didn't see it. But there *could* have been fights. The way Stephen talked with that other guy, it *could* have gone to fangs right there. And there's gonna be trouble later about it, am I right? Huh, Stephen?" She stared at him until he nodded.

She thought some more. "Partly it seemed strange because I couldn't really figure out why everyone was there. It felt like a business meeting or something, but all I saw was this conversation. The Camarilla doesn't get together just for tea-time or anything, does it?"

Stephen started to say something, but Sir Harold broke in. "No, Miss Elspeth. Had you and your guide come earlier, you would have seen the business portion of the evening. Queen Anne—"

"Hey, what's up with that?"

"I beg your pardon?"

"How come you got a queen instead of a prince or whatever?"

"She prefers it that way, and so far every challenger who'd depose her in favor of some other regimen has failed. We have a queen as long as she desires that we do."

"Gotcha."

"As I was saying before you interrupted..."

"Sorry."

"Very good. Queen Anne spent almost precisely two hours on the business of the domain. There were disputes over rights of access to favored hunting grounds, a question as to whether one of the city's newly created progeny was showing proper mastery of his responsibilities and, if not, what sanction might be levied against his sire, and so on. There was some discussion of possible Sabbat infiltration, as well," he said with a speculative look at her.

"Wasn't me."

"I believe you. The infiltrators in question, if they exist at all, are of a different breed in any event. I will spare you the whole tale of the Docklands dispute. Suffice it to say that yes, there was business to do and it was done. You arrived at the point where the remaining business is done privately, in whispers and code phrases in the midst of apparently innocuous conversation and the contest of appearances is the way we do the business of status assessment."

"Right. And there was all that other stuff, with the Gay Pride crowd..."

Sir Harold raised a hand. "Excuse me, Miss Elspeth. Do you refer to homosexual-rights advocates, or is this some American usage I'm unfamiliar with?"

"Yeah, that's what I mean."

"Then I'm at a loss. There are members of the domain in good standing concerned with such matters, but they do not bring contemporary politics into Elysium."

"But we were in..." El paused to look at the sign. "Oh, yeah, at the Earls Court Exhibition Cen-tre." She said it "sentree."

Stephen laughed heartily. "Come now, El. Remember your lessons. Elysium is the institution, which can convene anywhere."

"Oh, yeah. Okay, anyway, those guys and the creepy chicks with the pins, you must have seen them."

There was a moment of silence, then sharp, harsh laughter from both of the men. Each of them attempted to answer, only to succumb to fresh amusement. Stephen managed to regain his composure slightly ahead of Sir Harold. "El, those were the *Tremere*. Don't you have Tremere *antitribu* in the Sabbat?"

"Kinda. I mean, yeah, just not where I was. But I didn't see that thing as their logo. I used to hear that England had a bunch of queers. Does magic, you know, take gay tantric or anything?"

"No, child. That's a symbol of the union of fundamental forces under the magician's will."

"Are you saying that *isn't* a sex thing?"

"Yes."

"Okay. Anyway…they were all tense around Sir Harold and a few other people, and they had the kind of look that to me means 'I lost a fight and I'm gonna get back and win the next one.'"

"Stephen, have you related to your charge the history of the Queen and the Tremere?" Sir Harold demanded. Stephen shook his head. "Then I must congratulate Miss Elspeth on her perspicuity."

"My what?"

"You see things clearly."

"Cool. Anyway, there's all this stuff going on that *is* just like the fights we'd have around a big rite, it's just papered over with some politeness. The people in there seem just as messed up as the ones I ran away from. I caught little bits about Mithras and something about a fight with werewolves and diablerie this and justicar that, and it all sounds to me like the same old shit. I'm looking for a place that *isn't* just the same old shit. I don't really like being a vampire, but I'm not gonna go kill myself over it. I just don't want to get it all used up in stupid shit, you know?"

"I rather think I do," Sir Harold answered in an expressionless tone. El stared suspiciously at him, searching for some sign of a trick. "When I was a mortal man, I gave my devotion to two great causes. One died when I was still of middle years, and the other lasted only a few months after I drew my last breath. Now I hope only for survival. I want some day to stand on the surface of a cool, dark Earth on which the Sun no longer shines. To that end, I need above all security. I see the same turmoil you do, and it concerns me just as it does you."

He was going to continue, but El interrupted. "Either of you smell something strange?"

Neither did.

She looked around, but saw nothing out of place. The bouncers were still on duty; nearly all the other vampires had dispersed, apart from a little knot a block away (the women in wool dresses, she thought); no mortals roamed the streets at this hour. Then she looked up, and saw a misty form coming their way at faster than walking pace, gliding purposefully along above the streetlights.

"There," she pointed. "You see that?"

"Yes," Stephen said. "I think that we'd do well to be on our way home, where I'm better prepared to receive this sort of company."

Sir Harold bowed. "Madame, sir, it's been a very interesting evening, but I believe that I'll take my departure now. If you are on the brink of conflict, I wish to be well away. This is not the hour for a new mystery of any sort." He gazed calmly at El. "Whoever you are beneath the mask, I hope that you will remember me with a certain consideration when you act against London's undead."

El flinched. "Mask?"

"Please, madame or sir, don't insult my intelligence. It is a marvelous disguise. I don't know if you took the soul of an actual young Sabbat refugee or if it's remarkable impersonation. I doubt that anyone who hadn't lived as a traitor for decades on end would have noticed. Nor do I wish to know the details at this time. Good night." Sir Harold turned the corner, seemingly casual in his movements but almost immediately lost in shadows.

El looked worriedly at Stephen. "I do something wrong?"

"I think not. It's just him. Now, what's this about that?"

"Let's maybe head on out?" El felt relieved as Stephen led her back in the direction of their hotel. They walked steadily, and the absence of nearby pedestrians concealed just how fast they were moving.

Stephen surveyed the available shadows. "I take it you can hide yourself in darkness? You know the basics of our special affinity with shadow?"

"Sure."

"Good. Then I think we should perhaps make the rest of our journey away from prying eyes." He slid smoothly into the angles of a battered mailbox; she followed.

Less than a minute after they left solidity behind, the streetlights along the entire block flared more brightly, banishing nearly all of the available shadows. A faint whiff of blood descended over it all, until a momentary downpour of rain washed all lingering smells behind. Stephen watched the display and sent the thought to El, "Some ghost is unhappy with us. Time to go." Together they slid through the remaining shadows into one of the battered shops along the road. Once away from the street, they moved more quickly, with darkness prevailing almost everywhere, and in a few minutes they were back in the hotel room.

As she regained her material form, Lucita let the mask of El fall. She felt El's voice fade into the depths, ready for use again if need be, but slumbering. There was a series of rapid pops outside. Lucita peered out and saw the three nearest street lights shattered. "Someone's on to us, Stephen. Time to go, I think. Give me direction." Immediately she felt an intuitive sense for a small house in West London.

Again in shadow form, she slipped into the adjoining room where Angelica lay sleeping. The state of Stephen's wards showed that someone had tried and failed to force entrance, once from the street and twice from the hallway. Lucita extended her shadow-self around Angelica and a single suitcase, abandoning the rest to help foster the image of desperate flight. (Not just image, but she was willing to let their pursuer act on the belief in panic even when, as now, there was uncomfortable truth in it.) Then it was into the Abyss.

Outside time
The Abyss

A stiff wind blew up from nowhere, rising endlessly into nothing. Its direction shifted without rhythm, drawn toward outlets Lucita couldn't sense. The sharp edges of the void winds suggest columns like the fingers of some enormous hand. Her soul-self shivered in remembrance of the great thing her sire had summoned and lost control over. The Abyss was a peculiar realm, and she couldn't be too confident that it was altogether gone: it might survive as a single entity, or pieces of its memory and drive might now be embedded in other things, which would be glad enough to hunt her down and destroy her. Very little of will was ever lost for good here, where there was no substance to erode it.

Shards of will whirled up and out of the wind. Stephen's steady mental beacon seemed almost obscured beneath the tumult of pieces of Abyss awareness, reminding her of mosquitoes and gnats she'd encountered in the Louisiana bayou. So far the pieces didn't seem to have any particular intent toward the travelers; that could change at any moment, and she sensed Stephen's knowledge and concern paralleling her own. Angelica slumbered on.

Lucita wondered if anything was responsible for the tumult, and if so, what. Sometimes, she'd heard, the Abyss had activity for no reason apart from itself. She remembered trying to explain the experience to Anatole, and his answer consisting of quotations from the book of Job. When she demanded if he thought the Abyss was in some sense equivalent to God moving in the deeps, he said, "Of course." They hadn't talked about the matter again for a long time after that.

On the other hand, some big applications of the clan's shadow power could and did create effects in the Abyss. There had been tremendous storms in the year that ended with the Antediluvian's destruction. (If he was gone. If they were ever gone. The fear stirred again in her that she would always retain her sire's mark, and if he could do that, what might not the founder do?) Storms flourished the year Cappadocius perished, too, despite the insistence by Lasombra elders that they had nothing to do with the Giovanni coup. If this void weather were related to something in the material world, it could be most unpleasant. She resolved to investigate when she had some free moments.

There. The location she sensed with Stephen's memory drew near. Far "ahead" there was something powerful, not quite charging them but gathering its forces for some undoubtedly unwanted attention. Lucita was relieved to step out of the Abyss, back into the world.

Friday, 7 April 2000, 11:02 AM
West London

Angelica didn't realize she was a prisoner at first.

She woke to late morning sunlight and a gorgeous view, northeast across parkland toward the heart of London. She didn't quite remember where she was, and stirred to find herself wearing most of what she'd had on the previous day, tucked in carefully into a queen-sized bed with what felt like silk sheets. Red wood panels glowed in reflected sunlight, setting off the stark white of the sheets and comforter. There was no furniture other than the bed itself, not even a chair, she saw as she spotted her shoes and windbreaker neatly folded in a corner of the room.

Jumbled memories of the party last night sloshed in her mind as she got up. Judging from her attire, she hadn't gone to bed with anyone else, and that at least was a relief. She'd tried pick-up partners back in her city days, never with good results. It was vaguely reassuring to find that her libido apparently retained a bit of control even when her higher functions all went wherever they'd gone last night. The first door she opened led to a fully furnished bathroom, and she took the immediate opportunity to get clean. There were peculiar chilled patches on her skin, almost like precursors to frostbite, but warm water and some expensive lavender soap returned them to normal temperature.

The first clear sign of trouble came when she tried to open the other door. It was locked, without any obvious way to unlock it from this side. She tried tugging, pulling, slipping in a credit card, even getting out her pocket screwdrivers and going to work on the bolt plate and hinges, all to no avail. Someone else would have to let her out.

So she knocked.

To her surprise, the door opened within seconds. In the hallway (with the same red wood paneling, she saw in a quick glimpse) stood a man of indeterminate years whose features bore a strong resemblance to Stephen, the man who'd met her at the airport. He wore a dark suit and lightly tinted glasses.

"Hello," she said in her best professional voice. "I'd like to thank Stephen for his hospitality, if he's up, but it's time for me to be on my way."

"You're not supposed to be up." His voice came out smoother than those sheets, polished and calm.

"I didn't know there was a timetable. In any event, I *am* up, and I need to make my return flight, thanks very much. So if you'll just let me past…"

Her effort to barge past him didn't work. He stuck one arm in front of her, and running into it was like running into an iron bar. She barely had time to see four more doors, two on each side of hers, and stairs leading down at one end of the hall, before he flung her back into the room. A single twitch of that arm sent her sprawling.

"You mustn't leave. The master hasn't authorized it." Angelica couldn't hear any hint of strain in his voice, despite that amazing feat of strength.

Now she began to worry. "Thank you for your concern…" She paused in hopes that he'd provide a name. He didn't. "…whoever you are. I'm sure that you mean well. But I am a guest here, and it's not your place to keep a guest from leaving. So I'll just be on my way."

"No."

"No?"

"You will not be on your way. It is my place to keep you from leaving. You are not a guest. I do not mean well in any sense that would make sense to you. I am not concerned about you. You are wrong in every particular."

Fear spread through her chest with icy tendrils far colder than those spots on her skin. "This is kidnapping."

"In a sense."

"In a *sense*? What *else* would it be?"

"Hunting. Destruction of your will. Experimentation. Worship. The master has many interests, which he does not always divulge to me. I don't need to know his end to know that the means to it require your continued presence until he gives leave otherwise."

Something strange was happening to the man's features.

144

No single feature changed in a way she could pinpoint, but he become altogether more ominous. He seemed to loom larger, despite remaining where he was. Angelica felt herself on the brink of a full-blown panic attack, the sort that hadn't crippled her since refugee days. "Stay," he said. "I will bring you food. Do not try to escape, or it will not go well with you." He somehow slid back out of the room without his legs moving, and the door swung shut. She heard a key turn in the lock outside.

Angelica sobbed, despite her best efforts to fight back the tears.

Andrew looked over his new pack's handiwork. Not bad for a group still learning how to work together most effectively, he thought.

Niccolo might be—scratch that, *was* an utter imbecile, but he could follow orders when given clearly, and he turned out to have a real flair for mechanical work. It only took him a few minutes with simple tools and a truck stolen from a farm supplies shop to turn two cattle crossing gratings into a nice little spring-loaded trap on one of the side roads.

Barry did a great job of completely shattering the will of a crew trying to perform night repairs on a phone cable junction. He had them utterly cowed and willing to take any orders, while leaving them enough will to not sound like robots.

Roxana screened off the area around Andrew's project with a minimum of fuss. She didn't just conjure straight blackness, but a subtle fading into black that masked the road from the highway without making it obvious that anything unusual was going on. She also had enough mental presence to quietly turn away drivers' thoughts about the road, again without hammering home the idea that they were being manipulated.

With a few brief passes over blood taken from the tourists they snagged off the freeway the night before, Simon Peter could speak into a metal cone a little like a gas mask and have it come out as radio or telephone signals. Andrew was skeptical, but Simon Peter took it in good cheer and performed enough different operations to convince the ductus. Andrew would really have preferred that the magician look somewhat less like a Looney Tunes version of the young David Byrne, but talent goes where it goes.

Tonight they were ready.

Tracking wasn't something Andrew felt particularly competent at, but he certainly wasn't going to tell his packmates that. If they could pick up any of his concerns through their Vinculum bonds, they were welcome to the knowledge; otherwise it was his secret. When Cardinal Timofiev gave Andrew the assignment, what else was a new bishop to do but nod and go along with it?

The paperwork trail that began with Lezinski's files led them on alternating bouts of road trip and records searching. Andrew began to wish passionately for a ghoul he could assign to the office work part, after the third round of poring over old tax and property rolls in search of "K", Konstantin, or anything else suggestive. When the pack finally got its break, it didn't even come from human records at all. Consultation with a couple of nomadic packs who used the desert as hideout between forays into California cities turned up stories of a cantankerous Lasombra with a desert stronghold. He wasn't precisely Sabbat, but was at least willing to observe some of the formalities; rumor had it that he observed developments in California for an elder somewhere else. He seemed precisely the sort of odd-man-out with whom Lucita preferred to deal.

Andrew didn't really expect anything to come of this stunt, but it was something to do, something to bind the pack together with some constructive experience. Actual leads would be welcome fringe benefits.

So here they were. Barry led off, getting information from his phone crew victims about the not-necessarily-marked side roads leading off into the desert. The pack scouted out half a dozen routes for their ambush, finally settling on the one that seemed to run most directly into rocky, completely undeveloped land. Barry worked with Niccolo, or rather, he directed the victims to work with Niccolo, on rigging an ambush. Any vehicle driving along that road would be pinned down and torn up in a matter of seconds, its tires spiked and most of its undercarriage run through. While they worked their mechanical arts, Roxana performed a series of rituals to block off the road's junction with the main highway in layered shadows. Andrew tested the results, and was pleased; even with the blood linking him to Roxana, he could barely see the side road.

As Andrew drove, Simon Peter worked his own blood magic, laying out lines around their car's cell phone and drawing smoky trails in the air. His first effort at signaling sounded horribly fake, but with some refinements, he convinced Andrew that, yes, he wasn't boasting too much about his command over broadcast transmissions. Well, that wasn't precisely true. He *was* exaggerating—Andrew could tell the signs of false starts and repeated efforts—but he still got results.

Everyone was ready well before midnight. Andrew wrote out messages to send, and Simon Peter went into a trance while beaming them into the hills where Lucita's maybe-ally was supposed to dwell. "Mr. K…Mr. K…the lady calls…trouble in Los Angeles, she cannot come…Mr. K…Old Scott Road junction…Mr. K…" The rest was a matter of time.

Konstantin liked to keep a police scanner on most nights, just to keep aware of what trouble there might be around him. He hadn't survived this long by taking unnecessary risks. It wasn't any big surprise when the receiver crackled to life. This was the time of year when increasing numbers of idiotic would-be outdoors aces got themselves into trouble, and when would-be drug kingpins tried blazing new routes around choke points in existing distribution networks. The area's police forces were pretty good, and Konstantin expected any report of trouble to be followed in fairly short order by the terse summary of resolution.

This wasn't anything like that.

The signal wavered. Konstantin suspected that the operator was twiddling knobs without having much clue what any of the labels meant. A little more jiggling and the thing wouldn't have worked at all. Then there was the content. Mr. K? The lady? Trouble in Los Angeles? Konstantin knew the names of all the other permanent and regular temporary residents in the area, and he was the only Mr. K present at the moment. It could be for someone else, but the odds seemed somewhat slim for that.

Lucita had left him heading east, up toward the Rockies. But then that was a week ago. She could easily have flown or even driven around to the west. Would whatever she was after take her into that mess in Los Angeles? Well, yes, it might. Konstantin remembered the fear in her, and her anger at his insight. She could have gone off to fight Cathayan vampires purely to prove her own martial prowess to herself, or have taken a risky, dangerous job, or have acted upon impulses outside Konstantin's sphere of knowledge.

Would she have sent someone technically inept to broadcast a clear-signal call for his help? That took more thought, and raised more suspicions. In sufficiently dire extremes, of course, anyone might have to serve, with a quick mental push to get rudimentary information into that hot brain and a command to move fast. Konstantin looked at the clock, and did the math. Yes, if Lucita had given the order about the time she woke, a fast driver could have gotten in position. Or perhaps the driver had come up the night before and needed some time for healing; that panicked edge might reflect massive blood burning after equally massive trauma. It might even reflect recently broken conditioning, Konstantin thought while remembering some victims of the Sabbat wars of the 1930s.

It was the combination of factors that made him decide to go check it out. He didn't feel comfortable ignoring it. It might well be a trap…but then anyone who knew or guessed enough to realize that a call suggesting Lucita needing help was someone who would find him one way or another. He'd never given sign, that he knew of, that he had any connection to or interest in Lucita, and that above all inclined him toward a provisional belief. He put on heavy leathers, gathered up a pair of .45 pistols and a pocketful of bullets, and set out in his Land Rover parked down the hills from his home.

The stars were brilliant overhead, while thick white clouds ringed the horizon. From space, this must seem like a clear spot in the midst of general cover. Konstantin thought about that, and wondered if it might indicate magical trap-setting at work, but there were no disturbances impinging on his psychic senses. Again, anyone who could manipulate the weather that thoroughly and not leave a sign would find him one way or another. He preferred to advance toward confrontation rather than try to flee a superior enemy, knowing that motion gives a certain strength of its own. No sense of impending doom tickled his back brain; neither did any real sense of confidence. He disliked the unknown, and hoped to make it known as soon as possible.

The call for help stopped half an hour after he began driving. He didn't need to look at maps to figure out which junction the caller had in mind—it was an obvious place to turn off for anyone who knew "he's in these hills" but not much more. So obvious, in fact, that suspicion rose again. Wouldn't Lucita give more specific directions, so as to make it clear that the messenger knew what he was doing? Then again, wouldn't she know how nervous he'd feel about strangers showing up on his doorstep, or anywhere close? Logic could only lead him in increasingly vicious circles on questions like this. Intuition told him to proceed—cautiously, carefully, but still to proceed.

Simon Peter took off the dark glasses he'd been wearing to "simplify the inputs" and looked around for Andrew. "I've got something."

"Yeah?"

"I'm getting some feedback from the calling."

"Can I get subtitles for that?" Andrew tried to strike a balance between aggression and interest.

"I can tell that the calls I'm sending out are being received, and that the receiver's coming this way."

"The loner?"

Simon Peter looked exasperated. "I don't know. Trying to scry through the link would take a whole different ritual, and I'm short on blood."

"Okay. This is new to me. How much can you tell about the receiver?"

"Not a lot." Andrew stared at Simon Peter until the magician explained some more. "It's one source, but I can't tell how many people are listening. It's moving pretty fast and way low, but that doesn't mean for sure that it's a car; could be a helicopter. But you can see for yourself in maybe fifteen minutes or so."

"Okay." Andrew strolled away with deliberate calm, and paced around the trap. Everything seemed in order. The others watched Simon Peter, with occasional glances toward Andrew just to see if he were getting upset over anything.

Silence returned. Andrew noted with pleasure that the pack members moved with almost-normal speed but attention to footing detailed enough that he had to really strain to hear them. They were taking their lessons well. Barry held one of the phone guys while Roxana cut his head off with three quick whacks from the Bowie knife she carried. Andrew started to object to the mess this would make, then paused to watch. Roxana, Barry, and Niccolo took turns drinking the head and body dry. When the whole corpse was blanched pale, Roxana wrapped it with a ball of shadow that thickened and compressed it into a small, dense bundle. Niccolo threw it in the back seat of the phone truck. It was clever and careful, and Andrew took a moment to quietly praise Roxana. He wasn't entirely sure, but he thought she might have smiled for a moment.

Her complexion now shot through with vivid slashes of fresh blood just beneath the skin, Roxana carefully enhanced a few shadows on the highway side of convenient boulders, providing enough cover for the pack and two or three extras each. It all looked very natural, but if the loner (if this was him coming) did suspect trouble, he'd have to waste a lot of time checking duds. Andrew settled down for the remaining minutes. He focused on enhancing his own strength and melding it with what his old pack had called "shadow stilts" and the newcomers just called "dark crutches." With the darkness to surround his twisted limbs, he could run with the best of them and kick down doors with no trouble.

There, a car was indeed approaching.

No headlights, Andrew noted without surprise. That was just as he expected: anyone capable of surviving out in these boondocks couldn't be too dependent on light in the first place. Up over one hill, down into the trough, up another; at first all Andrew could make out was the solid mass of the thing. Details came gradually, in gleams of starlight and a little gentle probing through shadows.

The thing was big, the mature older brother of a typical sports utility vehicle, built for real work with no regard for play. Andrew recalled reading about the general class of "mountain truck" back in his living days, vehicles built in small lots by veterans of vanished companies like Hudson and Tucker, men who didn't care to keep up with the competition and tried to eke out a living plying their craft for appreciative specialized audiences. This particular vehicle looked like it might have begun life as the mad dream of a tired tank driver who yearned for speed along with armor. Andrew was very glad, as the mountain truck came over the second-to-last hill, that they weren't going to try shooting at it, and that they had supernatural support for their physical traps. The truck was painted a light gray which contrasted sharply with the overlay of dust under the moonlight. Not many dings or dents, and Andrew wasn't sure if that meant the vehicle just didn't *get* them or if the owner fixed them promptly.

Just one person visible inside, from what the pack could see. It appeared to be a man, but the pack knew as well as anyone that appearances were usually deceiving. Simon Peter murmured something Andrew couldn't hear, but which sent the driver into a fit of banging on the dashboard where a radio presumably was, fiddling knobs and looking frustrated. Close enough now for Andrew to see the long hair, lean but tough build, and ageless maturity common to so many vampires.

The carefully wrecked phone company car lay half off the road, with the still-living technician unconscious inside. The truck slowed to a stop, the driver braking with the obvious intent of getting out some distance away, maybe fifty feet. Unfortunately for him, the trap was more like a hundred fifty feet away.

The springs went first, shoving spark plugs and bolts up through a thin layer of dark-shrouded dirt toward what would have been all four tires on a car not quite so long. As it was, they ripped half a dozen holes in the front tires and sent a shower of debris into the undercarriage a foot ahead of the back tires. Puffs of smoke showed where the exhaust pipe was punctured. Immediately the car began slewing, and the driver's jamming on the brakes only made it start to spin.

The second wave of attack began. Two massive capacitors with feelers sprang up out of the dirt and discharged their loads right into the truck's frame. Anything that was even mildly flammable on the bottom half of the car burst into flame. Sparks flew in a shower out of the dashboard, and the driver jerked up his hands in evident pain and surprise.

shards

The third and last wave of attack had just one component: a hastily welded mass of cattle-guard prongs, forced up by small explosives taken from seismic monitoring sites. An irregular grid of solid steel bars jammed into the truck. The drive train shredded in a lethal hail of gears, and slight differences in strength at the ends of the grid gave a little extra impetus to the truck's left side. It rolled sideways, then end over end, then sideways again. To Andrew's relief, the rolling wreck didn't burst into flames, but the acrid stench of gasoline signaled that it could only be a matter of time before an explosion would light up the night sky.

Andrew and his pack were on their way towards the wreckage before the truck stopped rolling. Roxana dropped their local cover, while continuing to maintain the cloak isolating the whole scene from the highway, so everyone had good lighting as they crossed the irregular ground. Some of the roadside bushes, showered with sparks and gasoline, began burning along the way. Andrew leaned around them; Niccolo made a show of jumping over the ones in his way. Niccolo and Simon Peter on the passenger side, Barry and Roxana on the driver side, Andrew looking under the hood at the windshield, they pulled in unison. The shredded doors dropped behind the vampires, while shards of very much un-safety glass tinkled down to the dirt and gravel. Andrew himself grabbed the barely conscious driver and pulled him across the glass, out into the open.

Andrew spoke for the first time since the action began. "Check the truck. I want to get this one up for questioning." He used four shadow arms to hold the guy still (not that there was any resistance, yet) while dragging him over to the remains of the phone company car. The pack members did a thorough job shredding the truck's interior, finding nothing of interest and leaving no space for anyone to hide in any material form larger than microscopic size. Just as they finished, two rumbles gave warning of impending trouble. They backed away in time to avoid anything more than singing when at long last the truck did explode. Andrew suspected from the size of the fireball and level of shielding around the fuel tank that it must have been something rather more potent than straight gasoline.

The loner lay dazed, just barely conscious. Andrew still kept the bonds as strong as he could make them, just in case. (And if the loner were a lot more than he seemed, it might not do any good anyway.) Time for some questioning.

Saturday, 8 April 2000, 1:00 AM
Bushy Park, West London

Lucita had entered Angelica's room more than an hour before, and observed quietly as part of the shadows. She hoped to use the pilot for the rest of her search, and needed to see how the woman dealt with adversity. Stephen's ghoul told her and the master of the house about Angelica's show of resistance and crumbling; Lucita found it a little disappointing, but then there were uses for very malleable people as well as more stubborn ones.

Angelica woke from a tearful slumber shortly after midnight. Her aura radiated fear leavened with encouraging traces of anger. Lucita watched as the pilot took careful stock of her possessions, spreading around everything pointed (keys, nail file, a small knife, jeweler's screwdriver) into separate pockets for possible use as a weapon. Then Angelica made a second pass to check for loose pocket flaps and anything else that might make a convenient grabbing point, turning her collar in, tucking in pants. Lucita recognized the movements of experience, and wondered just where the pilot had done her dirty fighting. Once she was secure in herself, Angelica examined the room carefully. She didn't touch the door or windows, but felt around them and examined them from various angles, looking for security measures and any exploitable weaknesses. All of this passed in what was, for a mortal, remarkable quiet.

After making two complete passes through her room, and spot checks several more times at key points, Angelica sat down on the bed to wait for whatever came next. Lucita continued to watch as Angelica pursued a variety of tasks which kept her lightly occupied but not too heavily distracted: buffing and trimming nails, putting her hair up in a close braid, unraveling the bedspread's hem and checking for concealed layers. Lucita saw the anger in Angelica's aura grow, crowding out other emotions, and watched as fatigue dimmed it all. When the moment seemed right, Lucita drew herself out of the shadows.

Angelica didn't speak. She clutched her scissors and knife and charged. Lucita put her hands out, each one seizing one of Angelica's and forcing the woman down to her knees with simple twists. "I will speak with you."

The woman continued to struggle, Lucita noticed with a certain admiration. "I will speak with you," she said again.

"You're going to kill me. Get it over with."

"When I decide you should die, you will die promptly. In the meantime, will you listen?"

"You want my soul, and it's not yours. Though I walk through the valley of the shadow of death I will…"

"Stop that." Lucita spoke with the tone of command, and the psalm dried up in Angelica's mouth. Nothing she tried to repeat from Scripture could take form. Other words were fine, only the Bible was denied her.

"You come from Hell. Take me now, if you can, or let me go."

"I have spent a very long time staying out of Hell. I propose to keep on doing so, and I have no desire to send you there or anywhere else in the lands of the dead. Listen."

"How can I refuse?" Despair washed through Angelica's aura and her body. Her posture began to slump. Now was the time.

"Cardinal Networks. You know the name."

That caught the woman off-guard. "Yes, of course. Are they part of your scheme?"

"I created the company, two centuries ago, to help me in traveling. Then it was a matter of carriages and ships. It's still a matter of ships, but now trucks and planes as well."

"Why *me?*"

"I didn't choose you. That was…"

"Then who did? Was it the other devil, the one at the airport? The one in the hall?"

"My administrative assistant chose you. She looks for people with talent and few attachments, who show the personality traits she knows I look for."

Angelica thought about that. It was all starting to sound increasingly unlike the fiends that the preacher had described in church long ago. Surely the devils don't have secretaries.

"If you think you can cow me, your 'assistant' didn't do her job right."

"Just the opposite," Lucita explained. "She looks for people who seem likely to remain courageous and clear-headed in the midst of difficult circumstances. My existence has too many moments of…excitement, and they often call for a measure of self-determination. You showed yourself the right sort of person just now, with your defenses and scouting. That was very good." She saw Angelica try to hide a flinch of surprise. "Yes, I saw it all from the shadows." Lucita shifted her stance slightly, less poised for fight now, more like a human soldier's "at ease" pose. Angelica relaxed slightly in response—probably without realizing it, Lucita thought.

"You fly planes." Lucita waited for Angelica to acknowledge the statement, with a single nod. "You enjoy flying planes." Another nod. "You want to fly planes in challenging circumstances, with the freedom to ignore petty concerns." The nod came more slowly this time. "I want you to fly planes for me."

This wasn't what Angelica expected. She didn't want anything at all to do with the devils, or whatever they were, and she worried that an offer of the one thing she might consider doing for them was a temptation or trap. Her soul, if it was there, gave off no warning signs…but then that was the whole point of temptation, wasn't it, to overcome resistance and win acceptance? "What if I refuse?"

"One of two things. You might or might not get a say in which of them it is. The first is that we kill you. One of us would drink your blood and dispose of your corpse somewhere nobody would ever find it. You'd go down in official records as one more rootless vagabond, probably up to no good, who ran into more trouble than she could manage."

Angelica drew on memories of standing firm as a child in the face of official interrogators and death squads, trying to speak calmly. "And the other?"

Lucita simply stared at for a moment, then said, "Circle." Angelica rose without conscious thought and began walking in a circle in front of the bedroom door. When she realized what she was doing, she tried to stop. And couldn't. She could turn her head, swing her arms, move any part of her body in any way as long as it didn't interfere with the circling. The more she struggled, the less she could even envision the sequence of actions necessary to stop it: it was now a given in her universe, as fundamental as the need to breathe.

But then the fiend didn't seem to be breathing, either.

"What is this?" she thought to ask, after minutes of futile struggle.

"Willpower," Lucita answered.

Angelica gave up and surrendered to the circling. Now her body dragged itself around and around, the command extending so far as to hold her spine erect even as her shoulders and neck flopped. "This is worse than death."

"Some find it so," Lucita agreed. She was about to continue her demonstration of the options available should the pilot refuse to cooperate, when the window suddenly squealed. Lucita turned to see the misty form from earlier in the evening pressed up against the glass, a gaping maw and taloned hands emerging sharply and clearly from the body's fog. Twin scratches ran the length of the window, and the panes visibly buckled as the thing pressed against them.

There was no time for conversation. Lucita scooped up Angelica under one arm, strode into the hall, and barred the door as best she could. "Stephen!" she called out. "We have a problem!"

Stephen was standing at the bottom of the stairs by the time Lucita reached the top; his bodyguards stood close behind him. "Yes? What kind of problem?"

"The ghost from the Centre is back. It's clearly hunting me in particular. I need to get out of here without attracting its attention, and I need to know whether you and your knights here can take care of it."

"I believe we can. At least, if we can see it, I suspect I can cow it into flight, and perhaps force it to reveal something useful about who sent it. A closet necromancer in the London court…very interesting…but that's for another time. Yes, there's a way out through the basement that will let you make your way far from here." Stephen was worried, and didn't bother hiding it. "Do you think there will be follow-ups?"

"I haven't the foggiest idea," Lucita said. She could hear more scratches on the window, but there was no sound of shattering glass yet. The ghost might be very determined, but it seemed to lack much tactical judgment. "I suspect that it was a spur-of-the-moment venture from someone who wasn't entirely sure he recognized me. It doesn't have the calculation of a well-planned assault on a notorious independent elder." She looked down at Angelica, who squirmed with increasing vigor. "Stay calm." The pilot immediately went limp.

Angelica couldn't control her body, but her mind remained alert for the moment. The conversation struck her as even stranger than what had happened so far. Someone was attacking the female demon with a ghost, and she and her male companion sounded like they were reviewing shopping lists. They did move along, down the stairs, through two halls to the kitchen, and down into the cellar, but it all felt detached somehow. Were they insane as well as evil, or what? She couldn't make sense of any of it.

Stephen came to a halt in a remote corner of the cellar, next to old wine racks. A simple square metal plate lay in the floor. "Give me a hand," he said to one of the ghouls. The man stepped forward, and the two of them hefted it up and over, revealing a ladder descending into darkness. "Down you go, m'dear," he told Lucita.

"Are you sure you'll be all right?"

"Oh, I think so. My experience with ghosts is more theoretical than practical, but I have strategy on my side. And I look forward to finding out who of my fellow subjects of Good Queen Anne turned this thing loose. I believe someone has just given me substantial leverage." He didn't actually rub his hands, but that was simply because one still lay underneath the plate.

"Thank you," Lucita said simply. "I'm sorry to have put you to this inconvenience. I didn't expect your hospitality to face such a violation, and I will make amends when I can."

"No doubt, but we can discuss reparations another time. Go now." He handed her a small flashlight.

Lucita went. When she reached the first landing, still carrying Angelica, Stephen and the ghoul put the plate back.

"Light our way," she told Angelica, and the limp pilot did her very best, as with the other commands she'd been given. Together they made their way through a brick-lined channel, ever deeper into the bowels of the city.

Lucita had heard about the opportunities for sanctuary beneath London, but hadn't quite realized just how vast they were in the way of industrial revolution, war, and breakneck-paced construction. They went through few very lengthy passages, and she recalled Stephen's remark that the city's permanently tunnel-dwelling vampires (and others) claimed contiguous stretches for their own. The route Stephen had described led through obviously hand-clawed tunnels and even right up under street level on occasion, as well as through office building basements and chambers full of unfamiliar equipment. Lucita wished she had time to stop and examine her surroundings…perhaps another time.

Finally Lucita paused in front of a metal door at the end of a wood-paneled corridor. On the other side there'd be a parking garage, and she could get a car to take her to the airport and Angelica's plane. She set the pilot down. "Enough." At the word, Angelica found herself again in control. She huddled on the floor against the door, the strains of moving involuntarily combining with simple fear to overwhelm her.

Lucita squatted next to the cowering woman in one smooth motion. She drew the pilot's gaze to her own with one finger pushing under the pilot's chin: not hard, not threatening, but firm and allowing for no resistance.

Lucita's anima rose in her mind and launched itself across the intervening space, into the depths of Angelica's mind. She lost awareness of the outside world while examining the palace of Angelica's memories. Well, memory bungalow, perhaps— mortals simply had neither the time nor the power to build truly elaborate edifices in their inner selves. Only the passage of centuries made for really interesting structures. It took less than a hundred of Angelica's heartbeats for Lucita to edit out the memories of contacts with Lucita's organization before the flight to London, and a few from later. There was no particular reason to expect that someone might later be in a position to rip through the pilot's mind for background clues, but why take chances? Angelica would never notice the losses on her own, and it would simplify matters. As far as Angelica was now concerned, this all followed from the London party she thought she remembered attending.

When all was ready, Lucita opened up a vein on her wrist with another smooth swipe of one fingernail and held it up to the pilot. "Drink this, it will calm you."

Angelica now had no memory of the demonstration of how thoroughly she could be dominated, though Lucita allowed her to recall the fear at the thought of an anonymous, never-solved death. As Angelica saw it now, the choice was between death and service, and Lucita had accepted her demand that she retain free will during the service. Lucita had no intention of doing any such thing, having watched too many of her comrades perish at the hands of unbound servants, but she also realized that servants who believed themselves free were much less prone to revolt than those who thought themselves enslaved.

Angelica's conscious mind told her that the vampire gave her a glass of tap water. It tasted sludgy and warm, but she attributed that to her own fear. Her dominated mind replaced the blood's opacity with an imagined view through the glass, as she drained it on down. Lucita had prepared memory blocks in advance, so that Angelica didn't feel the blood diffuse through her system with its gifts of abnormal strength and resilience. She was allowed to feel a fresh jolt of something like sympathy for the vampire. This wasn't so bad. Yes, she had to watch herself or the end would no doubt come swiftly but painfully. But after all, the vampire was giving her the chance to do precisely what she wanted to. It might even be a good opportunity….

Lucita had long since given up feeling anything resembling straightforward interest in results when it came to binding mortals to her service. They were, after all, mortal, and if she didn't take them this way, the end of all freedom and choice would come soon enough some other way. In a world with so many billions of them, no one could possibly matter that much to the scheme of things. For Lucita, it was all as emotionally demanding as choosing the right luggage or repairing some useful bit of machinery—it took the same sort of care as did work with any volatile or otherwise dangerous substance, and for the same self-preserving reasons. She didn't know yet what she would want to do with the newly-made ghoul once this set of trips was over, but there'd be time enough to decide that later.

Once the blood was well diffused, Lucita stood for the final time that night. "So it's agreed. Come, we have work to do." Angelica rose as well, her fear falling away unnoticed.

shards

Saturday, 8 April 2000, 4:20 AM
80 miles east of Sicily, Italy

The cargo ship *Delta Mummy II* had seen better days. Right after World War II, it was bright and tightly maintained, part of a small fleet operated by an Egyptian consortium trading in luxury goods and valuable components salvaged from Axis military hardware. Twenty years later, when the consortium finally collapsed in a terminal welter of embezzlement, *Delta Mummy II* and two other ships from the same fleet went up for bankruptcy auction to a would-be drug kingpin from Ethiopia who fancied himself a builder of a new African dynasty. Two years after that he was one more anonymous body in the Nile, and the ships changed hands again, and again, and again, never staying with any one owner more than five years. One of the companion ships went down in an Indian Ocean storm in 1975, the other burned for insurance money (ineptly enough that the ensuing investigation finished destroying that owner's shaky business) in 1993. Now *Delta Mummy II* sailed under a partnership, half owned by its officers and some of the investment-minded crew and half owned by a small network of American art dealers wanting a reliable channel for smuggled art.

On this particular night, the ship's main holds were filled with 45,000 tons of natural gas, loaded at half a dozen small outlets over the course of the week for ease in getting past customs. Buyers all along the Mediterranean coast of Spain and France would pay premium prices, since they would still come out ahead without the maze of European Union and national taxes, inspections and regulations. Side compartments carried a ton and a half of mediocre-grade heroin and twenty-two slabs hewn from a recently discovered classical tomb before the discovery was officially reported to the antiquities authorities. The risks were substantial, starting with the ship's unfortunately thorough compliance with the international stereotype of smugglers, but the payoff would be good. Two more trips like this and both halves of the partnership would have cleared their debts and hold true profit, free and clear.

Captain Biruni peered out into the darkness with a slight twinge of discomfort. He'd worked on *Delta Mummy II* on and off, under various owners, for fifteen years. In that time he'd seen his share of weird phenomena, the sort that many people in illicit trades encounter in the corners of the world where respectable society's lights seldom shine. He was not a superstitious man, simply one aware that the world held quite a few things that made no sense in any reasonable framework he knew of. Many sailors took omens seriously; he didn't, and hadn't since the trip surrounded by oracles of doom which netted him his first hundred thousand dollars and his first wife. Doomsaying, he knew, usually served some undeclared agenda on the part of the doomsayer. He wasn't as sure as some of his officers that Mossad was buying out fortune tellers in the Nile Delta and using them to spread doubts intended to hurt Egypt's economy…but then he wasn't quite sure they were wrong, either.

Ordinarily he'd be asleep at four in the morning. Tonight he couldn't rest; he kept having nightmares filled with imagery right out of the old horror movies he'd seen as a child on family trips into the cities of Turkistan and Azerbaijan. He wasn't about to tell the third mate that, so he just said, "Can't sleep so well," as he poured himself a cup of the surprisingly good coffee the night watch crew brewed at the start of their shift. Cup in hand, he paced the front half of the ship, ending at the bow where he could lean and watch the waves go by. Every half hour or so (deliberately on a slightly erratic schedule), a two-man patrol passed him by on their sweep for pirates or other trouble. He gave them a salute and a moment's chat each time, following up on old reports, inquiring after relatives, doing his part to remind the crew that their captain was still on the ball despite getting a little old.

All the while, the Mediterranean coursed by at a dozen knots. It wasn't as bad as when Biruni started his career and there were rafts of pollution and garbage so thick you could just about walk from Libya to Italy. But even now, after decades of sustained effort at cleanup, broad swathes of water glistened with the sheen of oil or dumped chemicals, and thick mats of

shards

netting tangled with everything from Styrofoam to discarded soup cans rolled along. Biruni started a tally, and discovered that he saw one significant indication of pollution every ten to fifteen minutes. That impressed him. He had no love for untamed nature, remembering the soul-blasting winters and skin-charring summers of the steppes where he grew up. Humanity couldn't subdue the world enough to suit him, and while garbage wasn't quite the sort of triumph he hoped for, he'd take it over endless emptiness. He felt connected to the rest of humanity in these moments of garbage passing, not quite so alone in the depths of the sea.

When he had woken, around 1 a.m., it had been a clear night with crisp, sharp moonlight. Now the sky was growing gradually darker: not cloudy, just hazy and obscure. He suspected that if he went in to the radio shack and did a little monitoring, he'd find that Mount Etna was at it again, emitting the fine ash and smoke which sometimes heralded major new volcanic activity. Biruni had sailed through the outskirts of eruptions before, and knew that *Delta Mummy II* could handle just about anything short of lava flows in the immediate vicinity. For now he wasn't sufficiently motivated; let the darkening night do as it would, it was just one more projection of his gloomy mood. Only if the guards reported anything really unusual or showed some signs of difficulty in patrolling properly would he rouse himself and go check.

At 4:20 he decided to indulge in at least a little dread. It took actual effort to turn away from the bow and from the view of blacker-than-black ocean, and start towards the bridge. Once he wasn't looking at the water, the rest came easier, and by the time he stepped up onto the bridge itself, nobody could have guessed that he felt anything other than simple fatigue. Third Mate Farouk had the wheel, and the bridge to himself; the other five sailors on duty were all back in the lounge, watching TV or dozing. That suited Biruni, who didn't want to incite a panic or start the crew wondering if the he were going mad at last.

Biruni stepped up to look over Farouk's shoulder at the instrumentation. "The water seems a little sluggish tonight," he said in what he hoped was a relaxed tone of voice. "Any reports of spills?"

Farouk flipped on the autopilot. (Biruni suspected that it had been on until the moment Farouk heard the captain coming, but this wasn't the moment to push that issue. Finish the trip and ditch the lazy bastard then.) The third mate stood almost a full foot taller than Biruni, but with a skinny slouch that compared unfavorably to the captain's weathered muscle. "Nope. There's no report of a leak or wreck anywhere in the area. Over in Algeria, sure, they've got a couple of vents they can't quite stop, but you wouldn't notice that here."

That was true enough. Still, Biruni persisted. "You're listening off the line as well?"

"Yes," Farouk said with a grin. Both men knew that the official reports covered only a small fraction of what really might affect shipping in the Mediterranean. The vast array of unofficial channels, custom-spread frequencies, in-house word codes, and other means of informing peers without getting officials involved was "off the line" in smuggler jargon. When Farouk first joined the crew, he'd been reluctant to place too much weight on off-the-line traffic. Once he grew comfortable with it, he was still reluctant to let the captain know about it. Biruni had spent years convincing the third mate that, yes, really, it was right and good to look off the line and to admit doing so. "Some hassles off the coast of Yugoslavia or whatever they're calling it this week, and there were two unreported sinkings over on the far side of Sicily from what sounds like badly handled munitions. Still nothing you'd see here."

In a way it wasn't what Biruni wanted to hear. "Thanks. Make a note for the log that I think we've been brushing up against something. Any news of Etna acting up?"

"Not as of the start of the shift, anyway. Deliseaux's on second shift, he's the volcano buff, and if there were anything going on he'd still be on deck hoping for a view, pestering me to go take a closer look. I figure with him around, I don't need to check the news myself." This time Biruni grinned along with Farouk. "Honest, Captain, nothing to tell you."

"Okay, message received." Biruni refilled his coffee cup and headed out again.

It was darker still now, and Biruni noticed something odd. The waves were getting stickier and sludgier, even as the breeze from the west picked up a cold edge. There were no little whitecaps like he'd expect. In fact, it was damned hard to see anything outside the ship's own lights. Biruni looked up just in time to see something he would really rather have missed. The whole sky was dim, as if filled with soot. But a solid sharp edge of blackness swept overhead from west to east, isolating the ship and captain in absolute darkness. Now there really was nothing to see but what the running lights illuminated. The wind grew colder and stronger.

All at once Biruni wished he had superstition to fall back on. In the face of the death of light, it would be reassuring to have some prayer or invocation to say, something beyond "Damn." Unfortunately, that was all he could think of, and he wasn't even sure who he'd like to have damn the darkness.

As he spoke the single curse, the ship shuddered to a halt. Biruni had never heard the sound of screws being ripped off a ship while the shafts were still turning, but that horrible, sustained screeching from behind and below could scarcely be anything else. A series of terrifying metallic shrieks raced through *Delta Mummy II* from stern to bow, as pieces of drive shaft and steering mechanisms, suddenly forced to stop by some outside power, tore themselves to pieces. Surely it could only be a matter of time before something caught fire, Biruni thought.

There were shouts from the bridge. Biruni turned around to see the entire shift crew gathered around Farouk, pointing at various gauges, flipping knobs and dials, trying to fix things or at least get some result from their efforts. So the captain nearly missed the arrival of his own death. Only the muffled crunch of bow plates compressed by dark pressure alerted him to look forward again.

Against a background of absolute darkness, nothing showed of the thing itself. Biruni could see it advance— whatever "it" might be—by the marks it left on the ship. He started to lean forward to see what was pushing against the bow, but before he got there, the thing had reached the bow. The bow lookout stand bent under the weight of incalculable tons, or perhaps under the strength of something that could push that hard, and then disappeared into the blackness. The anchor chains soon followed. There was a pause, during which Biruni heard sounds of the dark thing passing down to the anchor reels and filling those spaces, then its advance resumed the pace of a slow walk.

Biruni felt his grip on sanity loosen. He couldn't doubt the evidence of his sense, but this made no sense at all. This wasn't even a religious moment: this wasn't demons or angels or totem spirits or anything else, just darkness come to life. As he tried to make some sense of it, he stumbled against a stray rope. "Damn," he thought again. He felt a stabbing pain in his left ankle and knew he must have sprained it in the fall.

No time for standing efforts now, he thought, and turned to crawl as far back as possible. Power failures below caused the deck lights to flicker, then extinguish. Only half of the emergency lights came on, and they were dimmer than he'd expected. An intangible mist seemed to fill the air, making everything hazy. He kept running into pieces of the ship he didn't normally think about: tool chests bolted to the bridge bulkheads, electrical outlet covers, small vents. The crumpling behind him grew louder and closer.

In the end, he didn't quite have time to turn over before the moving darkness reached him. The mass landed on his back and left side, and descended so quickly that there was no time for blood or viscera to spatter. All that was left of Biruni was an irregular thin mass of leaking tissues to tumble down into the Abyss. Within ten minutes, the rest of the ship and crew were drifting through the void with him, and within another ten minutes there was no terrestrial consciousness left among any of the pieces.

The ball of darkness, more than a mile across, quickly collapsed into nothingness. No one had seen it in its phase of intense activity except its victims on board *Delta Mummy II* and the ghouled servants of the shadow magicians, piloting an inconspicuous yacht not far away.

More than a hundred miles away and well underground in their stronghold, the magicians watched through the servants' eyes as typical manipulations of shadow prepared the environment for the great summoning. The sacrifices were all ready in the Castle of Saint Rafael the Archangel, and this time all went well. In the midst of the darkness they'd made at sea, a hole opened into the Abyss, and two great creatures of that realm rose to accept the sacrifice of water, metal, flesh, and mind. The magicians weren't quite sure what the creatures would make of the ship's cargo, since they couldn't list it among the sacrifices, and hoped that there wouldn't be a problem with it as there'd been with the first attempts. It seemed that the creatures were willing enough to take a little of other things along with the quantities and substances enumerated for them.

If the magicians had breath, they might have gasped in pleasure at the sight. There, for the first time in centuries, the wilderness of uncreation had emerged onto the surface of the world. It couldn't last long, yet, but now the magicians felt confidence.

It wouldn't be long now before they could open the great door. And through it would walk Lasombra Itself, the Great Darkness, and It would lead them in the final conquest of the world. The end was near, and nobody knew it but them.

Saturday, 8 April, 11:15 PM
Over the Atlantic Ocean

Lucita relives the destruction of her sire, again and again, and each time she perishes with him: dragged down by Leviathan, crushed beneath falling rocks and left to face the day, betrayed by the Assamites, drained by Monçada in his frantic final bid for strength.

Then she glides through the air like the highest of clouds. She soars toward the Mediterranean, with the delta of Sicily centered in her view. She descends from what they now call the stratosphere. Now she can see only the southern half of Europe and Saharan Africa, now only coastline around the sea, now only Sicily itself. She recognizes the castle. She never went there very often in her early nights, and then it was not a place she ever wished to go again.

It is the stronghold of the Lasombra Antediluvian.

It's not as she remembers: her dream is not building it just out of memory but out of (she is aware on some level) extrapolation and desires from other souls linked to hers through the Curse. Much of the rubble remains. The new construction is mostly around the periphery, and there is a brand-new wing whose proportions show the concerns of mathematical magic. It is impossible for Lucita to judge the wing's height, without the sun or convenient lights to cast shadows. Indeed, she realizes suddenly that the whole site is in pure darkness and that she's seeing with an intellectual awareness that she only interprets as sight. She feels undead souls moving within, gathering in groups and then dispersing.

She floats down into the more-than-night darkness, close enough now, it seems, to reach out and touch the great castle…

…and it splits apart to reveal a single giant eye beneath. It blinks once and focuses on her. She feels herself pushed up by a wind from the Abyss, which rushes through the eye. Pieces of the shattered castle tumble up into the sky even faster than she rises; before it shrinks too small for her to resolve, she can see that the whole castle has been cast into the wind, leaving behind only bare ground.

Now she floats high above the world again, and can see it spinning faster and faster, as though it had snapped off its hidden axle. The sun remains behind it, and giant clouds rise higher and

shards

higher, far beyond the atmosphere, to screen it out. Now there is night everywhere. Fires break out in the cities as mortals panic. The Antediluvian eye continues to stare up at her, blinking once with each rotation. It slumbers in the Abyss. Or rather it slumbered, as it is now awake.

Lucita woke in blood sweat.

She took what felt like too long to orient herself. Ah, yes, the cabin of the plane they'd provided for Angelica. She could feel the pilot up ahead, the first vampiric blood still working its transformations in her mortal frame. Sometime soon Lucita would need to instruct her in the proper use of her new strength, and search for signs of other potential in her, but that could follow in due time.

She should speak to Angelica about their current trip, too, but that could also wait. Instead, she sat in one of the big plush chairs and dialed Stephen's number. One of the ghouls answered. "Lenoir residence."

"This is your master's recent guest. Is he available?"

"Yes, ma'am. Hold please."

Then a click, and Stephen's voice. "Yes?"

"Lucita, Stephen."

"Ah, good to hear from you." He exchanged a quick series of interrogations and responses, drawing on their personal backgrounds, to establish that both were who they claimed to be. (It wasn't infallible, she reflected, but anyone who could find out enough to pass the challenges was probably going to win anyway.) "So where are you now?"

"In the air—"

"That's what they've been saying of you as long as I've been around, I believe," he broke in.

She chuckled. "True. I meant, however, that I am traveling in an airplane, on my way to Eleuthera."

"Eleuthera…please tell me you're not going to try meeting with those disgusting pirates of Kleist's."

"As a matter of fact, that's precisely what I plan. What's your concern?"

"They're *savages*, m'dear. They have that tedious American zealotry, even the ones that didn't come from America, and they are utterly humorless in the pursuit of what they think their duty is. I fully expect that they'll try to clap you in irons or some such and haul you off for the powers that be to examine."

"I'll remember that."

"Please do. I would hate to mourn your passing for so stupid a reason. Why on earth do you want to get tangled up with them, anyhow?"

"Partly because they are, as you said, zealots. But they'll talk with me, or at least so I'm led to believe. I can scarcely risk returning to London at this point, and I feel it appropriate to spend some time at a Camarilla court. If it has to be one that puts to sea with big guns, that's the price I must pay. I need perspectives not my own."

"But surely…"

"Yes, Stephen, I have considered the alternatives, and none of them strike me as particularly satisfactory."

"Very well…"

"But enough of that. Did you manage to deal with the ghost?"

"Oh, yes. I sent it running off in fear before it could do much more than smash up some of the vases."

"Do you know yet who sent it?"

"Not for sure, but I have some solid leads already. I believe that one or another of the artists at court has necromantic connections, but it will take some fieldwork before I can say for sure. There's…but you don't want to hear me tell the sad tale of Vittorio Giovanni and how he met his end in 1785. I'll tell you about it some other time."

"I look forward to the opportunity. In the meantime, take care of yourself. My world is not so rich in allies that I can afford to dispense with even one, Stephen."

Once Stephen rang off, Lucita set about replenishing her funds.

She had an account with the Bank of Normandy dating back to the Franco-Prussian War, allegedly a backup fund for Rhineland merchants who wanted to make sure that a sudden shift in borders wouldn't deprive them of all their assets. She sent a ghoul or other human in to add funds every couple of years, and to make a withdrawal every ten to thirty years, so that there was a pattern of activity. Sometimes there'd be a dozen or more transactions within a couple of years, and other decades the account wasn't touched at all. It all looked very plausible. This had been a quiet decade for the account, and it was about time for a little action in any event. She authorized a series of electronic transactions, the last two on time-delay for completion several weeks from now.

Lucita wondered if she should contact Willa. Surely Willa would notice the activity and want to investigate. But she also had her mistress' instructions not to attempt contact, and until Lucita knew what her own plans were, she didn't want to involve Willa. For all her admirable qualities, Willa was useless or worse in any sort of fight or personal conflict. There'd be time for that later, too, Lucita promised herself. She'd let Willa in on the story once she knew what it was.

"East." It was the first thing the old vampire had said in almost four hours, and Andrew had to suppress the urge to jump.

"East, you say?"

"East."

"Very good. Now, that wasn't so hard, was it?" The elder didn't say any more, but Andrew didn't press the issue. He wished once again for the full range of torture equipment and supplies available in Mexico City or even back home in Portland, and he was proud of how his pack had made do in the aftermath of their raid. The wreckage was still there for the police or whomever to worry about; the interesting machinery, along with the victim, was now arrayed in a gully a dozen miles away, well away from the road. Konstantin was trussed securely.

Andrew had to admit some admiration for the elder's determination. He had to know that he'd be leaving this situation only as ash. Nonetheless, the elder gave out as little information as possible, as infrequently as possible. By this point he was, so to speak, only half the vampire he'd been— thoroughly hacked and bled, barely enough for satisfactory diablerie remaining. His will to resist remained almost intact.

"Barry?"

"Yesss, bosss." Barry shuffled over in what he imagined to be a good imitation of Igor or some other hunchbacked assistant. It wasn't. Andrew would correct him on that, but later.

"Got the maps with you?" Andrew's tone apparently conveyed enough disapproval to get the point across, as Barry stood up straight.

"Right here."

"Great. So, if the bitch went east from here, how many options are there?"

"Just a sec. Let me count…looks like one, boss. Route 15, on into Nevada."

"Thanks. Now, if you'll leave me with the gentleman for a few minutes?"

"Sure thing." Barry drew way back, and motioned the others around to the far side of the truck.

"This is it, old-timer," Andrew said when he was alone. "Any last words?" Konstantin merely glared at him. "Okay, then." Andrew made sure that what was left of the elder was well chained down and bent to suck out what was left of his blood.

It took longer than Andrew would have imagined. The blood just kept coming and coming and coming. Where was it all stored? Andrew hadn't really believed the old myths about super-concentrated elder blood until now. The rush was indescribable and unprecedented. All the pleasures of his mortal and immortal existences rolled together didn't compare. He trembled, and had to brace himself to avoid plunging off before finishing the deed.

Flashes of Konstantin's memory echoed in Andrew's mind: an old friend in Russia, snow in Colorado seen from an airplane cruising low over the slopes, rain in the desert and the night blooms after. Deaths, many of them, some wanted, some accidental. Lucita telling Konstantin, "Cardinal Networks." Konstantin's worry for Lucita and rage at himself for such an end as this. That anguish only reinforced Andrew's pleasure. If this didn't finish soon, he might explode.

At last the flow slowed. Then there was nothing at all. The body and soul were equally drained. Sunlight would take care of the rest. Andrew rose shakily. He hit his shin on the converted cow-catcher, and erupted in a wholly unexpected bout of frenzy. Burning much of his newly acquired blood in a sudden outpouring, he shredded the metal framework, tossing the body aside like a rag while seeking his revenge on the evil inanimate thing that had distracted him from the moment. He managed to regain control only after completely destroying Niccolo's handiwork, down to individual nuts and bolts broken in half.

So this was diablerie. No wonder the practitioners of the Path of Caine made it their central dogma. A boy could get used to this, he thought to himself and laughed. "All right, beloved packmates!" he shouted. "Eastward ho!"

Tuesday, 11 April 2000, 2:07 AM
Gunnison County Airport
Gunnison, Colorado

There'd have to be a fire, Andrew decided. And they'd have to be careful about it, so that there'd be no detailed investigation of the corpses. He felt wistful for a moment, wanting so much to confront this town's herd of kine with the reality of the secret masters among them, to inspire the fear and dread that should be all humanity's lot until the time when the capacity for feeling left them altogether. It was so satisfying to stand, or rather float, in the midst of such carnage, feeling blood lapping around one's feet and hearing the soft sounds of bodies collapsing in the first stages of decay. But this was not the time or place to make their stand.

"Are we sure of their story?" he addressed his pack. With a swift curve of his wrist he pointed at each of them in turn. Niccolo smiled. Roxana held up a stack of printouts with her usual calm. Barry nodded vigorously. Simon Peter had his mouth full, and tried to say "Yes" around it, with limited success.

The night after Andrew devoured Konstantin, they rose to find racing storm clouds overhead, which suited Andrew perfectly. The pack had never rehearsed clean-up routines very successfully, and he had been hoping for weather to be on their side. A little flash flooding would go a long way toward complicating any human investigation of the crime scene.

Much to his surprise, the actual clean-up went very well. Each pack member took responsibility for one quadrant of the area and went to work, scooping up everything that could fit in the service truck and breaking up the rest. Then they worked together to roll the loner's truck back upright and loaded it with everything it could carry. The remaining chunks of metal were strewn around and buried quickly but thoroughly. After two hours of work, the site was essentially pristine. Barry drove the service truck to a tricky bend in the road a dozen miles away and rammed it into a cliff face at high speed. Simon Peter,

Niccolo, and Roxana joined Andrew in pushing the loner's truck to a steep gully already starting to fill with water, and then over, down into the canyon. It bounced four times on its way down and caught fire as it landed on shallow, protruding rocks.

Simon Peter broadcast a few fake signals from the telephone repair guys as the pack headed east. There'd be nothing to trigger an investigation until the next day, and by then the evidence would have seasoned a little bit. All was going very well.

Andrew had the name "Cardinal Networks" but not a great deal of insight into what it meant, beyond the faintest of recollections on Konstantin's part that the network moved Lucita. The pack stopped in at every airport and town center along the way, looking for charter services of any kind. They took turns more or less at random, trusting in fate and diablerie to give them the clues they needed. In the greasy-spoon café at Mesa Verde's airstrip, two young guys reflected on that great custom charter job they'd seen up at Gunnison, and the pack was off again.

Sure enough, the flight records here (now wet with blood) just about reeked of Lucita's hand. Cardinal Networks? That was so obviously a reference to the late lamented Monçada that Andrew figured it *had* to be a deliberate invitation. Which in turn meant that she was expecting pursuit, and had probably set up defenses. Perhaps they'd just been lucky so far…best to get out of the building and take care of the evidence.

Andrew decided to take care of the fire himself. He and the others each took a couple of bodies downstairs, but then he sent the pack out to search the area for any more clues. "And no more killings for now. I can take care of bodies if I have to, but I'd rather not." He looked carefully at the pack, realizing how close they all were to blood frenzy. "If you kill anyone, you'll have to settle with me, and I don't think any of you is quite ready to challenge for leadership, are you?" That sunk in. They left him alone.

First he propped the bodies up against the fire doors, as if desperately trying to push their way out. Then he went outside and knocked over a few 50-gallon drums of fuel oil and soap, just enough to keep the fire doors from being able to swing out. Then it was back upstairs to wipe up as much of the blood as he could, to check for loose fingerprints from the pack— just a few, fortunately, and all easy to scrub off, since vampires don't generate skin oils and only leave prints on surfaces already oiled or otherwise prepared—and to gather up strewn paper into as close a semblance of the situation before their attack as possible.

He wondered idly if he regretted slaughtering all the tower crew when they refused to answer the questions shouted by a demented quartet who'd forced their way through locked doors. As he scooped up fluttering forms, he decided that he didn't. They would have had to die anyway. It's just that he wished he hadn't given the pack such a thorough indulgence; on the heels of the ambush and the bus game, they might get careless. It wasn't enough to be a superior individual when sufficiently powerful hordes of the kine gathered in response. Oh, well, either the pack would learn or they'd perish, and either way the average quality in the Sabbat would go up. Andrew simply hoped to avoid being involved directly in any perishing.

The tower room wasn't exactly *clean* when he felt done, but it was tidy enough that the fire crews wouldn't find its state suspicious. Time to find an excuse to start the fire. In the basement he found something that made him laugh out loud. Some fool had actually left oily rags near the furnace! It was such a classic cliché. Clearly fate demanded the burning, he thought. He didn't even have to throw a match, just push the rags a little closer to the furnace.

They lit in seconds. He felt the great fear rise within him, the fear all vampires have for flame and its capacity to sear them into Final Death, but he fought it down long enough to see that the fire was well underway. Back upstairs he pushed flammable objects close to furnace outlets and kicked over a propane tank. By the time he strolled outside, half a dozen small fires raged on the first floor, and things were spreading rapidly. As he watched, sparks wafted all the way up to the control room, where the first loose papers caught. The rest would just be a matter of time.

"So, London?" Andrew turned to find Simon Peter beside him, also clearly enjoying the mounting fire and murmuring softly.

"Are you sending out false air traffic control signals?"

"Yup."

"Clever. I should have thought of that. I owe you some special consideration next time we're dividing the haul. That's good thinking." Andrew watched Simon Peter smile in a calculating way. "Anyway, yes, London. At least that's what these plans indicate, and I don't see any sign of forgery. While the hell would she go to London?"

"Beats me. Old friends? The urge to drink warm beer? Not my department. Maybe she wants to have Camarilla badasses do her in."

Andrew saw a faint grin run across Simon Peter's face, and smiled himself. "Somehow I think that if she were going to throw herself into destruction's way, she wouldn't do it there. No, I think she's after something. Or someone. After what our friend Konstantin said, I'll bet good money she's got another contact there and wants to go whine at him for a while."

Roxana and Barry came up as Andrew spoke. Roxana looked skeptical. "You think he told us the real story?"

"Oh, indeed I do," Andrew said, sustaining the smile. "He was well and truly broken there. She's on one of those guilt trips that seem to overcome pawns once in a while. She'll spend the next few nights asking 'But is it all worth it?' and 'Am I just a pawn in some ancient parasite's scheme?' Being the fool she is, she'll decide 'Yes' and 'No' in that order, instead of the other way around, and then she'll get back to killing other pawns and feeling superior in her independence again.

"No, the real question for me is, do we want to go after her?"

Niccolo looked puzzled. "Why wouldn't we?"

"I'll use small words." Andrew sometimes got tired of holding Niccolo's hand on anything involving logic or subtlety. "She isn't staying in one place very long. She goes here, then there, then over there. We could fly to London just in time to find she's gone someplace else. Or we could wait and see..."

"Oh, I see," Niccolo broke in. He either didn't choose to respond to Andrew's little insults, or (likely as not) he had missed them. He didn't seem to do very well with the nuances of English. "Maybe we can shave a leg off of our pursuit."

"Something like that."

Simon Peter mulled. "If you can get me to a good access point, I can settle in to monitor official traffic in London. Disasters, crime, anything out of the ordinary, and I can ferret it out of the general flow."

"Sounds good. Let's clear the scene, settle in, and get started with that tomorrow." Andrew paused. "But let's enjoy the fire a few more minutes, first."

Tuesday, 11 April 2000, 9:45 PM
Ocean View Inn
Harbor Island, Eleuthera, Bahamas

Archon-Captain Alejandro Kleist cut a striking figure, particularly in the midst of a typical tourist crowd. His ancestors had been Spanish and German, and he showed features from both sides; he wore his long black hair in a platinum ring decorated with the badges of half a dozen patron saints. He looked out at the world through piercingly sharp blue eyes tinged with silver; Lucita would have thought them contacts if she didn't have reliable descriptions of them from others. He moved with the easy grace of a swordsman and seaman, and Lucita recognized the telltale signs of concealed weapons in his coat, slacks and shoes.

He entered the dining room as if he owned it, scanned the room, recognized her, and walked over with something less obvious than a stride. In one smooth move he shed his coat and sat down in the chair opposite her table. "I don't approve of you," he said without preamble.

Arranging this meeting had taken careful diplomacy. They knew of each other, of course: the archetypal independent and the paragon of Camarilla loyalty among the *antitribu*, the assassin and the most-honored official. They'd never met, though, and Lucita had to make her approach through intermediaries: first an information broker in Miami of uncertain lineage, then a deal with one of the city's Setites, a way of reaching Kleist in exchange for certain files retrieved from a hit performed twenty years ago. All of this took substantial radio time and occasionally the cryptographic help of a radio man of Angelica's acquaintance. He wasn't very happy about shifting to a night schedule, at least not until realizing just how big the bonus for his help would be. Then things went smoothly.

Finally Lucita spoke directly to Kleist's executive officer, an American sailor named Randall Thomas about whom she knew very little. "Let him specify the place and inspect it beforehand. I will have my aide do the same, and he can monitor her progress if he wants. I'm willing for him to feel secure."

In the end they worked out a meeting at one of the island's luxury hotels. It was close by the docks, and apparently Kleist and his crew were regular guests. Their alleged research vessel *Black Aegis* could even be found, so the Setite had said, in postcards available in Eleuthera gift shops. The hotel was furnished in a style Lucita perceived as a mixture of modern American upper-class kitsch and quite careful Provençal elements. It was a headache waiting to happen for her, though the guests seemed to enjoy it all. She moved about in a sea of happy emanations.

Lucita listened calmly to his declaration. "You don't have to, as long as you're willing to speak with me a while."

Kleist had more to say. "You are such a perfect example of why the Sabbat rules our clan so thoroughly. You've spent your whole existence doing precisely two things: indulging in petty grudges against your sire, and assassinating any Kindred with enemies willing to pay your fees. You have never at any time acted with the least concern for the state of our kind as a whole, or for the welfare of our clan, or indeed for anything except your own self-interest. You have consumed the fruits of a great many Kindred's labors directed toward allowing us all to continue existing, and you give back nothing except final death. You refuse to resist the Sabbat yourself, and remove those who would do the duty you shirk.

"If you were to meet me under any other circumstances, I'd destroy you out of hand and feel I'd done a good deed. Tell me what you want, but expect no sympathy."

She paused for a moment. He seemed through for the moment. "Do you have more to say before I begin?"

He waved a hand dismissively. "Now that you know where you stand, say what you will."

"Tell me about your work, Captain."

"Archon-Captain, to you."

"Tell me about your work, Archon-Captain."

"Why?"

Lucita spread her arms to encompass the scene. "Archon-

Captain, this is a world I know very little about, and I want to learn more. I'll explain why in return for your answer. For now, tell me about what you do, and what it's like to do it."

He stared at her. She held his gaze. "It's not a trap. Surely you have enough awareness to sense my intent?"

"Frankly, no. At least not in your case. I've seen reports of some of your attacks on Camarilla figures, and I have no delusion about your ability to cloak yourself, and cloak that seeming, and cloak the result again. Please don't waste my time with such things. I have a ship to tend and cousins to destroy, and this meeting is worthwhile only if you refrain from pointlessness."

Lucita had cultivated a very human-sounding sigh for such occasions. She delivered it, startling him. "Very well. Do you need the explanation first?"

"I do."

"Do you know that Monçada is gone?"

"So reports have said. Is he?"

"He is."

"Good riddance. If there's a Hell, I hope it's very happy to have him. What does that have to do with you being here insulting my knowledge of your condition?"

"You said it yourself. I've spent nearly a thousand years doing what I could to stop his schemes. It never worked as well as I would have liked, but in any event, it's done. I assume that I'll be uncovering plots he set in motion for years to come, if Gehenna doesn't descend first, but he won't be initiating anything new."

Kleist nonchalantly put his hands on the table. It would have been a great gesture of his forsaking access to weapons for anyone who couldn't make the darkness become new arms. Still, Lucita appreciated the thought. "Very touching. The great warrior maiden confesses her failure."

"You're trying to provoke me. You're good at it, too. I recognize the legacy of your teachers in Seville. I'm not sure if you realize that I sponsored the first authors of your textbooks on rhetoric."

He blinked. "I did not. My apologies for using such an obvious ploy."

"Accepted, Archon-Captain. Suffice it to say at this point that I want to know what it's like to have a mission. I know about your kind as adversaries and obstacles, but very little about what you think it is you do, or how you feel about it. Say, for the moment, that I am one of our clan's independent souls who wants to know what the Camarilla has to offer. Why do you serve them, and what do you gain in return?"

Kleist spoke slowly and somewhat hesitantly at first, gathering enthusiasm as he got underway. "The justicars are the practical authorities in the Camarilla. They have a very broad mandate to ferret out violations of the Traditions and the sect's prohibitions." Lucita nodded. "Each justicar chooses one or more archons to help out, almost always a member of some other clan who brings a perspective and abilities that complement those of the justicar." Lucita nodded again.

"In 1942, shortly after the Americans entered the war, Justicar Xavier approached me. Did you ever meet him? I expect not."

"I never had the pleasure."

"Heh. I doubt it would have been very enjoyable for you. In my case it was different. He knew of my work mediating between our clan's *antitribu* and the Camarilla, resolving conflicts peaceably and promoting joint ventures on matters of mutual interest. He found that interesting, and told me that he wanted the Camarilla to stop being, in his words, 'such a Club of Seven and more what we like to tell everyone else it is.' I would be—again, in his words—'Apostle to the Others.' That suited me, as I felt I'd gone about as far as I could without more authority, and this kind of offer presumably wouldn't come along very often."

Kleist paused to look at the approaching waiter. "Do you want to deal with this, or shall I?" Lucita waved an acknowledging hand. Kleist looked up at the waiter with an absolutely serious expression, ordered one of the more expensive wines, and delivered a small mental nudge to refrain from disturbing them further.

"Now then." He gathered his thoughts again. "1942, yes. As his duties allowed, the justicar trained me, and by 1950 I earned his approval. I've been doing the same sort of work ever since. Even though he's withdrawn from the Camarilla now, the consensus of the remaining justicars is that I should continue at my post until such time as they and their overseers decide whether a replacement for Xavier is called for and if so what that individual's brief should be."

"Tell me what a year of that is like."

The waiter brought their wine. Each pretended to sip it until the waiter moved away; Kleist then wrapped the bottle in a dimness that hid how full it was. "It would all be different if I were on land, of course. Some of the other archons specialize in types of environments or in geographical regions. I am interested in the sea. I look after ports, and after the ships that move between them.

"The Masquerade is a fragile thing at the best of times. In practice, if we punished every vampire whose actions created a serious risk of mortal discovery, we'd quickly depopulate our kind. We—that is, the justicars and archons—wield great personal authority precisely because we must exercise broad discretion. The Camarilla is as much an attitude as an organization, and certainly much more like a community than like a government. We have to instill respect and trust in our subjects as well as fear, or we risk starting the Anarch Revolt all over again. I realize that loners like yourself seldom care about this, but in the end you would notice not only the loss of customers but the end of all sanctuary."

Lucita gave no visible reaction. There'd be time to argue later, perhaps. Kleist paused, saw she wasn't going to respond, and continued. "I look at anomalies. When there are reports of strange deeds on the waterfront, I go to investigate, and if I find careless vampires, I do whatever is necessary to make them careful again. That can be as simple as cautionary words and a little advice. Often there's a struggle involved, and I fight as necessary to win. When the offender is new to unlife, I seek out his sire and make the tradition of progeny work on my behalf. Sometimes I go to the local prince or sheriff to recruit help. Occasionally, perhaps two to five times a year, I must destroy the offender outright. I regard that as a success for the survival of the community as a whole, but as a failure for my own ability and for that locale.

"In between port times, I sail. My own ship goes forth several times a year to raid Sabbat-controlled vessels. We escort weak Camarilla-controlled vessels with important cargo, either with that ship out there—" he pointed out the window at the *Black Aegis* "—or with another arranged for the occasion. Sometimes we perform research on the Camarilla's behalf, mapping out possible aquatic havens and the like." He paused again to study Lucita's reaction, but found little on which to fasten. "Finally, when necessary I assisted Justicar Xavier in problems that required more power than he had in himself or resources he happened to lack direct access to. Presumably I will do the same for whomever the new justicar proves to be."

Lucita remarked softly, "Your routine is less different from mine than you might wish to believe."

"How so? What does a rootless vagabond have in common with a respected authority of the largest sect of Kindred?"

"Spare me the labels. You roam around getting into trouble and then doing what you see fit to fix it. You spend most of your time, according to your own tale, out on the road or at sea, doing what catches your interest. You just happen to have the labels which earn you the trust or at least the support of others."

Kleist snarled, very briefly. "I act for the safety of all Cainites, yourself included. You indulge yourself. You drift without duty; I move in accordance with specific instructions and obligations." Lucita shook her head and affected a sorrowful expression. Kleist fought to regain composure. "You said yourself that you only know us as antagonists. You do not know what you're saying, literally, when you talk about us that way. Come, if you dare. Sail with me on my next assignment and see for yourself."

This was the point toward which Lucita had steered the conversation all evening. It was crucial that she not let on how much she wanted that invitation. Coolly, she answered, "You'd trust me onboard your ship?"

"Cousin, I trust you no farther than I could throw you in broad daylight. You are without honor or principle beyond the merest self-interest. I do think that I can appeal to your vanity and curiosity, and rely on them to guide you toward the information I want you to receive."

"I'm touched by your confidence in me."

"If you want to play games, I can leave now and never speak to you again. The only way I can deal with you at all is with honesty. I have no interest in playing Elysium games with someone like you."

"I see."

"You should. Now, do you dare to step onto the *Black Aegis* and find out what it is I do, or do you prefer to spin idle metaphors?"

"When you put it that way…"

"Watch yourself."

"…I accept."

Kleist stood with Lucita on his ship's bridge, and felt great pride in the ship and its crew. It was a gorgeous, warm night, with the earlier showers now gone and clearing clouds streaming across the sky. Shoals of luminescent plankton rose near the surface, making the sea gleam with a life like nothing on land. Dolphins fed on the glow alongside strange fish rising from the deeps after their favored prey. This was part of Kleist's world, and unfamiliar to Lucita except as obstacle to overcome as quickly as possible on her way to her goal.

The captain entertained no delusions (so he thought) about his standing relative to her. He wasn't her inferior in innate potential, thanks to his ancient sire. But a thousand years of energetic existence must have given Lucita an advantage in practice. He'd been a diligent study of shadow manipulation almost from the night he died, but she'd had five times as long. He very sincerely hoped that he wouldn't have to fight her.

The executive officer saw things a little differently. Of course Randall Thomas seemed *always* ready for a fight. Kleist was never quite sure how many of the XO's stories were accurate, how many exaggerated, and how many purely fabricated. He did know that the XO performed very impressively in the line of duty, and that his record constituted a formidable argument about the foolishness in the general Camarilla prejudice against Caitiff. Kleist would much rather have a "clanless" vampire who could do the job than any quantity of fools with good pedigrees and no demonstrable abilities.

Thomas had put it to Kleist this way, two nights earlier: "We have nothing to lose. If she makes trouble, we've got 88 experienced fighters within 270 feet at all times. If she decides she's unimpressed, we can make changes faster than she can sell out our secrets. And she might pick up some clues along the way, right?" Kleist was more doubtful, but agreed that the experiment was worth performing.

So here they were. Kleist could see Lucita visibly relax as the ship quietly cruised out into the Atlantic, even surrounded by hostile individuals and a largely unknown tactical situation. Kleist himself didn't feel the clan's inclination toward the sea; his own attraction was simply the continuation of the fascination with the sea he'd had in mortal life. Standing on the bridge of a ship responding to his orders was for him the very essence of independence. His masters were far away, and he liked it just fine that way. Even Xavier, so fine a master in many ways, was nonetheless embedded in the scheme of things as Kleist's superior, and Kleist did not willingly bend his knee or submit his mind to anyone else's lead.

"What did you do with your ghoul?" he asked, as much out of formal courtesy as any real interest. Tradition said that specific inquiries showed the host as attentive to his guests.

"She's staying at the inn," Lucita answered, not looking at Kleist. He saw her taking a careful inventory of the hatches and gangways along the top deck. Well, let her; it wasn't like the information was likely to do her much good, and if she felt more secure that way, so much the better. "She had to work very hard on our way here, and needs the rest more than she needs to see this."

Kleist nodded. "Very well. Shall we tour the ship?"

The *Black Aegis* was a custom job from stem to stern. It began with the plans for the US Coast Guard's *Famous*-class cutter, but once *antitribu* naval architects were through with them, only the general proportions remained. Almost all the distinctive surface features could be removed and exchanged with alternatives, giving the entire hull and superstructure significantly different profiles with a few hours' work. The options for modification even extended to anchor chain and rudder designs, though internal refittings took a little longer. Most of the time she sailed as a Bahamian research vessel with prominently positioned instrument arrays for probing tropical storms. A 76-millimeter automatic cannon at the bow and smaller machine guns on each side lay concealed in what looked like stacks of packing crates.

The captain began to win a measure of respect from Lucita as he described the sources of the funds that paid for all this. He had a ledger summarizing the outlines of the process: so many millions of dollars in bank certificates and other currency from this Sabbat ship, so many meters of fiber optics pulled out of a Lasombra yacht before scuttling, and so on. The *Black Aegis* was not only the means of victorious strikes against the main clan; it was testimony to previous victories, and a lot of them. Kleist, Thomas, and their crew had done perhaps more than she had in the last century and a half to interfere with the clan's collective business affairs.

Thomas bustled up with a handful of radio intercept printouts. "Here you go, sir. Got those ass-cannoning choad monkeys pinned solid this time."

Lucita blinked. Thomas' tone was clear enough, but the vernacular completely passed her by. She must have been more obvious than she thought, because he smiled at her. "Fuckwits, ma'am, and a lot of them. It's a whole can full of assholes all needing a little double-barreled enema action."

She could make out part of the last sentence. "You've located someone you've been pursuing."

"Damn straight. I hate these goddamn bastards so much, I've been waiting for the chance to feed them through the meat grinder a little and blow hot tar into the scrapings."

Lucita gave up and turned to Kleist. "Archon-Captain, I'm clearly missing something."

She thought for a moment he might laugh in her face, but he retained composure. "This is one of the XO's personal projects. He's been hoping to identity a band of aquatic Sabbat ever since we ran into them three years ago. They only surface when they've got enough loot to warrant a trip to some convenient port for sale. I assume from Mr. Thomas' expression that he's intercepted communication between them, their current hostages and their transportation, and one of their usual fences."

Thomas nodded vigorously. "Shall we give the lady a show, sir? Let her see what *we* can do with a bunch of meat Popsicles waiting for the jiffy-pop treatment?"

Lucita made a stage whisper. "He wants to show me how you fight?"

Kleist finally lost control for a moment, with two short laughs. "Yes."

Lucita studied the crew as they went to work. Auras showed that about half of the…88, she thought…men were ghouled. The unghouled ones seemed to lack many of the technical shiphandling skills: they were muscle, a familiar style of mercenary apparently assembled from all up and down the Americas. The ghouls were an even mixture of Caucasians and Caribbeans of African descent, and they were clearly the ones who actually made *Black Aegis* run.

The readying cycle was impressively smooth. Lucita suspected that there must be regular drills. They surely couldn't see combat *that* often, could they? Kleist had said "a few times a year", and this showed a lot more practice than that. Small openings in dummy equipment domes and the like let firing teams load weapons and even do rudimentary targeting on instruments without spoiling the illusion. It looked like less than a minute's action would remove the covers and let the weapons come to bear. Lucita could see how it was that Kleist's ledger listed so many profitable hauls.

Kleist directly instructed the teams reading the main gun, while Thomas circled the deck endlessly and oversaw everything else. They seemed to be the only vampires on board other than Lucita herself, and they'd cultivated respect, fear, and devotion as necessary in everyone else. Nobody ever, ever got in their way or showed unwillingness to carry out an order. Lucita felt a brief pang of nostalgia for long-lost estates and the patrician lifestyle.

Thomas and Kleist went over the intercepts. Apparently there were certain code phrases they recognized as belonging to their targets. Triangulating based on signal direction and data about expected docking times didn't take long. *Black Aegis* turned to head nearly due north, aiming to intercept the raiders twenty miles on. Kleist and one of the radio officers began sending what looked like a straightforward stream of technical reports on local current conditions with an occasional mention of something tantalizing, like metal-extraction filtration tests.

The crew arranged themselves in squads, actually performing various scientific tests, with weapons at hand. Like the gun readying, the dispersal showed Lucita that the crew had practiced all of this. The ship slowed from 12 knots to slightly more than seven, in keeping with its research vessel persona.

Wednesday, 12 April 2000, 11:00 PM
Ocean View Inn
Harbor Island, Eleuthera, Bahamas

Angelica had tried to sleep, but found that it just wasn't forthcoming. She was certainly tired enough for it, but somehow sleep wouldn't come until the early hours of the morning. Nor did she feel comfortable leaving the hotel; something told her that it was important she remain close at hand, within reach of a hotel summons if not actually in her own room the whole time.

She couldn't quite make sense of what was happening to her. The...vampire. And there was part of it right there. Angelica still, after all she'd seen since leaving Gunnison, couldn't quite fit the reality of undead blood-suckers into her view of everything else in reality. It didn't fit. More than that, it was an offense against much of what she thought she knew, what she'd learned in church and home as a child that survived the hell of war and flight, what she'd learned in all the years since then. She'd been required to accept amoral men and women and the motiveless miseries of the natural world, and one of the necessary consequences of those lessons was that everything had boundaries. It all stopped somewhere.

Except that Lucita and her kind kept going past the point where all people stopped.

There were times, of course, when a sensible woman had to question her perceptions. Angelica knew what fever and famine could do to the senses, and to the mind's ability to interpret what they sent. This wasn't that. Angelica was certainly tired but nowhere near the brink of exhaustion, and she was getting much better than adequate fare. She showed no signs of disease. Nothing in her self-appraisal offered her any hope that this was all just an extended hallucination.

The fact was, unless some unexpected relief came, that the world wasn't just different than Angelica had imagined, but *radically* different. It might have been easier if Lucita and Stephen and the others were pretty much all the vampires in the world. A handful of them would still have been an offense against the nature of the world, but more in the nature of an anomaly—the sort of freak event that gave rise to stories of miracles and Fortean events. Angelica knew that the world sometimes broke in peculiar ways, perhaps just due to chance. If enough things happen, then the things that only happen one time in a million can happen pretty regularly, and rarer things at least occasionally. They were troublesome but not particularly significant.

It was much worse for there to be so many of them. Did every city hide one of them? A dozen of them? Angelica imagined thousands, perhaps millions, of the things, behind every shadow. Lucita had given only vague answers on the flight from London when Angelica asked if there were vampires in Africa and Asia. In the absence of hard information, the pilot was fearfully inclined to imagine the worst.

Nor did Angelica begin to understand why she'd gone along with Lucita through all this. Two transatlantic flights didn't explain this peculiar enthusiasm she felt. In a couple of weeks she'd have to make arrangements for her bills or she'd lose the apartment, the hangar space...and she couldn't quite make herself care about any of it. No matter how much she hated and feared the thing that Lucita was, Lucita herself commanded Angelica's allegiance.

She needed to understand what was going on. And there didn't seem to be any way to gain that knowledge without continuing this journey.

As that thought echoed around her mind, she tried to imagined herself deciding not to go with Lucita anymore. Enough. Going home. That was it. The thought fell flat. It slipped out of her mind almost before she could conceive it. It wasn't until she started to write a list of possibilities that she realized she'd conceived and lost it at least five times, without remembering doing so.

A chill worked itself into her bones. Could she actually do anything but obey?

Thursday, 13 April 2000, 2:22 AM
Cutter *Black Aegis*
75 miles northeast of Eleuthera Island, Bahamas

"Two thousand meters and closing," the radar operator said. Kleist acknowledged with a brief grunt. Thomas grinned.

The marauders' "raft" proved to be three small barges lashed together and powered with half a dozen engines apparently removed from mismatched ships. Lucita studied the arrangement through binoculars, a touch impressed by the ingenuity while noting the vast array of vulnerabilities. The marauders clearly didn't plan for anyone attacking them on their own turf.

The radio crackled again. "Research vessel," someone said with a thick Cuban accent, "hold course and prepare to receive boarders." Kleist smiled along with Thomas this time as he acknowledged that message, too. The marauders were by now convinced that they had the *Black Aegis* completely cowed.

It had started half an hour earlier with the two Zodiac inflatable boats. They came zipping out of the north to circle around *Black Aegis* and fire off a great many rounds of semi-automatic rifle ammunition. Kleist told the crews to refrain from returning fire. The Cuban radio man came on the air a few minutes later to explain that *Black Aegis* would be "escorted" to a rendezvous point with a larger band, who'd strip it of valuables and set the crew loose in lifeboats, as long as they didn't attempt to resist. Any would-be heroes would die. Kleist did a fine job of sounding terrified as he agreed to the demands.

Now came the moment that, Lucita could tell, everyone on board looked forward to. *Black Aegis* slowed its speed as directed, and turned to run parallel with the raft, chugging along at a steady two knots on a west-northwest course. The Zodiacs raced along *Black Aegis*' starboard side, tossing up cables which extended from large winches bolted to the raft. The raft and cutter converged in three-foot jerks. Soon the Zodiacs had to move out of the way to avoid being crushed. The inflatable boats sped out from between the two larger ships, and then zoomed around to run along *Black Aegis'* port side.

The first marauders came climbing up in pairs. They were a mixed lot, a few with obvious lineages—particularly the Nosferatu who didn't bother concealing their deformities— but most potentially of almost any clan at all. Lucita knew from long experience that vampires could adapt themselves to almost any situation where they might find prey, but this bunch startled her.

Fully half of them seemed to have transformed themselves, or arranged for others to transform them, for existence underwater. She remembered childhood stories about the creatures of the deeps who preyed on incautious sailors, and now here the beasts were. They had huge, bulging eyes with distorted, irregular pupils and complex glassy lenses. Their arms and legs ended in fins or tentacled masses. Lucita was no stranger to using tentacles, but in her case they were merely pulled from shadow and let go again; these things were massive and permanent, pulsing with infusions of vitae and looking terribly organic. Their skins varied wildly: some scaled, some leathery, some covered in algae and even barnacles. Reflexive fear made her draw back a step.

The others were no more human. There must have been Gangrel among them, she thought, for animal features to be so prominent…but then perhaps they'd shared blood and shared curses with it. There were seven-foot tall rats and five-foot tall upright dragons, and creatures that Lucita recognized vaguely as coming from more recent horror images in the popular media. One pack seemed to take pride in displaying themselves as murder victims, loaded up with cleavers and other murder implements, which they'd draw as they approached the fight.

As they turned to receive a fixed gangway that would allow many more marauders onboard, Kleist opened a bridge window and shouted "Now!"

The crew on the 76-millimeter cannon ripped off its coverings manually, while it wheeled around to face the raft. Its first shot went long, throwing up an impressive splash fifty meters beyond the farthest barge. The marauders froze in place, then scattered in a panic. Smaller weapon covers blew off as their respective crews went to work. The first volley mowed down two-thirds of the marauders on *Black Aegis* and knocked out long swaths in the crowd of raft-borne marauders waiting to board. Behind them, the cannon's crew cranked the barrel lower and reloaded with amazing efficiency.

After that it was slaughter.

Somewhere along the line, Lucita realized, she must have succumbed to frenzy. She regained her mental poise some unknown moment later, her mouth filled with another vampire's blood and her feet wet with gore. She looked around to find her hosts recovering from similar excesses, both of them looking very pleased with themselves. Only a handful of marauders still seemed to be intact, and all of them were under guard. Gunfire wouldn't kill a vampire (except for particularly good head shots), but it would certainly slow the target down long enough for an attacker to apply more permanent means. *Black Aegis'* crew had ripped up chunks from the barges themselves to use as stakes, and wrapped the mooring cables around marauder necks and pulled them tight for decapitations.

Sharks filled the water, feasting on the rich, exotic blood of so many vampires. Lucita watched them, thinking to herself, *You don't know the first thing about being real predators.*

Thursday, 13 April 2000, 9:50 PM
Ocean View Inn
Harbor Island, Eleuthera, Bahamas

Lucita sat at the same table she had to meet Kleist. This time Angelica kept her company. Kleist and Thomas had supplies to arrange and other duties to do; they would meet up with the women around midnight so that Kleist and Lucita could carry on their discussion of the merits and drawbacks of Kleist's Camarilla affiliation.

Angelica was ravenous, and worked her way methodically through three courses of seafood dinner while Lucita looked on and pondered. *Can I trust you?* Lucita pondered. *I suppose so. The blood bond seems as strong as ever. Perhaps even more so. Do I want to trust you? What risks do I run confiding in you?*

If anything, Lucita found Kleist's existence even more disappointing than Stephen's. The latter's routine included grace and culture, a modern echo of the aristocratic life to which she'd been born. She had no particular desire to adopt the many artifices the London Camarilla seemed to require, and even if she chose to, there was no guarantee of what anyone else would do. However, granting the most favorable outcomes possible, it would at least have rewards. Kleist, on the other hand, walked through mud and sailed through sewage without, as nearly as Lucita could tell, recognizing it. Nothing in his self-description gave weight to the role of savagery and amoral ruthlessness in his routine.

Back when the Camarilla moved from muttered speculation to actual organization, five hundred years ago, Lucita had listened to speeches about how vampires in alliance could overcome their baser impulses. They could not only survive but flourish, invent or reinvent a genuine night society, where there'd be culture as well as force, and the end to the Anarch Revolt would lead into a renaissance for unliving minds. She'd doubted the claims then, and little of her experience in the intervening centuries gave her reason to reconsider. This voyage with Kleist had been the last nail in the coffin of her hope for something more than rhetoric. There was no answer for her here.

No one in the restaurant would see anything except that the ageless woman in black was very, very still. Being voluble in her despair would not have been conducive to her survival, and Lucita was very, very interested in surviving. But for what? The Camarilla, that great white hope, wouldn't even make a good enemy, much less an ally. The Sabbat? Hardly. Lucita was just the sort of elder that Sabbat ideology described as the enemy. She might still think of herself as the young victim of elder manipulations, but to someone Embraced a week or ten years ago, there was little difference between her and some veteran of the Roman Empire.

If the institutions failed, perhaps it was time to consult some individuals. Her sire, her nemesis, was gone. Her dear counselor was gone. But her compatriot, her ally, was not. Time to travel east.

Andrew fumed.

Where the hell had the bitch gone this time? Once they had the lead on Cardinal Networks and Angelica Tranh, it was easy enough to establish that she'd been to London, and then left again promptly. The Caribbean sighting was firm, with both the plane and Lucita documented on the ground. He had a feeling that there was a connection between her presence and the big raid on the packs that Andrew's sire Conrad liked to call the "Sea Goons," though he couldn't prove it.

He spoke to the pack about going to London and shaking down a few randomly selected neonates for information. In truth that was just bluster. He knew better than to stick his head into the meat grinder of a thriving Camarilla court. It wouldn't work, and it would just win them all painful destruction. No, they had to leave London alone and try the Bahamas. But Lucita had left the plane on Eleuthera and taken herself and Angelica somewhere else. Where? They could be anywhere, practically. Simon Peter had managed to get at various passenger manifestos, but there was so much tourist traffic this time of year, without any other evidence it was impossible to figure out which seemingly mundane couple masked a fugitive vampire and her ghoul.

While they continued to scrutinize the news and vampiric rumor mills for leads, Andrew led his pack back along the bitch's trail. After a couple of false starts, they'd found this guy. He had the stench of victim about himself, and a little persuasive effort by Barry and Niccolo left his soul in shards for them to poke through at their leisure. Sure enough, the bitch had used him years ago, and again more recently. And what was this? Yes, an air tank needing recharging, a little sand to sluice out of the boat when she returned it: she had a cache of some sort out there, and had dived to it. Andrew suspected it was contact information, and suspected as well that there might be more there.

Finding it was another matter. The wasted hulk of what had been Jerry certainly couldn't object to their taking a couple of his boats, and every night the pack split up to run sonar and magnetometers in search of anything interesting on the gulf floor. Nothing relevant turned up, just as Andrew expected, but at least it was something to do. When they were done, they'd sink the boats and Jerry with them.

Saturday, 22 April 2000, 10:55 PM
Bushy Park, London

"Ah, Sir Sydney, good of you to come. A touch early, even." Stephen smiled broadly at his guest, a dour little vampire in immaculate evening dress.

"Indeed, Mr. Lenoir, on occasion a cab actually performs its duties as expected and then a bit more. I trust this isn't an inconvenience?" Sir Sydney Elling's voice rasped unpleasantly. Not for the first time, Stephen wondered if the man were simply immune to his own voice or if—pleasant thought, this—he spent his nights in perpetual torment, his blood crying out for beauty and receiving only such harshness.

"Not at all, please come in."

Sir Sidney handed his coat and hat to one of Stephen's ghouls and followed his host upstairs to the supplemental library. "Am I the first, then?"

"I beg your pardon?"

"Am I the first you have consulted about this find?" Collector's lust made the little man's frame practically quiver.

"Oh, yes, indeed you are. The moment I uncovered it, I thought who might give me best advice, and your name came immediately to hand."

"Good, good. Let's see it."

"But of course." Once they were both seated at the library's teak table, Stephen opened up a portfolio and withdrew half a dozen sheets of well-worn vellum. They'd been repeatedly erased and reused, but as palimpsests went they were fairly well-cleaned. The final writing was all in a single hand, hastily transcribing something in medieval Latin.

Sir Sydney bent to scrutinize them, his eyes and nostrils flaring. Then he closed his eyes and ran his fingertips across the surface of the sheets, all before actually reading them. "Tell me the provenance again."

Stephen was fascinated by the sight of a master diviner and scryer at work, but reminded himself of his underlying purpose. "Yes. As you remember, I had a guest earlier in the month. She had to make a rapid departure, and in her absence I found myself at loose ends. Last month I went to the auction at Jarndyce's, and secured several volumes from the Cunningham collection. You remember the story there, I presume."

"Oh, yes." It had been in the literary papers: a small collection of books which had survived the 1666 fire by being wrapped, by unknown hands, in soiled diapers and towels. They'd come to light in a building demolition. The restoration work was particularly tricky, with one of the restorers commenting, "You know, normally when we say that a volume is a piece of shit, we're being metaphorical." But the work had proceeded, and the early results were attracting impressive prices. Many of them went to collectors known to donate to the technical universities, as there was widespread interest in the forensic side of the matter—looking for the consequences of the fire and what amounted nearly to fossilization.

"Well. I opened up this 1650 folio of Mallory, and these sheets fluttered out. I could tell at once that the handwriting was medieval, and that puts it well before my field of expertise. Hence I decided to consult you."

"Very wise. And have you handled them?"

"Only as you see here, with sterile gloves, on this table with this lighting."

"Very good." Sir Sydney bent to his task.

It was after midnight when he looked up again. "Mr. Lenoir, this is very peculiar. There are a number of anomalies at work here."

"Oh?"

"The vellum and ink are of Eastern European origin. Somewhere in the vicinity of the Black Sea, I should say. The actual style of the writing, however, is distinctly Western. The text itself, alas, is very obscure. I can make out a few theological terms—it is some kind of apocryphal text, I believe—but there appear to be terms that I suspect are transliterations of one of those Balkan dialects. I can make very little of it here. May I take it with me?"

"Hmm. Perhaps so." Stephen stood up. "But let's take a moment to stretch. Have you seen what I've done with the armory?"

"I have not. Show away." Sir Sydney rose and followed into the room where Lucita had faced the ghost. "Sir! This is not your armory! What do you play at?"

"Why, I play at inquisitor, of course." Stephen raised his voice slightly. "Now." Two of his ghouls emerged from the spacious closet and pinned Sir Sydney's arms.

"What is the meaning of this?" Sir Sydney squirmed, but couldn't manage to wrench himself free.

Stephen gathered up an image of the ghost as he'd seen it charging down the hall, hungering for the blood of his guest. He compacted it into a hard, dark knot of terrible recall and impressed it on to the fore-psyche of his guest. The reaction was what he'd hoped for.

Sir Sydney was good, certainly, at deception. One wouldn't survive to his age at a court like London's without it. But even masters sometimes slip. When he saw in projected memory the thing that had trailed Lucita, there was a single moment of bright and clear recollection which he didn't quite manage to suppress in time.

"Thank you, Sir Sydney." Stephen forced himself to remain calm, though he yearned to shred the bastard. "You know whereof I speak, and I know that you do, and we can dispense with the pretence. You have violated my hospitality, and all that is necessary for you to do now is explain why."

"Mr. Lenoir! Do you have any idea who you sheltered under this roof!"

"I believe I do. I introduced her at the time. Do you have any questions about that?"

"You fool! That was no 'her' at all!"

"What?"

"That was the notorious pirate of your clan, Alfonso Lopez!"

"What?!?"

"Ah, Mr. Lenoir, you've been deceived. I felt something uncertain about your guest, and took many opportunities to probe 'her' from across the room."

Stephen felt a chill along his back. "I see. And you found…"

"I established to my own satisfaction that 'she' was indeed an imposter. It was a most excellent deception, but not one that could resist my expert eye."

"Did you inform anyone else of your insight?"

"Very nearly, but no. You see, I continued to study 'her.' It was very difficult; as I said, 'she' was very good. I felt a moment of utter bewilderment—perhaps an active resistance, even— and then it all became clear to me."

"That you were looking at this Lopez?"

"Oh, yes. You see, he hijacked one of my vessels more than two centuries ago, and denied me certain relics I'd sought for my own ends. I swore that one day I would have revenge on him. I don't know what brought him to the court that night, but there was the object of my desire. So I acted!"

"Pray tell, Sir Sydney, how *did* you come to have a ghost at your command?"

"Ah, well…."

"Or rather I should say, what did you trade to some passing Giovanni for tutelage in necromantic lore?"

"Mr. Lenoir!"

"Do you deny it?"

"Alas, no. But you make it sound so vulgar. And also so wicked. The truth is that I received a query shortly after the war about the occult portion of dear departed Prince Mithras's personal library, and it included an offer of mutual assistance. I long ago realized that necromancy could be of substantial use to me. Why waste time in guessing when I could consult the creator himself?"

"Indeed." Stephen still managed to avoid destroying the miserable wretch.

"So you gave your tutor the books he wanted—"

"She."

"The books *she* wanted—"

"Not quite."

"Eh?"

Sir Sydney managed to look pleased with himself despite the current trouble. "You see, I traded her clever forgeries, which I'd helped the prince identify some years earlier. They are not entirely valueless, but they could not quite teach her what they purported to."

"I see. And she didn't return seeking revenge of her own?"

"Not yet, at least."

"Remarkable. So that's how you happened to be capable of summoning a ghost."

"Yes. It was the victim of some ghastly sensational murder or another, and quite willing to go after someone I told it was responsible for deaths of the same sort."

"So you violated my hospitality because you thought the woman I brought was in fact this man you're obsessed with punishing."

"I had no intention of violating your hospitality! I simply neglected to instruct the spirit for that eventuality."

Now Stephen did lose control. He fell on Sir Sydney with fangs and claws extended, pulling huge chunks out of the man's body and scattering them around the room. By the time he recovered, he and the ghouls were covered in gore, and they were well and truly alone.

Sunday, 23 April 2000, 3:30 AM
Somewhere beneath Mexico City

There were times, Trasaric believed, when he could almost feel the sanctity leaking down from above. The sensation was worst on Sunday mornings, when the faithful gathered to pray to their one god. He discussed the matter with his unliving masters from time to time, and found that opinions differed. Warriors either flat-out disbelieved in the power of any mortal god or feared it intensely and believed it far stronger than Trasaric did. The devout believers generally acknowledged the reality of divine favor among the living, unless they held to creeds which reserved divine attention for vampires, but they came to no agreement about how far such influence could flow. Scholars and sages gave answers that Trasaric couldn't begin to understand, full of talk about the nature of the pleroma and essential versus inherited versus developed features of vampirism.

In any event, here it was Sunday morning again, and Trasaric felt edgy. He'd been waiting all evening to do a fitting for Cardinal Mysancta, only to have her (or him, or it, as might be) cancel at the last minute. Now Cardinal Timofiev wanted to consult with Trasaric about "a matter of fashion." Trasaric didn't expect that the little monk had suddenly developed a desire to dress sensibly, and couldn't readily imagine what could be up.

Timofiev arrived on time, somewhat to Trasaric's surprise, meeting in one of the mirror halls that littered the Sabbat's warrens. Trasaric saw himself moving alone in the endless reflections, while listening to Timofiev's footsteps behind him. "You spoke of a matter of fashion, Eminence," Trasaric began. "How may I serve you?"

The Cardinal laid out a scheme for Sabbat packs infiltrating the Camarilla forces occupying the cities gained but lost again in last year's sieges. It was elegant, showing the Cardinal's predilection for layered misdirection, and Trasaric was glad to be called in. The aesthetic challenges were delightful. Trasaric would actually end up doing some field work, studying the styles prevalent in the American Camarilla and working out durable but suitable-looking gear, along with instructions for the infiltrators…"Pardon, Your Excellency?"

"I said that we will of course also benefit from the information we get from Monçada's rebellious childe."

"Ah. Of course, Eminence. How is that search going?"

"As well as fate allows."

"Of course, of course. And what does fate allow your little band to achieve?"

"So far they have primarily uncovered and punished deceit. They find signs of the childe's movement, but the hunt goes slowly. I believe that victory will come when the childe attempts to make herself strong."

"Very good, Eminence."

"You distrust the omens, Trasaric, but this is because you are not part of the true society. You think to yourself, a great hunt should go to great warriors. You wonder why we do not send forth Talley, or Black Wallace, or other proven veterans of our crusade. But I say to you that this force is like a mouse bearing the plague into a fortress. Battering rams cannot reduce its walls, for the defenders are prepared against mighty assaults. Only the small can make it through the chinks in their defenses, and with disease undermine them all."

"Of course, Eminence."

"You will see in due season, Trasaric."

"I look forward to it, Eminence."

Monday, 24 April 2000, 11:45 PM
Somewhere beneath Mexico City

Andrew paced through wet tunnels, his legs strengthened by shadow, filled with rage he couldn't discharge. The hunt was going nowhere. It had been going nowhere. If it didn't start going somewhere, the grand lords were going to decide that he and his mission were both failures. And Andrew didn't much want to face that fate.

After a very long time alone, Andrew heard running footsteps. Long before the runner came into sight, Andrew knew that it was Barry Morn with his distinctive half-step run. Andrew stopped to compose himself.

"Andrew!"

"Got that one right. What now?"

Barry had learned from experience that a particular style of dry sarcasm was Andrew's way of covering rage or frustration. He proceeded carefully. "We have a lead."

"Did the Blessed Lucita heal the sick again, or what?" Andrew was annoyed with Barry for getting so worked up over this kind of thing. Lucita impersonators were thick on the ground, or at least common enough to keep hunters busy. In addition, Lucita made a handy boogey monster on which to blame ill fortune and the consequences of a vampire's own stupidity. For a month Andrew and his team had crossed the hemisphere again and again, always finding…well, just about anything except their quarry.

"Better than that. But maybe you want to come examine the evidence for yourself."

"Is this an admission of incompetence or an effort to distract me?"

Barry really, really hated that kind of question. He settled on honesty for his answer. "Neither. It's just that I think you're more likely to be persuaded if you see the evidence firsthand. If I tell you, you'll keep finding reasons to disbelieve it."

That was sharp. Andrew smiled. "True enough, I suppose. All right, lead on."

There wasn't much left of the messenger. It looked like he'd been staked at least twice in recent memory, and beaten up on other occasions. He hadn't had the opportunity to properly feed in some time, either, and his body was consuming itself from the inside out. Administering a lot of blood quickly might help pull him through. Or might not. First he'd have to prove himself useful.

"So. You're a sailor boy." Andrew started off his interrogation with an insult, and followed it up with more, hoping to gauge the strength of the man's resistance. In addition, Andrew wanted to know just where the man seemed strongest. He looked young enough that he probably hadn't formally committed himself to any of the Paths of Enlightenment…unless, of course, like Barry there he had some secret motivation. Best to go carefully until the spiritual battlefield was clearer.

Questioning proceeded slowly. In the end it turned out that he had three useful pieces of information.

First, Bishop Guiterez's pet project, the "kingdom of the sea" as he liked to call it, was history. The messenger was one of no more than half a dozen survivors, and he'd made it only by spending two whole days and nights as a chew-toy for sharks. (That explained the wounds Andrew hadn't been able to figure out.) The messenger had seen the bodies and could describe them vividly, his aura quivering with fear and the desire to pass the awful truth along. It was a most efficient slaughter. If Guiterez wanted to continue his scheme to build a wholly aquatic base of power, he'd have to start all over again.

Second, the raiders were some Camarilla commando named Kleist and his crew. But they were accompanied by someone else. The messenger had been in one fight with Kleist before and knew others who'd fought him as well, over the years. It was common knowledge in the "kingdom of the sea" that Kleist sailed with just one other vampire and a crew of mortals. This time, though, there was another vampire. A woman, with the most impressive shadow powers the messenger had ever seen….

"I see. Thank you, Barry."

"Wait, you haven't heard the best part."

The messenger had pulled himself out of the sea on Eleuthera to prey on tourists and build up some strength before seeking out the great sanctuary in Mexico City. While there, he saw the woman again. She was walking along the beach, talking with a mortal woman. ("Some Chink," the messenger said, and then flinched when he remembered the priest Tanakawa standing behind him. Tanakawa took it without obvious response.) They were making travel plans, and the messenger heard them discussing a flight to Bermuda and then "on their way."

Andrew wheeled around. "Barry, have you checked this out?"

Barry grinned broadly and held up printout of Simon Peter's passenger lists. "Two tickets in the name of Katherine Scott from Eleuthera to Bermuda, and from there to Lisbon. Two tickets from Lisbon to Rome to Doha, Qatar in the name of Maria Cadamon."

"*What?*"

"Yes, really. 'Monçada' with the syllables flip-flopped."

"God damn. What next? Pig Latin? If the bitch is out to commit suicide, the least she could do is throw herself at *us*, right?"

"Should I book a flight for us, Ductus Emory?" Barry trotted out the formalities for the sake of the interrogators.

"By all means. As soon as possible."

Barry flipped up one wrist and pulled out a wad of papers from his sleeve. "We'll be leaving in two hours."

As they drove to the airport, Andrew asked, "What would you have done if I'd said, no, let's take some time, or no, let's take another route?"

"Sold the tickets to some desperate sucker, I suppose. But you didn't."

"No, I didn't."

part three: trials

Saturday, 22 April 2000, 1:40 AM
Leonardo da Vinci Airport
Rome, Italy

Lucita could not, of course, express her fear to Angelica. Had the thought to do so even occurred to her, she would have dismissed it as being equally appropriate as a wish to flap her arms and fly to the moon. It was the ghoul's place to take orders, and Lucita was glad to see her settling into it. Soon, Lucita hoped, the last of that irritating independent streak would disappear, leaving behind an admirable combination of subservience and technical excellence.

Angelica did a fine job handling the travel arrangements. At some point in the future, perhaps, Lucita would give her a freer hand, but one thing at a time. For now it sufficed that she could take instructions and carry them out, and negotiate good compromises when necessary.

This next step would be interesting: What *would* Willa make of Angelica now? After all, if things went well, they might be associates for quite some time.

As Angelica spoke on a cell phone acquired for this one call, Lucita reopened the telegram she'd received almost a year ago. It was from Dubai, United Arab Emirates, and it said only this:

There'd been no signature, and no need for one. Lucita did not believe that Allah called her, or indeed that He ever would. But her need was as great as a divine mission, and she could think of no one left in the world more likely to offer solace and advice than her old comrade, Fatima al-Faqadi. She hoped that Fatima would receive her even without the conviction of holiness.

```
ON RETREAT IN AL HEJAZ STOP
COME WHEN ALLAH CALLS STOP
```

Lucita had picked up an atlas in one of the airport bookstores, and thumbed through it, assimilating all the details she could. Al Hejaz was not a town or nice compact region. It was hundreds of miles of barren mountains, broken by occasional streams, with the narrow coastal plain and then the Red Sea to the west and the great deserts to the east. People did live in the midst of the wilderness, where oases permitted; most of the space belonged in practical terms to no one. There one could find, with some searching, pilgrims and fugitive criminals and lepers and all other sorts of outcasts. It was just the place for a devout vampire to try and commune with her God without presenting a tempting target for the clanmates bent on her destruction.

"Good evening, thank you for calling Metterlinch and Associates. May I have your identification number? …I see…to whom am I speaking? …Ah, yes, Miss Tranh. I remember speaking with you…I beg your pardon? …I see. Well, never mind, perhaps the recollection will attend you at some other time. What service may I perform for Madame at this time? …I see. One moment while I verify the availability of that account. Perhaps you are not aware that this is a difficult time in the Gulf states. Their governments have imposed rather onerous restrictions on the movement of certain classes of wealth in conjunction with diplomatic ventures intended to…no, I rather thought you wouldn't be informed on such matters…are you still there? Very good.

"I can transfer the funds Madame requests, but only with a 48-hour hold for what's described here as 'verification of independence' of the transaction. Please inform Madame that I will therefore have the standard package transferred from Bahrain to her in Doha at local noon on Wednesday the 26th. Yes, I am sure that this is inconvenient. You may explain to Madame that I have done my best…thank you and goodbye, Miss Tranh."

Willa did not sigh; she'd never cultivated the art. She did stare wistfully at the phone, wishing strongly that some mishap would remove that damnable Yankee ghoul so that Madame could choose a better one.

Thursday, 27 April 2000, 9:55 PM
Four Seasons Hotel
Doha, Qatar

It had become too much. Angelica had to ask. "Ma'am…"

Lucita looked up, a thin sheen of moisture along her hairline. She was counting bills delivered by the last courier, but her hands held their position so she could resume later. "Yes?"

"Ma'am, you look more uncomfortable than I've ever seen you. Ever since we landed in Qatar. It's like you're sick all the time or something."

"You wish to know what ails me."

"If something does, yes, so I know what to do about it."

"Very well." Lucita pondered, realized she'd never had the opportunity to conduct this particular experiment, nor heard about anyone else doing so. "Close your eyes. Turn around slowly." Angelica did so with perfect obedience. "Do you feel any unusual sensations, any variation in your condition?"

"No, ma'am."

"Interesting. Now, face south. Yes, that way. This time with your eyes open, turn around slowly, looking out to the west, until you face due north." Perfect obedience again. "Do you notice anything?"

"I don't think so, ma'am."

"Interesting." Lucita pondered for a moment. Did Angelica need to know? Yes, she might very well. "Although you carry my blood, you are nonetheless mortal, and not fully subject to the curse." She felt the thought rise in her ghoul. "Forget that about the curse. Another time for that. You are nonetheless mortal. We who have passed beyond mortality are aware of some features of the living world, feeling their power. There is something in the Arabian desert that roars like the rising sun, all the time, and it makes me unsettled. Some of my kin say that it's strongest in the holy city, but I have no knowledge of such things nor interest in the investigation."

"So is there anything I can do?"

Lucita smiled. Such a practical thing, a ghoul's devotion. "No. Merely watch and perform your duties carefully. Soon enough we will be on our way to a land where the sun rests more quietly at night."

Saturday, 6 May 2000, 11:55 PM
King Abdul Aziz International Airport
Jiddah, Saudi Arabia

It was very yellow. It was by far the yellowest plane Angelica had ever flown. It was also built like a brick, with a bare minimum of streamlining. The wings, stretching out from the plane's roof, looked like ironing boards. She didn't care. As of ten minutes ago, it was hers to fly.

This wasn't actually the first time she'd flown a CC-138 Twin Otter. Half a dozen years ago, on vacation in the Inland Passage, a bush pilot trying to get into her pants let her take his Twin Otter for a spin along part of his semi-regular route resupplying scientific outposts on the islands. (He never did get to sleep with her. For some reason even the explicit declaration "maybe if you bathed" didn't sink in.) That plane had floats, of course, and used broad open channels for takeoff, narrow little inlets for landing. But it looked like this one would handle the same way in the air. Angelica knew that it could get down to around 60 mph before stalling out and had a range of just under a thousand miles, which made it very well suited for the search Lucita was talking about.

And talking about and talking about, come to that. She'd exhaustively and exhaustingly covered all sorts of details on their flights here. Only the demands of daytime rest quieted her down. Angelica didn't feel particularly comfortable about the vampire's enthusiasm. It reeked of desperation—sometimes literally reeked, in fact, as little rivulets of nearly black blood seeped out from her eyes. Fortunately for their privacy, a few well-placed terms of medical jargon kept away prying questions about the ghastly emissions. Only Angelica had to deal with them. Lucita's condition reminded Angelica more than anything of the malaria cases that had raged among some of the boat people.

The emptiness Angelica felt during those nights alone, while Lucita sailed with *Black Aegis*, faded once Lucita was back in the (cold) flesh. The intellectual reservations remained, however. Angelica was torn between wanting to know just how far demons (or vampires, or whatever they were) had infiltrated the visible world and fearing what the answer might be. She decided that for now she'd rather not know the details of the phone calls and e-mail messages Lucita sent from their hotel rooms. Nor did she want to know who the couriers were who arrived the next night with brief cases full of cash, credit cards (forgeries, apparently, but good ones), and identification papers for half a dozen nations. All Lucita said was, "Burning bridges shed a lot of light, for a while."

On her own, Angelica could have gotten from the Bahamas to Saudi Arabia in one ghastly long day. Lucita preferred to make the journey in steps. Arranging first-class cabins that could be closed off during the day was just a matter of money, but when Angelica brought it up, Lucita brushed off the suggestion brusquely. "I don't need to stick my head into any more bear traps right now." So they stayed in airport hotels each day, and each evening Lucita made more calls, so that at the next airport there was another drab little man (or woman) waiting with funds.

As they rode through the air, Lucita explained the parts of her plan that Angelica would need to know, and reviewed them from time to time to make sure that the pilot understood.

Angelica felt a hesitation about this flight she couldn't explain, and which she knew disappointed her mistress. The weight of that disappointment lay on her chest like a stone fallen from heaven, but there it was. Despite the changes in herself, Angelica remained a good pilot with experience in bush flying of many kinds, while Lucita's experience was with dealing with the personalized hunt at ground level. Angelica wanted to engage in a systematic search by map grid, and nearly rose to the brink of objecting when her mistress insisted on a more intuitive and meandering route.

"No, I don't know precisely what we look for. I shall simply know it when I see it." And, of course, in the end that was enough. There could be in Angelica no lasting doubt of Lucita's rightness. The pilot just hoped that sometime soon she would understand enough to know why her mistress was right, as well as enjoying the certainty that she was.

Jiddah wasn't what either of the travelers expected. It reminded Angelica of Singapore: almost all modern construction, laid out in a master plan that gave a great deal of attention to traffic flow and commercial floor space and none at all to street-level shadows or air flow. Even at almost midnight, the interior of the city was like an oven, as the breeze off the Red Sea collided with the front rank of skyscrapers and scattered. The airport was cool, but the offices where Lucita had to do her business, just a few hundred yards away, weren't. Angelica kept a bottle of water in her hand almost constantly, taking sips every few minutes; Lucita was freshly appreciative of not sweating herself.

The plan was simple: land in Jiddah, stay the day in an airport hotel, buy a plane the following evening, and be off to Al Hejaz. Lucita had made this kind of arrangement countless times before, from Singapore to Montreal, and she was prepared for a certain amount of difficulty finding the right seller. She was not prepared to spend three entire nights without success of any kind, nor for the variety of excuses offered: everything from conveniently absent prior customers to local religious festivals prohibiting commerce of some sorts (the duties differed in each account, and in some cases were allegedly penance of a personal nature) to simple refusal to acknowledge the women's presence.

Twice Lucita began to force her will on a particularly annoying merchant, and each time she immediately felt a cautionary dread. The same feeling struck whenever she tried to obfuscate her appearance into a male form. There was something at work here—in herself or in the city, she couldn't tell which—which led directly from power to misery. So she relied on her skills of bargaining developed across centuries and continents. Angelica sometimes tried to help, but it didn't seem to do much good, and by the end of the second night they agreed that Lucita should proceed as the sole speaker.

In the end they found their man at the very back of a long row of warehouse offices. Aram Kanikhurian, "Master of Aviation," according to his sign, had pictures of planes available for sale on a cash-only, no-questions-asked basis. Most of them looked like they'd been through wars, and probably had;

Angelica asked a few pointed questions about flights to supply Eritrean rebels and government forces, which the dealer equally pointedly ignored. A couple of the planes seemed in better condition, and Lucita arranged to meet the dealer at the airport the next night. She and Angelica immediately went to the airport themselves, but found the dealer's hangar space locked tight and decided against breaking in.

The pair strolled along the waterfront, watching oily waves break on white sand leave rainbow halos beneath sodium lights on their way back out to the sea. Parts of the Red Sea were supposed to be pristine marvels of natural beauty. This wasn't one of them. For Jiddah's city fathers, commerce trumped all other concerns, and quick commerce at that. One day the tides of fortune would turn to some other harbor, and they aimed to get all the wealth they could in the meantime. The police scrutinized the two women carefully, as with all the other visitors, since it wouldn't do for there to be any whisper of complaint about the safety or harmony of Jiddah's public spaces among international travelers. Half a dozen cops gave them cards with various emergency contact numbers, just in case anything went wrong.

"Tell me about where we're going," Angelica said as the 6th of May became the 7th.

Lucita promptly said, "It's not where, it's who."

"Um, you want to meet with someone. But he—"

"She."

"But she's in some place out there in the mountains. My job is to fly there, and I should understand as much as I can about her, to know what sort of place she'll be in."

"Capabilities, not intentions."

"We're not going to war with her, are we?"

Lucita thought about that. Her initial glib answer died in her throat as she considered the possibilities. "No, we're not. She may not welcome me, but this won't be a grand brawl."

"Good. So I don't have to worry about heavy armaments for the plane."

"No, I don't think so."

"So tell me about the target."

"She's another old-timer, from the time when Islam was

222   shard

young. We met as strangers, then as enemies, then as occasional allies. Unlike me, she always remained close to her clan...." Lucita spun out the image of Fatima as she knew her. Angelica imagined a figure out of fairy tales, a beautiful woman with an aptitude for war, her skin darkening with the centuries as the blood curse had its way with her, rising in the councils of secret masters in the Middle East, most recently striking the decisive blow against Lucita's own sire.

"She's important to you, then."

"One of the most important people left in my world. Maybe *the* most important."

"So what is she doing *here?*"

"I'm not entirely sure. There have been strange stories about upheaval among the Assamites. I'm reasonably sure that some very old member of the clan is active again and trying to reshape the rest for some purpose, but beyond that, I couldn't say. I know that there have been many more Muslim Assamites seeking sanctuary lately. Some of them do what Fatima did, and go to ground somewhere. Others go out wandering. Some, I gather, end up with one or the other of the sects, but I didn't think to ask Stephen about it and my usual contacts don't have much to say."

Angelica would have been deeply fearful, if it weren't for her absolute confidence in Lucita's ability to navigate them through the troubles safely. (Where did the confidence come from? But no time to think of that now.)

The planes in the side hangar fully lived up their photos, Angelica found. Of the dozen Kanikhurian showed them, she doubted that more than half of them would fly at all, or remain in the air for more than ten minutes if by chance they managed to take off. Of those remaining, three of them looked like they wouldn't hold cabin pressure, or had defective landing gear, or both. The CC-138 was the only one in the lot that looked capable of going anywhere. Fortunately, it was well suited for the kind of flying she expected to be doing.

Not so fortunately, she must have let on in some way that she was pleased with the plane. She'd wanted to keep her expression and manner calm for this, to make bargaining easier. Kanikhurian sensed her interest and dragged out the process for more than an hour. Lucita thought she'd reached a deal only to watch Kanikhurian back away again three times, with many intermediate climaxes and failures. In the end, though, Lucita secured the plane, and its license, and access to airport fueling facilities. He offered to supply false identity papers, forged money, and other such goods, but Lucita declined them all. (She whispered into Angelica's mind, "Accept none of them. I suspect that he'd immediately report us to the police.") The deal went through honestly and above-board, with clean cash in exchange for papers that passed the authenticity tests Angelica could apply on short notice.

So here it was. It was a long way down from the jet that Cardinal Networks lured her in with, but at least it was a plane and it would be hers to command, for the duration of the search. While Lucita went off to handle the paperwork around fuel purchasing and flight plan filing, Angelica gave the (her!) plane a thorough inspection. This was going to be a long night.

In the end they decided to wait one more day. Angelica didn't finish her inspection until nearly 4 a.m., and Lucita's efforts needed half an hour more. If they took off then, Angelica would be exhausted and Lucita would have to immediately get herself into shelter. Instead, by waiting another day, they were leaving rested and ready for a full night's searching.

Within a very few minutes they were outside the major air routes. In the clear dark skies, it was easy to trace those routes. Jets left crystal-white contrails that almost shone, running to Cairo and Riyadh and Amman. Oil derricks lit up the Red Sea with landing lights and exhaust flames. A few highways flickered with the headlights of cars and trucks winding their way toward distant cities. Elsewhere the night held sway. Lucita felt very comfortable in the midst of it all; Angelica was still a creature of the day, and felt isolated from the world.

"Wouldn't I do better to search while you sleep?" Angelica asked at last.

"No. Fatima couldn't know for sure whether I'd be alone or not, and would plan on the assumption that I was. So whatever her sign is, it's something that I can see at night."

"All right."

The coastal strip gave way to hills, and then to genuine mountains. Instruments showed that many of the crests were over 8,000 feet, and as steep and rugged as anything Angelica had ever seen. There were many narrow canyons with nearly vertical slopes, completely unsuitable for landings, and a few strips that looked barely wide enough for the Twin Otter to come to rest on. A handful of lights sprinkled the mountains like fallen stars: some campfires (singly or in tribe-sized groups) and some electrical. The talk Angelica had heard at the airport suggested the usual mix of withdrawn people, from tradition-minded natives to smugglers. There had been tales of cannibals in the hills, and while Angelica was *mostly* sure they were just talk, her own experience of life in the gravest extreme made her cautious of dismissing them altogether. She hoped they had no mechanical troubles this trip.

Three times Angelica spotted something unusual, and each time Lucita dismissively told her to check it out, with a manner indicating that the vampire already knew it wasn't what she was looking for. In a canyon that petered out in a foothills landslide, an irregular dark mass proved to be a row of black cargo containers, smashed and clearly dropped from a great height. They weren't leaking or labeled, and Angelica couldn't tell what they were. She took pictures and flew on. An hour after that, something glinted halfway down a moss-covered slope. Some very careful angling let her pass right overhead only a few dozen feet overhead, and she could see that it was a jeep pinned by a boulder fallen from father uphill. Wind and perhaps fire had polished it smooth in places. Finally, less than hour before it'd be time to scout the day's resting place, there was a perfectly straight black strip two feet wide, running up over one hill, down to the next valley, and up the next slope. Angelica crested the second hill, only to find a cluster of dumped toxic waste barrels. A straightforward leak must have sterilized or mutated whatever grew in the black strip. Lucita did not say "I told you so."

Tuesday, 9 May 2000, 11:40 PM
King Abdul Aziz International Airport
Jiddah, Saudi Arabia

"Goddamn you!" Andrew shouted as he slammed Kanikhurian against a hangar wall. "We don't even want you, we just want the bitch! So tell us where the fuck she is!" Behind him, he could hear the pack chuckling. This was the kind of "investigation" they liked, with a lot of killing people and breaking things.

Kanikhurian was barely conscious as he slumped to the floor, for the fifth time since the pack arrived, and he bled from wounds to his head, arms, torso and genitals. He still had breath to say "fuck you." That was it. Something in Andrew snapped, and the Beast within him poured out in a continuous wave of fury. Part of his mind watched with calm detachment as his hands gathered up the almost-corpse, as his teeth tore at eyes and ripped them out of their sockets, as his hands moved up to rip out the screaming tongue, as his shadow-wrapped legs smashed all the major bones in the man's feet and worked their way up to knees and thighs. Short of dismemberment, it was about as thoroughly incapacitating a death as Andrew could manage without specialized tools. The movements meant nothing to Andrew. When Kanikhurian hit the ground one last time, it was with a far more fluid thump, a plopping rather than a fall.

Andrew realized a moment too late that he'd made a ghastly error. Best not to let the pack know it, at least. "So much for that," he said with what he hoped was jaunty confidence. "She'll be back. We can mount our ambush here."

"Are you sure?" Even Barry had his doubts.

"Sure enough." Andrew groped frantically for rationales. "She went into the desert with a plane that can carry a lot of cargo. She'll need to bring it back, and here she already has contacts." He gestured at Kanikhurian's body. "*Had* contacts, at least. We can pass ourselves off as him and a few customs officials, take the goods, and then take her."

The others mulled it over. Apparently it was good enough to assuage them for now, and Andrew figured that after a fight with Lucita they'd either be triumphant enough to banish all doubts or so thoroughly destroyed that it wouldn't matter.

They were closing in. They all knew it, too. Those long weeks of fruitless search and nights of inactivity had completely given way to a bustling schedule of travel and interrogation. Andrew was pleased at how restrained, relatively speaking, they'd been. No more public places awash in blood, just select bodies. It had been worse since Qatar. They all felt constantly uncomfortable and the lead had gone dead for a while. Too much time went by before they picked up the trail, and it took much violence and intimidation among independent charter pilots to find the old man who remembered flying the two women to Jiddah. He'd never learned their names or indeed much of anything beyond the facts that their cash was good, and that they sat mostly talking in what the old man thought was probably French.

So they landed in Jiddah two nights ago—right about the time Lucita and her ghoul were taking off, Andrew realized later, but he didn't bother mentioning that irony to the pack. Sharpened by their experiences in airport-vicinity hunting, the pack spread out to observe the sleaze that flourished just beyond official sanction. No matter what ideals she might profess, in practice Lucita seemed to spend a lot of time among lowlifes, and such people were quite willing to spill everything they knew when confronted by undead monsters. Andrew instructed the pack not to kill anyone except in immediate self-defense, but otherwise to go wild with intimidation. He suspected that the city's secret byways would echo for some while to come with stories of the things that came out of the shadows at fliers and those whose businesses let them fly.

After a couple of dead ends and false starts, they'd found Aram Kanikhurian. He proved just what they wanted. When Andrew described Lucita, the old man trembled with a recognition visible even to those who couldn't read auras. A little gentle questioning—actually gentle questioning— revealed that he'd seen her feeding shortly before her departure and figured he was damned for consorting with demons.

Andrew smiled. "Right you are, sir. Eternal damnation begins right here, while you're still alive. But tell us what we want to know and Hell may be relatively light for you." Then the torture began.

Well, here they were. Andrew really did hope that Lucita would return. It made at least some sense: She now knew Kanikhurian and could consolidate her dealings so as to avoid bringing any more mortals than necessary into her confidence. Time to think about what in the hangar would make a good trap.

Sunday, 14 May 2000, 12:00 AM
Castle of Saint Rafael the Archangel
Sicily, Italy

There were eight of them this time, on the roof of the tallest remaining tower. It would have been unbearable for them under even the weak light of stars, so their allies called forth mist to hide the sky. The castle floated in its blanket of darkness and the magicians could imagine themselves in the early stages of their final triumph, as the Earth's bonds dissolved and the Abyss claimed all.

Their strike against the world was going well now. It took more sacrifices too often than they could afford, but they knew now how to unleash the Abyss deep beneath the ocean's surface. The same principle should work for openings within caves, but something interfered; a trio of the cabal continued to study the problem. In the meantime, all the cabal's members rejoiced in the growing force demonstrated by the things that answered their summons. Their repeated breaches in the wall of creation, concentrated in the middle expanses of the Mediterranean, created a current of attraction within the Abyss, and as it flowed ever deeper, stronger (and stranger) powers rose to strike at the painful universe of created things beyond.

Surely, the magicians agreed, it could only be a matter of time before the Antediluvian heard their call and spoke with them. And then the world would end.

The magicians had little interest in the details of the modern world for their own sake. Human society was not and could not be anything more than a collection of irrelevant changes which would in turn be swept away, and the physical matrix of society was so much detritus cast up by the blight that was creation. The world concerned them mostly as a source of interference at this point, when the great work was underway but not yet secure. It was an obstacle, the mob as much a problem and much the same kind of problem as a storm or earthquake. Their masons kept the castle strong; their agents observed the world and dealt with problems as they arose.

Tonight's reports were encouraging. The great herds of humanity knew that something peculiar was going on in the Mediterranean. Rumor attributed the disappearances to pirates, but also to more exotic explanations: monsters of the deep, secret government experiments, alien interference. The magicians liked that, and instructed their agents to feed such rumors.

The last agents filed downstairs a few minutes before midnight, leaving the eight alone in the mist. It took only seconds to redraw the summoning circles where the closing hatchway left small gaps. Starting with the outermost ring, five concentric circles faded from the castle's native black stone into a flatter, purer blackness. The eight stepped in and descended slowly out of sight, the blackness becoming increasingly yielding toward the center. The nested gates kept the Abyss wind from blowing and allowed them a quieter passage.

In the darkness outside creation, the eight felt the swirling turmoil created by their rituals so far. They sent their wills up and away, into the calmness of the void, and let their minds open to the subtle echoes of the Abyss' inhabitants. It took work to cut through the screams close at hand from all the mortals (and a handful of vampires and other denizens of the night society) sent into the void against their wills. Some had died in the shadow creatures' assaults, but a great many still lived, their bodies failing only gradually, and it all made a tremendous amount of useless hubbub.

children

The concept insinuated itself into the eight minds from somewhere very far away. Excited, the magicians tried to get some sort of bearing on it, searching for any kind of reference mark against the Abyssal background on which to focus.

children i sleeping waking come

The thoughts were too obviously appropriate to be anything but their vanished master. Each of the eight had sometimes wondered, in private moments, whether this process was all just some ghastly exercise in self-delusion and denial of the reality of Gratiano's act of diablerie. Now they *knew*, in their innermost selves, that it was not.

children i come not yet you return prepare

The voice cut off abruptly. No amount of calling or searching brought it back.

Lucita smiled. As she'd suspected, the sign, when it came, was obvious enough.

The valley was small, and nearly perfectly circular. Flying at this particular angle, Lucita could see how that particular combination of ridges resembled the stylized crown favored in her clan's heraldry. It wasn't obvious, and would likely have escaped her notice from almost any other viewpoint, but it was there. And it was like Fatima to do that, trusting to fate or Allah to see that her friend would see the sign if and when she needed to.

"There," she said and pointed.

Angelica turned to follow Lucita's finger and did a double-take. "All right, that's certainly something. Do you want me to land?"

"Of course."

Lucita looked on with rare impatience as Angelica circled the valley, established it was indeed wide enough for the plane to land, scouted out a relatively good approach, and finally began her descent. Faint white lines—veins of quartz, Lucita thought—ran through the "crown" to mark a landing path, but Angelica preferred an alternative angle; she came in almost due east to west to take advantage of a gap in the mountains to the east for a little extra descent before the actual landing run. At the last moment there was nearly a disaster, as the plane rolled over crevasses not visible in the night and nearly got its wheels caught in them. Angelica managed to put on a brief burst of speed, then a series of rapid, shallow turns to shed the excess. She taxied to a stop mere yards short of crashing into the cliff face that defined the valley's western edge.

Lucita was out of the plane even before it came to a complete halt. By the time Angelica secured the controls and stepped down, Lucita was moving in long loping strides, clearly searching for signs of current or recent presence.

And there she was.

A woman stood at the northern edge of the valley. The nearly full moon shone down nearly as brightly as a streetlight, and without the distorting, monochromatic hue of a sodium lamp. Lucita suspected that even Angelica could make out at least some features, and to the vampire it was all perfectly clear. The woman waiting was taller than either Lucita or Angelica, and her hands and neck held the Assamites' dark sheen where they extended beyond her pristine white robe. Lucita wanted to run to her, but she made herself slow to a walk, and at the last moment to pull herself into a formal bow.

"Hello."

It was her friend. Lucita would have known those eyes anywhere, and the robes held few secrets from someone trained in the best use of supernaturally acute sight. She knew Fatima's lines and curves, the particular angle of her left heel as she stood at rest but ready to leap if necessary. She knew the hands that extended from the long white sleeves, how they hooked and curled while their owner thought of other things. It was she.

Fatima reached up to pull back her hood. Her long black hair was cut short now. Her gaze was alert, concerned, but not warm. "The peace of this place be upon you and those who travel with you. Welcome, Lucita, to my sanctuary."

Lucita turned briefly to look at Angelica, who was walking carefully across the valley's sharp outcroppings. "She is my pilot, serving me while I travel this time." She remembered the formal phrasing. "I speak for my companion, and pledge that she brings peace and not conflict, gain and not loss, good and not evil, into your home. What she does here, it shall be as if I did it, and there shall be no account left unreckoned when we depart."

"It is good. Be welcome, you and yours." Fatima still didn't smile, but she shifted her weight slightly, away from the ready-to-lunge stance toward a position of less immediate preparation for attack. "Come in. The night won't be long."

The cave opened into the northeastern side of the valley, where dawn glare couldn't reach. Fabric dyed the colors of valley stone hung in three layers across the entrance. No one passing overhead could have seen that there was anything beyond the apparent back wall of a shallow niche, and even someone on foot would have had to come quite close to discover the truth. The night was quiet, but Fatima took no chances. She stopped motionless for a moment, and Lucita heard all sounds fade away. She couldn't remember whether she'd explained to Angelica about how Assamites could do that, but decided that if not, the ghoul would nonetheless learn soon enough. Sound returned as they entered the cave.

There. They were in. Fatima lit the nearest oil lamp and paused to let her guests examine the scene.

The main chamber was no more than five feet wide, but at least thirty feet long. Long-ago residents had hewn niches out of the rocky walls. Angelica realized after a moment that the niches were most likely originally for internment of devout hermits, and wondered whether Fatima or someone else had removed the bodies. She remembered the mounds of corpses cleared from cemeteries the victorious armies wanted for their own purposes in Vietnam. In any event, the cave was now completely clear of dust, animals and insects—apart from Fatima herself, only a few lichens occupied it now.

The niches along the left wall were all completely barren. The right-hand ones were given over to a library: books and scrolls filled some, while others held writing supplies. In between the niches, long scrolls held careful calligraphy of Arabic passages (from the Koran, Angelica presumed). At the back of the chamber, a stone slab closed off a passage running downhill toward unknown inner chambers.

"It's not the palaces of old," Lucita said, and immediately regretted her glibness. What was it about Fatima that always brought out this crass, facile side? She was, after all, born to a higher station than Fatima and more skilled in aristocratic arts. Somehow she always ended up sounding, at least to herself, like the vulgar one.

Fatima simply nodded. She took off her outer robe and hung it on two hooks so that it spread out and covered the first left-hand niche. Beneath it she wore a black tunic and trousers, with soft black sandals. As she moved down the chamber to light more lamps, she was very aware of Lucita's person studying the black skin that was part of her Assamite legacy. "This is a place for contemplation, and I'm here to study the world and my soul. It serves me very well." Her voice came out softly, with just enough air so that it would carry to her guests, and she deliberately chose a neutral accent. Only her gentle soprano pitch kept her words from sounding inhuman and intimidating.

"How much of the world can you actually see from here?"

"All of it. Or at least enough of it to remind me of it all." Fatima frowned. "But this isn't the time for that, yet. Dawn will be on us in scarcely more than an hour, and both you and I must rest by then. We should arrange the accommodations for your entourage."

Lucita could feel some confusion in Angelica. Apparently the use of terms like "entourage" made her feel like she was part of an unseen group. She'd have to explain more of the Traditions to the ghoul another time. She remembered from adjusting Angelica's memories in London that the mortal did have experience with ceremonial greetings at extended length—as a child she'd paid formal visits to grandparents before the war swept across her home. So there would be a point of familiarity. Lucita was also slightly touched and a little amused to notice that Angelica felt her mistress was acting hastily. She worried about the vampire's state of mind and feared the intentions of their hostess. If anything, Fatima's resolute calm only made it worse, reminding Angelica of psychotic torturers in her homeland. That, too, would need to be addressed in the future.

"Angelica can use the plane," Lucita said. "It's got space for us both to rest in. Shall I join her, or do you have a place here for me?"

"I prepared one for you precisely the way I prepared one for me," Fatima answered and gestured at the empty niches.

"That's it?"

"That's it. It's sufficient for what you and I really need, after all."

"Are you so sure that peace of mind isn't necessary?"

"We will talk more about that later." Fatima's tone did not invite response.

Lucita looked at the niches, then at Angelica. Without hearing any words, the pilot nonetheless developed the distinct desire to step outside, and not to return until half an hour after sunset. During the day, she realized, she should rest, and study the plane, and conserve her energy. She should be ready to leave at a moment's notice, but under no circumstances should she stray outside the valley. If she felt restless, she could remove the trails of her landing gear. Yes, that would be wise. With a final look over her shoulder, she stepped on out.

"Have you really slept this way the whole time you've been here?" Lucita asked once they were alone.

"Yes, I really have. Does it bother you so much?"

"It looks like an invitation to nightmares and despair, if you must know. Yes, it bothers me. The symbols of where we sleep are important."

"And yet you're the one who came around the world to seek me out, not vice versa. Do I look like a woman in the clutches of nightmares and despair?"

"Well…no."

Fatima didn't precisely smile, but the muscles of her face relaxed more than they ever had. "Child of Aragon, childe of Monçada, trust the tradition of hospitality. Not the story about vampire traditions we tell the young ones, but the living tradition of hospitality. You are my guest, and I do not condemn you to bad rest any more than I would condemn myself to it."

Trust wasn't something Lucita gave willingly. But then perhaps that was part of the problem… "Very well."

So she lay there in her chosen niche, halfway back the length of the chamber, and listened to the sounds of approaching dawn. The gathering dew collected on plants and outcroppings of rock and trickled down around the cave. Nothing moving came inside the cave itself, but insects and burrowing mammals moved around it, skirting the water's channels. Birds of prey swooped out of the pre-dawn sky to catch rodents seeking shelter before the day grew hot. Every few minutes an airplane passed by far away, far beyond any mortal's ability to detect. As her cursed body drove her to sun-fleeing sleep, Lucita gradually became aware of the cave as a safe place and of the outside world as dangerous intrusions best kept at bay. She marveled briefly at the reversal before all conscious thought ceased.

The sky was dark again. Lucita and Fatima sat across the valley from the cave entrance, beneath a deeper overhang, and watched the stars rise over the valley mouth. While they slept, Angelica had moved the plane up against the steepest cliff she could find and strung netting to mask the plane's outlines. No thorough search would be fooled by the disguise, but it should at least cut down on casual intrusions, and there was something to be said for knowing that any visitor had made a determined effort to get there. The pilot now dozed fitfully in the plane's main compartment, her sleep slightly augmented by gentle suggestion from Lucita. The vampires had the little world to themselves.

"What do you do for food?" Lucita had fed before they left Jiddah and could go several more nights without blood if she had to, but she was curious.

"I leave the valley, of course."

"And?"

"And Allah provides."

"What does God provide you, though?"

"You must have seen that these mountains are by no means empty."

"Yes. Angelica kept finding signs that she thought might be yours, but they were all from people's ventures."

"Sometimes, when the world is rich in irony, Allah provides me flocks of shepherds. There are some very rich pastures further north, where springs keep the canyons green, and in season I take from the men who guard the sheep. Other times I feed on the smugglers, bandits and escaped convicts. Twice I've fed on scientists, and twice on tourists. I don't starve."

"I see." Lucita looked down the valley. "So if I had to feed in a hurry and Angelica weren't available, I would…what?"

"This isn't really the question, is it?"

"What?" Lucita swung her gaze back to Fatima, who

showed the same calm reserve as ever. "What do you mean?"

"I mean that you're letting a particular piece of detail eclipse the larger scene. You want to know how I survive and what I do."

"Well, yes." Lucita could produce a blush on command, but chose not to. Her words would suffice to indicate embarrassment to one who knew her so well.

"I came here because I had to go somewhere. I had to go somewhere. Alamut was dangerous—" She paused to hold up a cautionary hand. "I'll explain that, but later. Alamut was dangerous. I needed time to think and remember and pray. At first I settled as close to Mecca as I could get with my cursed blood, but it didn't work. There are too many people, too many complications of all sorts. I wandered north until I found this place, marked it out for you with stone stones placed on the ridge, and settled down. That was ten months ago. As you can see, I'm not wasting away."

"No, you're not. You look as fit as ever."

"I should. Do you see those marks?" Fatima pointed. Lucita looked, thought, and looked again. She realized that what had seemed minor natural cracks were in fact the marks made by hand and foot blows, running from the valley floor up more than thirty feet toward the crags above. "I may not have the training floors and precision instruments, but I use what I have."

"And what do you do when you're not training?"

"Pray. Question. Read. Write."

"You told me once that I had the art of giving perfectly truthful answers which said nothing. That sounds like one of them to me."

Fatima looked startled. "Is it?"

"I think so. What would you say to me if I'd given you an answer like that?"

"'Pray what? Question what?' Yes, I see. Very well." But she sat silently for many minutes. When she began again, Lucita was surprised all over again. "When I pray, of course, I pray as the Koran instructs. Five times a day, or rather a night, and on all the other occasions I'm supposed to. No, don't interrupt yet." She hadn't looked at Lucita, but Lucita suspected she must have moved in some small way that alerted her host to impending speech. "I read the Koran and Hadith and works of the law and memoirs. I write out my own experiences. I question…everything, I suppose."

"Why are you doing this?"

"Let me answer with another question. How much do you know about the state of Haqim's children?" Lucita remembered that the Assamites tended not to call themselves "Assamites," preferring instead to associate themselves as the family of Haqim, their clan's founder. It was a very alien way of thinking for Lucita, to whom the Antediluvian founder was almost anything but a friendly father figure. "You see many things from the outside, I think, and I don't know what shows."

"I know that many of your Muslim clanmates seem afraid for themselves. The rumor mill says that some have even joined the Camarilla. I know that I encounter more independent wanderers from your clan than I ever have before, and I know that there are also many fresh Sabbat recruits from your lines."

"What do you make of it all?"

"I think there's a purge going on. The council must have decided that Islam is no longer acceptable, which causes the Muslims to flee, and it's acting brutally enough to make the Sabbat's 'kill your sire' nonsense sound appealing."

"Not bad."

"But wrong, I take it."

"At least in part. It's not the council. It's one individual."

"One individual has your whole clan in this much uproar? Did Haqim wake up after all and decide to put you all back on the straight and narrow path?"

"Close. Ur-Shulgi claims to be one of Haqim's own childer."

Lucita felt an arctic chill around her heart. The Sabbat took it as given that apart from the Antediluvians they'd destroyed themselves, the ancient monsters were still all out there, manipulating Cainites and humans alike toward the grand destructive consummation that would be Gehenna. The Camarilla claimed as a matter of policy that all the Antediluvians were destroyed or sunk into torpor from which they'd never awaken. Like most vampires who thought about it at all, Lucita had always assumed the truth to lie somewhere in between. But she'd always assumed that any active Antediluvians were active in ways and in places far removed from her own experience, so that she would never encounter them.

A vampire of the fourth generation, if such this Ur-Shulgi was, was altogether too damn close to the Antediluvians. Lucita had met others of that generation, of course, but this thing sounded—in both Fatima's description and in her evident fear—far more formidable than Lasombra's childer, Montano and Gratiano and the rest.

"Is…" The words died in Lucita's throat. "Is he?"

"I don't know. I don't think any of us can know for sure. I do know that he's strong enough to destroy everyone who opposes him. The Caliph is destroyed. The Vizier and the Amr have fled. Alamut is given wholly over to the ones who believe that they're preparing for Haqim's imminent return, when he will judge all in the blood."

Memories washed over Lucita: neonates in rebellion against their sires, princes at war with each other, the tide of blood attracting mortal attention, inquisition and secular hunting, the great diablerie within the Lasombra Antediluvian's stronghold…it had been a nightmarish time. She did not welcome the thought of it coming again, to any clan.

"Have you seen him yourself?"

"No. I don't expect I'd survive if I did. Much stronger vampires have already perished in the attempt."

"What precisely is this Ur-Shulgi demanding?"

Fatima pitched her voice lower, clearly imitating some male vampire. "Know, childe, that it is time for all Children of Haqim to forsake mortal faith. The end is upon us, and we must prepare for our appointed role. Give up the gods of men and honor in your heart only our Father who was and is to come. Do this or perish."

"And you…"

"I couldn't. No matter how much I feared for my existence, I couldn't abandon Allah to worship any of His creations."

"So you fled."

"Yes."

"What have you done since then?"

"I've asked Allah to give me the courage to do what I know must done."

"You want the courage to confront the Methuselah?"

There was no real humor in Fatima's laugh. "I do not ask Allah to make me stupid, no."

"What, then?"

"My brothers and sisters in the blood need to see strength turned to causes other than this delusion of purging all vampires for Haqim's glory. They need me along with the others. But I don't yet know what I should do. So I seek an answer. When it comes, then I'll go back out into the world."

"That's very convenient."

The rock on which Fatima had been sitting shattered when she smashed a fist into it. She didn't seem to notice; both the strength and the subsequent healing of broken bones in her hands came unbidden. "How *dare* you speak to me that way! What do you know of duty except that it's something you can exploit in others? When did you ever sacrifice your personal ambition for the sake of anything at all? Did you ever once submit in obedience to anyone, choosing any greater good over your own desires?"

Defensive reflexes took over for crucial seconds. Lucita ran a distance away at high speed, fell into a defensive crouch, and wrapped herself in concealing darkness. By the time she realized that Fatima was not in fact going to attack her, she was altogether geared for battle—a waste of blood as well as an embarrassment. She tried to maintain her poise as she dropped the defenses and came back to sit down next to her friend, but it wasn't easy. "I didn't mean to give offense."

"At least, you hoped that I'd overlook the offense." Fatima's voice was cold now, purged of most of its humane cover. It was very easy now for Lucita to remember just how effective a killer her friend was. "Did you really come all this way to mock me?"

Lucita swallowed, an involuntary response she'd last made more than a century ago to what had seemed like an inescapable death trap. "No."

"What, then? Do you want to recruit me for some new mission? Does the dear departed cardinal have an heir you'd like to remove?"

"No, nothing like that." Lucita looked up to see Angelica emerging from the plane with a worried expression. The noises of the not-a-fight had disturbed her rest. This was time for no subtlety. "Sleep again," Lucita called to her with the force of a mistress' command. Obediently, Angelica climbed back into the plane. "Nothing like that," Lucita repeated, half to herself.

"What, then? What brings you here tonight?"

"I have lost my way." There. It was out in the open.

Fatima made a snuffling sound that might have been a snort if she put more air into it. "Your *way*. What sort of way did you ever have?"

Now it was Lucita's turn to be angry. As she spoke, her anger bled out in subconscious commands to darkness. Shadows pulled themselves loose from the valley floor and swung around the two vampires. They shifted from irregular blobs into demonic figures from the folklore of three continents, and the air whistled in minor keys as they cut through it. In a moment the pair sat at the center of a tall column of angry shadows. "I didn't realize mockery was part of your holy meditation. You speak as if it was just me and my whims, but it's not so, damn it. I gave my existence to stopping my sire, on every front I could, in every way I could. I couldn't make him unmake me, but I could and did try to keep him from enjoying success ever again. I spent centuries acting out a practical atonement for his sins while you cheerfully carved your way through bystanders."

"But your duty was never more than pique."

"What?"

"You acted against one individual. While you did, his cohorts went about their merry way, and you never did anything against them unless someone hired you. This is not morality, this is a grudge. It's what my people train children to grow out of."

"You…" For a moment Lucita envisioned herself smashing her fists into Fatima's face while shadows pulled her wretched corpse apart. The intensity of it shocked her. The shadows around them instantly collapsed back to their natural forms, and all the fighting power within Lucita boiled away. "It doesn't matter. That's history now."

"Yes. You're not here to tell me that he's come back, I assume."

"No, he's well and truly gone, as nearly as I know. No sign tells me anything else."

"So tell me of your way, and how you lost it."

"The cardinal is gone. I can continue to clean up his schemes, of course, but then what?"

"You could…"

"Wait. You asked. I've been traveling, trying to see our kind from their own eyes, looking at the alternatives. Whatever you think of my calling, accept at least that I knew it wasn't like allegiance to another cause. So I've been seeing what it's like to hold some other tenet."

"And?"

"It's all lies."

"It is?"

"Everything anyone said to me about duty to a sect or cause was so clearly a cover for their own personal ambitions. Manipulators use it as an excuse to manipulate; fighters use it as an excuse to fight. Whatever it is they want to do, there's some justification for it in their various codes. None of them seemed any more conscientious than I am, and most less."

"Do you think the same of me?"

"I'm not sure."

"That is not the most reassuring thing you ever said to me."

"I don't really *understand* what it is you do. You follow the words of some mortal man…"

"No. I follow the words of God, given by the Archangel Gabriel, to a mortal man."

"So you say. I don't believe it, but at least I can tell you're submitting to a real discipline. But now, at a time when you say yourself your clan needs you most, here you are in the desert, speaking to nobody but me." Fatima looked pained. Lucita tried to sound apologetic. "I don't mean to doubt your honesty, but can you really tell me that your faith is making you any more effective in a time of need than my choices have?"

"I can, but not in any terms you would accept."

"Then no, you cannot. Unless you can make your God speak to me himself, I must act on what I see, and I see stillness at a time when you know motion is needed. This isn't any help to me. I could pick an ambition at random and get just as much use out of it."

Fatima trembled. "You cannot speak this way to me."

"We decided once that there would always be honesty between us. Are you recanting that commitment, too?"

"You admit that you don't understand what you're talking about."

"It's true. But I know what schemes are like. I see that your faith takes you out of the struggles most important to you at just the time when your enemy is consolidating his hold. You've crafted enough useful deceptions in your times. Can't you at least entertain the idea that this story, like so many others, is a trap for people like you?"

Fatima leaned back and closed her eyes. "There speaks the childe of Monçada, who has learned her lessons well."

"What does *that* mean?"

"Your sire was one of the best manipulators your lineage ever produced. He saw everyone but himself as dupes and pawns. You absorbed more of that outlook than you ever realized. Once you rejected his own convictions, you simply assumed that you'd never find anyone who was actually acting out of conviction rather than in response to manipulation."

"But I've searched…"

"And found just what you expected to, isn't that right?" Fatima opened her eyes just in time to see Lucita's nod, and closed them again. "You found that the Camarilla is in fact just what you and I decided it was long ago. The details may vary, but in essence you got what you went looking for. Then you came to me, and again you found what you expected to find."

Lucita clenched her fists again. "I didn't expect to find someone who'd attack my motives and soak herself in dogma…"

"But neither did you come prepared to accept anything I might have to say."

"What?"

"You knew that I had gone into retreat of some sort. You knew that I have always cherished the faith of my father and mother, where you rejected it long ago. You knew that there's been trouble among my family in the blood. You must have known that I'd be reexamining my decisions, and that either I would be freshly immersed in the will of Allah or altogether turned from it, since at times of crisis I commit myself wholly to a course until I see my way out again."

"Well, yes."

"But look. You brought no supplies. You made no arrangements to stay any period of time. Your whole plan assumes that you'd fly in, speak with me, and fly out. But if you thought you might want to hear the answers I have, you'd have acknowledged that it might take quite a bit more time to work it all through. You prepared for failure. You don't want to allow for the possibility of an answer that would impose the sort of external restraints you know the will of Allah does."

More than anything, right now Lucita wanted to flee the scene. This was not a charge she wished to hear or consider. She forced herself to stay.

Fatima ached to see her friend's pain, so manifest in every tight muscle and almost-concealed tremor. She also knew that if nothing jarred Lucita into a reappraisal of her own legacy, the course her friend pursued could lead only toward destruction or the acceptance of some other darker creed. "Your sire poisoned the well of faith in you."

"He was the most evil man I ever knew! And he was the most completely devout. How can I trust belief, when it lives so happily in someone like him?"

There. That was the essence of it. "The conviction that guided the cardinal was a counterfeit. But we do not counterfeit what's worthless, only what's valuable.'"

"That's the sort of smug rhetoric I'd expect from a rank neonate."

"If I'm so wrong, ask yourself why you're so afraid to consider the possibility that I may be right."

A long silence followed. The tension slowed eased out of Lucita's frame, leaving behind despair. "I wanted for so long to keep believing, you know."

"Yes."

"But I looked and looked, and I found those who manipulate and those who are manipulated. Everything I've seen tells me that we make faiths to trap each other, and that's all."

"You've seen miracles. Remember that time on the shore…"

Lucita waved a hand dismissively. "You and I could both be quite plausible goddesses if we chose to. We are the heirs of vampires stronger than ourselves, and they of vampires stronger than themselves. I remember the halls the Antediluvian walked down, how air and stone responded to its will as readily as my clothes follow my movements. I have no reason to believe that there's any power beyond our kind, or that if there is, that it means good for anything but itself."

"Reason. But what does your heart say?"

"My heart doesn't say anything! It lays there like the dead tissue it is, preserved by a power that makes death itself a tool for inflicting suffering on the world."

"Set aside the rhetorical defenses for now. You know what I mean."

"Yes." Lucita paused. "I wanted to believe. I don't know if I still do. I fear to give myself to anything answered in the unseen, because I look there and see puppeteers only."

"You believe I'm a dupe."

"I can't believe anything else."

"And are you so very sure that your disbelief is any less a plot?"

"Eh?"

"Your refusal to commit to anything beyond yourself ensures that you will never get the benefits of cooperation. You have individuals to work with, yes, but you will never have the power of an organization. When you perish, as we all must, your memories will go with you and no one will benefit thereafter. You leave behind no students, no legacy apart from your clients and their victims. What a convenient existence for someone who could lead armies if only she could get past her need to be queen."

This time panic did overtake Lucita. She flattened out and sank into the deepest corner of the niche she sat in. Once in shadow form, she moved in jerky leaps throughout the valley, careening off rises and flowing into dips, burning off frustration in nervous exertion. It was almost half an hour before something resembling clear thought returned. In the intervening time she was only dimly aware of the tangible world; currents within the darkness constantly captured her attention, and there were bass rumbles from far away that reminded her uncomfortably of an unwanted voice she couldn't quite identify. Reason returned to her like a hot rain, a few painful drops at first, then an escalating torrent in which she had to swim or perish. It was close: part of her wanted only to shrink from light and self forever.

Fatima was still sitting in the same place, and turned only her head to watch Lucita reassume human form. "I think you should go. This cannot do either of us any good."

"I agree."

They said nothing more as Lucita walked to the airplane and climbed in. Fatima heard her friend (her former friend, perhaps) mutter "Wake up, now" to the pilot, and the sounds of the pilot stirring to begin flight preparations. She watched from an absolutely motionless stance all during the plane's revving up, taxiing, and takeoff into the night. She remained motionless until all trace of it was gone. Then she returned to her cave, and didn't notice for many minutes that she was shedding tears of blood onto the commentary she'd chosen as that night's reading.

Lucita likewise remained very still once she'd roused Angelica. She swayed slightly as the plane bounced along on its way, but otherwise might have been some statue consigned to an art collector with a taste for medieval ladies. Gradually Angelica realized that there were twin red streaks running down her mistress' face, but she lacked the courage to say anything about. Sometime in the pre-dawn hours the trickle stopped, and Lucita removed the marks before settling down to sleep. She said nothing.

Monday, 15 May 2000, 11:03 PM
King Abdul Aziz International Airport
Jiddah, Saudi Arabia

In the end, it was easy.

Andrew spent more than an hour pacing around the hangar, studying the possibilities for concealment and lines of assault while thinking thoughts like "...be careful not to run into the jet fuel canisters..." Finally the realization sunk in. There were hundreds of gallons of high-grade fuel in tanks in the hangar, waiting to be adulterated with larger quantities of cheap oil of various sorts. There were strong hoses for getting the fuel into planes and pumps for moving it all fast. He smiled. The others flinched.

Once he explained his insight, they all relaxed. Barry said that he wanted a t-shirt that said "There's jet fuel. The rest is easy." Andrew promised to get a set for the pack.

Andrew tested the pack's reaction to a quick blast of fuel lit by a blowtorch. He himself had difficulty maintaining self-control in face of the anathema, and chose to let the pack see him flinch a little—he needed for them to feel free to be honest about this one, since they'd just get one chance unless their target had suddenly become much more incompetent. Roxana, the closest they had to an accomplished Abyss mystic, fared worst, spending nearly an hour as a cringing mass of darkness in the far corner. Niccolo retained his human form, and that was about all that distinguished his performance from hers. Simon Peter managed a more dignified withdrawal.

Barry kept it together. He trembled, yes. But he managed to pick up the torch and the fuel hose and aim the flame at various targets around the room. Andrew timed him, and found that he could wield the fire for at least three minutes. Andrew figured that if that wasn't enough, they were all in trouble.

This wasn't like the desert ambush, where the pack had thorough control over the whole environment. Andrew was excruciatingly aware of how many people there were just a short run's distance away, and knew that numbers could make up for a lot of innate human inferiority. They had to act quickly and then get out, with no luxury for art or indulgence along the way.

So the trap was a simple enough one. Roxana sat in the late owner's desk, with his corpse arranged on its scarred teak surface, entirely drained of blood and washed clean so that it wouldn't give off warning smells. Two hoses each ran into a 55-gallon drum of number 3 jet fuel, with the nozzles directly over the doorway like showerheads. Asbestos-wrapped cables let Barry sit on a palette a few feet away and wait for the opportunity to tug the nozzles open. A pair of blowtorches guttered quietly; every few hours one of the pack changed the fuel tanks for them. The hangar's fire extinguishing system was mostly bunched up on hooks right over the fuel nozzles, so that with a flick of one switch Barry could dump a *lot* of fire-retardant chemicals on the vicinity.

Then it was time to wait.

Sunday went by without word of Lucita or her plane. Simon Peter scanned the local air traffic control frequencies, both directly with his own magic and with the aid of some of the great many radio rigs Kanikhurian had stored next to his desk. There were two false alarms: one report of a CC-138 flying out of Medina, and one customer at the door. It didn't take long to establish that the plane was one owned by a local meat broker, with a solid trail of documentation for its movements. The customer was a big greasy Caucasian, who got as far as seeing Kanikhurian's body and stopped dead. Andrew sent him on his way with a mental shove, telling him to come back on Wednesday. This would all be over by then.

Small talk filled some of the quiet hours. "Hey, this is Chinese fuel," Barry said at one point. He pointed to the logo of the Red Leaf Brand of JPC's Nanjing Refinery. "How'd it end up for sale here?" They kicked around various possibilities without arriving at any particularly trustworthy conclusions. Probably it had been resold more than once out of a shipment intended for Iraq or Iran, but the packmates all realized how much of this part of the world was just a mystery to them. In other slow moments, they talked about past exploits. Niccolo described a very convoluted hunt for one of his sire's enemies in Spain during the Spanish Civil War; Andrew recalled the amusingly incompetent rivals for his bishopric and snippets of the state of the Sabbat in the Pacific Northwest; Barry and Roxana compared their instructors' approaches to the Paths of Night; Simon Peter told about the time he'd worked with a roving band of Lasombra who operated as a computer consulting service in their three-way sting against a Camarilla-backed publishing venture in California. None of it was particularly deep, but Andrew was glad to see the pack thinking of each other as perhaps more than drive-by companions.

Andrew secured the warehouse just before turning in for sleep at the end of Sunday night. He commandeered a passing baggage handler to write a sign in Arabic as well as English, saying that Kanikhurian was out of the city on business but would return Monday night.

Monday evening began like Sunday, but now they were all more on edge. Andrew took down his sign and made sure the door was unlocked. Simon Peter reviewed the logs and found an afternoon report of Lucita's plane on its way back to Jiddah after unspecified stops in the Al Hejaz. She must still have the pilot, Andrew realized. For a moment he considered destroying her at the same time they took Lucita, but then he thought again. The odds were very good she'd seen interesting things, and she should be questioned by vampires more skilled in subtle interrogation than Andrew and his pack. He instructed the pack that if at all possible, they should take the pilot alive. There was no particular need to go out of their way to avoid hurting her at all, but they shouldn't do anything that would require really major effort to fix, and it would be best to take her as intact as possible.

Barry frowned. "Someone's going to have to get her out of the way of the fire, then."

"Very true, if it goes that way," Andrew said. "Which means that if it's necessary, you'll have to do it and let Simon Peter or me run the jets and extinguishers. I just hope it won't be necessary."

They waited in silence.

Suddenly Simon Peter opened his eyes, ending a magical trance, and flipped on the radio nearest him. The pack listened to air traffic control make contact with the CC-138 and route it into the standard path for approaches from the north. The pilot, an American-sounding woman, made arrangements as she flew for an overnight berth as close as possible to the warehouse where the pack waited. She said that she hoped to sell the plane soon, and would make longer-term arrangements if a sale didn't take place immediately. The pack shared smiles about that. Sure she would. Then she was down on the runway. Simon Peter flipped off the radio, so silence returned. Roxana turned off half the lights, leaving the entry and her vicinity brightly illuminated while creating natural -looking shadows for the others to wait in.

Later, Lucita would recall that she felt no warning twinge. Her usually strong sense of impending danger totally deserted her. Did the ongoing grief about Fatima turn it off? Was there some Sabbat magic at work? Had fate decreed what would happen next? She never knew for sure.

The hangar was quiet as she and Angelica approached. Angelica was tired, having rested very badly indeed in the psychic shadow of Lucita's turmoil. By the time Lucita woke, she found that the pilot had already left their daytime shelter on the east slope of the mountains and started back toward Jiddah. It seemed at first like an act of rebellion, but then Lucita realized that it was the product of combined concern and self-defense. The further Fatima receded into the distance, the softer the edges of Lucita's despair, which in turn meant that much less pain echoing through the pilot. They should unload the plane as quickly as possible and get out of here to go…

Somewhere. Lucita didn't have the vaguest idea where she wanted to be now, apart from "somewhere else." Perhaps she'd think of something as they did their business. She could scarcely think straight, and the loss of blood through the injudicious use of her powers back in the valley and through mourning since then didn't help. Feeding would have to be a high priority, too. She almost fed on the pilot, before realizing that in Angelica's weakened condition, feeding would court serious trouble.

Once the plane was down and secure, Lucita took the lead in approaching Kanikhurian. She was too distracted to worry much about semblances or courtesy, and let Angelica scamper along behind as best the pilot could. The hangar wasn't so brightly lit tonight. A slightly lighter square marked where part of the door had been shielded from the dew and the afternoon's windblown dust by a sign now taken down. The door was unlocked. She pushed it open.

The first thing she saw was the strange woman sitting behind the desk. The second was the body on the desk. Kanikhurian had been killed and prepared very efficiently: no odors leaked to alert her until she was inside. Lucita whirled and saw three, perhaps four figures standing in carefully contrived shadows. Before she could act further, there was a pair of metallic clunks from overhead. She looked at the smell of liquid fuel. Half a dozen drops splashed in her face.

Then there was pain.

The first blasts seared her upturned face. Her eyeballs shriveled. Her mouth, open slightly so that her tongue could pick up any stray tastes, filled with flame that charred all the way down her throat. Her hair caught on fire. She couldn't scream, and fell over silently.

The flames continued to beat at her. From head to toe she was a solid mass of burning skin and boiling vitae. Her clothes were gone in seconds, and with what sensations remained to her she could feel where all the tissues from skin down had burned or melted so that her bones thumped on the floor. This was by far the worst agony of her thousand-year-existence, far worse than the sunlight she'd chosen to confront the year before, worse than any of the burning buildings she'd been in over the centuries. Pain filled the whole universe and pressed in on her with all the weight of creation. In seconds she would cease to exist altogether. Her last conscious thought was *what a waste*.

Angelica's experience of the ambush was even shorter than Lucita's. She was holding the door to open it when there was a bright light inside, followed by that rush of heat. Lucita's pain filled her head through the blood bond. She was scarcely aware of the door being flung open by the blaze, nor of it striking her to the ground. She passed out in agony long before Lucita's elder mind collapsed.

As soon as Lucita hit the ground and stopped moving, with an emphasis on the "stopped moving" part, Barry turned off the jets and turned on the extinguishers. Gooey white foam soon flooded the quarter of the hangar around the slumped body. He picked up a portable blowtorch just in case the target needed any remedial treatment and jumped down from his perch. "I think we got her."

"I think so too," Andrew said with tremendous satisfaction. "Niccolo, go check on the pilot."

The eldest packmate obediently waded through the melting foam and stepped outside. "She's out cold," he said as he dragged her back inside.

"Good. Tie her up and make sure she's gagged. Don't bother knocking her out again if she wakes up; we don't want to risk a concussion. As long as she can't make a nuisance of herself, let her watch." Andrew watched Niccolo long enough to see that his orders would get carried out properly, then turned back to the main event.

The body wasn't very interesting. Or at least it wouldn't have been very interesting to someone who didn't know who it was. Andrew could see tiny traces of healing happening even now: patches of charred skin flaked off, and broken ligaments relinked themselves over exposed bones. At this rate it would take weeks for the body to regain functionality, but the fact that it was happening at all impressed him. "Are we sure she's out of it?" he asked to the hangar in general.

Barry set down the blowtorch. With one swift blow he shattered a nearby crate and pulled out a slat while using his foot to nudge Lucita over onto her back. With his second blow he drove it through her heart and down hard enough to knock loose shards of concrete. "We are now."

"Very impressive."

"I've been practicing." Barry smiled. "I had a feeling that that stunt would come in handy sometime."

"It's always nice to have an extra margin of security."

Andrew relaxed a bit, knowing that even if Lucita did wake up now, she wouldn't be going anywhere. He poked and prodded her wounds, and saw no sign of conscious response at all. That was as he expected. Likely she wouldn't regain consciousness until someone gave her blood, and he had no intention of doing that until they were at their final destination. "Simon Peter, give the paladin a call and let her know that we've got the target. Ask her where she and the cardinal would like us to deliver her."

Monday, 15 May 2000, 2:25 AM
Somewhere beneath Mexico City

It wasn't as simple as picking up a phone and dialing direct, of course.

Simon Peter spoke to a contact in Sicily, who in turn connected him through a wireless network mostly used by drug smugglers based in Venezuela, who...Andrew lost track of the twists and turns about there. It took more than an hour of holding and speaking in code phrases and holding again to get Simon Peter to the person he actually wanted to talk with. Then he reeled off a message summarizing the ambush and providing contact points for further instructions.

The voice mailbox into which he spoke used storage space on a mainframe in Vera Cruz. Every half an hour it dumped its contents to another voice mail archive in Mexico City. The engine parts wholesaling firm which owned those computers had no idea that there was twice the stated capacity lurking in their basement, anymore than anyone suspected the private, heavily shielded cabling running down into the sewers. A convoluted network of disparate systems carried signals deep into the Sabbat's warrens for technically inclined vampires to study.

Without the right identifying code phrases, Simon Peter's message would have been dumped unceremoniously by the first vampire to examine it. Nothing in Sabbat doctrine gave much weight to prudence or temperance, and packs who thought they'd performed the greatest feat since Gratiano and Lugoj constantly called to boast. Before the warrens worked out a hierarchy of authorization signals in the 1930s, there'd been a bad time where angry superiors slaughtered a great many arrogant underlings. (Some observers said it was a contributing factor in the brief but bloody 1937 Sabbat civil war.) Now the scrutinizers preferred to err on the side of caution, discarding all traffic they couldn't clearly identify as worthy. Better, so the conventional wisdom of the warrens went, to require repetition of valid messages than to continue annoying

shard

authorities who had better things to do with their time.

Simon Peter and the others had been asleep for hours by the time the message made it to the paladin. It spent some more minutes considering whether this was misdirection to cover up a spectacular failure or simple ongoing lack of results, but eventually decided not. Bishop Andrew had been honest enough so far, and must know the consequences of failed bluffs. Best to proceed as if it were genuine. Very few emotions a human being would recognize still existed in the paladin's soul, which was almost wholly given over to one of the more obscure Paths of Enlightenment, but it could and did feel satisfaction.

The paladin found Cardinal Timofiev on the balcony of a gallery overlooking pre-Aztec ruins. Nobody was quite sure who'd built this little altar, but the cardinal seemed to find something very satisfying about and spent many hours gazing at it and the bones and fungus around it. The paladin spoke softly, so as not to break its master's mood too harshly. "Eminence. I bring news of success."

"Of course you do, my loyal paladin. Success is our lot, as the world spins in our favor. What success in particular do you wish to tell me of?"

"Bishop Andrew Emory sends word to us."

Timofiev jerked around. His eyes glowed—literally, the paladin realized after a moment, lit by the exercise of some arcane discipline of the cardinal's own design. "Lucita."

"Yes, cardinal."

"Show me." But the cardinal didn't wait; he snatched the paladin's transcription and read it himself. "This is wonderful."

"It is a tribute to your acuity in planning."

"Of course, of course, but never mind that. We must verify the information…"

"I have already sent off instructions about that." This was a lie, but a small one. The paladin could act as soon as it left the cardinal, and a little air of intelligent independence within the framework of submission wouldn't hurt.

"Good, good. Assuming it's true, and I shall for the moment, we must think where to convene the trial."

This was something new to the paladin. "The trial, Eminence?"

"Of course the trial, my paladin. Do you not think that Lucita must be held accountable for her actions?"

"Certainly, Eminence. It's just that I had thought you'd be attending to her directly. Personally."

Timofiev paced back and forth on the balcony. "That was my original plan, but it's become clear to me in the course of my meditations that this is not a task for me as an individual. Lucita's fundamental sin is her refusal to accept her family in the blood. We shall not dignify her rebellion with a response that treats her independence as a state worthy of respect. We shall instead treat her as what she is: a Lasombra, who does not escape the bonds that tie us all together. She is not the great rebel she thinks."

"Certainly not, Eminence. What sort of arrangements must we make, then?"

The cardinal pointed down at a rocky column near the altar, filled with water dripping down from above. "There."

"Right here, Eminence?"

"No, not here. I think it would be unwise to bring her here until and unless we are sure that she's had a change of heart." The paladin wondered about that. Did Timofiev actually expect Lucita to join the Sabbat? But the cardinal continued. "What I mean is a place away from the mortal world. She's too fond of it. Everything in the environment must remind her of her real nature and ours. We must go to a place the living do not, where she is constantly aware of being apart from the herd."

"Very wise, Eminence. And did you have a particular place in mind?"

"Thera."

"I beg your pardon, Eminence, but I don't know the name."

"Did you never study the classics?"

"No, Eminence. It wasn't encouraged in the curriculum where I lived and I've never felt the need since then."

"Ah, a pity. Thera is an island in the Aegean Sea. You do know where that is? Good. Its volcano erupted 2,500 years ago and created a calamity that affected civilizations throughout the Mediterranean. Some of our own history is tied up in that, as well as mortal affairs. There's a deep, sea-filled crater there. We sink ships in it from time to time, and sometimes they sink for other reasons. There's a whole warren there which we almost never use. We shall gather there."

"Very good, Eminence."

"Now let us consider who should sit on the seats of this Court of Blood."

Thursday, 1 June 2000, 12:40 AM
Yacht *Latter-Day Feast*
Off the coast of Santorini, Greece

The lords of the Sabbat do not come running from around the world on a moment's notice. It took extensive diplomacy, with frequent exchanges of messengers, direct conversations, implicit threats, and a touch of coercion to assemble a five-member Court of Blood. Most of these dealings took place in secret, though a few rumors began leaking out into the sect at large. "Lucita has been taken." "Monçada's destroyer will be destroyed." "Lucita has joined us." "Lucita refused to join us and will betray us all to the Camarilla." "Lucita is chosen as Monçada's heir." It all vanished into the background noise of sect rumor, which suited Timofiev very well. He proposed to say nothing until there was something much more definite to say.

Timofiev would sit on the panel himself, of course. This was his vision being worked out. His fellow cardinals from Mexico City, Mysancta and Menuven, would join him. That left two positions to fill, which he wanted to assign to Lasombra with perspectives very much unlike his own.

One of Timofiev's invitations went to Elieser de Polanco, a Spanish nobleman Embraced not long before Lucita. Elieser shared much of Lucita's background: He had been a knight in life, a valiant warrior in the *Reconquista* but capable of appreciating the strengths and beauties in Moorish culture, a gentleman in the full old sense of the word. He had known Cardinal Monçada, and while he did not share the late cardinal's faith, he at least respected the institutions of Christendom and held some measure of personal devotion. Elieser struck Timofiev as not entirely reliable in some ways, particularly that continuing interest in and attention to mortal society. But no one could question the don's devotion to Lasombra supremacy or the great cause of the Sabbat, even if as one of the founding Kings of Shadow he dealt with mortals rather than with the sect's most serious enemies.

The other invitation had gone out on a whim, and Timofiev was as surprised as anyone else that the recipient accepted. (Naturally, Timofiev knew better than to *show* surprise, though his paladin recognized the truth. Nobody else did, and Timofiev liked it that way.) In a clan full of inhuman and posthuman monsters, Zarathustra was still "one of the odd ones." When first learning of him, young recruits who knew anything about religion asked if he claimed to be the Zarathustra from whom the Zoroastrian religion sprang. No, he didn't; when he deigned to answer, he explained that he'd adopted the name as a soldier in Alexander the Great's army to show his devotion to that earlier man of wisdom and holiness. Nobody was quite sure that Zarathustra the Lasombra actually was 2,300 years old, but he was certainly around when the western Roman Empire fell for the last few times and nothing strongly suggested that he was embellishing his age very much.

Zarathustra had one, precisely one, driving interest: he claimed the city of Antioch, Turkey, as his own and guided it as he saw fit. His childer and their childer and so on down to the newest thin-blooded whelps were the only vampires allowed to reside for more than a month in the city, and outsiders who tried to sneak in and stay tended to meet with particularly violent ends. From time to time he agreed to sit on Courts of Blood, with no rhyme or reason Timofiev had ever discerned. He had no patience for either the Camarilla or Sabbat as institutions, but when he judged, he applied the principles of the other judges with merciless consistency and logic. Nobody really knew what Zarathustra's own opinions might be on the cases he presided over; he never spoke of his personal reactions, only of the interplay between evidence and the judging principles laid down at the outset of each particular trial. Timofiev had thought it might be interesting to get a very pure Sabbat-oriented point of view, undimmed by personal issues. Zarathustra apparently agreed.

So here they were, having arrived at Santorini by their various means. The yacht *Latter-Day Feast* belonged to a Greek businesswoman who hoped to buy her way into the Sabbat with favors and donations. It wouldn't work—some morning she'd be found floating dead and drained in a ditch somewhere—but the local archbishops were certainly willing to exploit her in the meantime. The crew were centuries-old ghouls, all individuals who'd been offered the Embrace and chosen not to accept it. They had proven trustworthy, intelligent, and were quick-witted, and probably safer when it came to transporting so many elders at once than a vampiric crew would be. The ghouls would be less inclined to engage in acts of diablerie on the vampires in their charge.

Timofiev and de Polanco were the more-or-less human-seeming members of the court. Timofiev wore his customary simple robes, while de Polanco shone in a black suit with silver threads. The Spaniard's hair was subtly blacker than black, enhanced with a little careful shadow play, and his black eyes were pupil-less pools of shadow. Nonetheless, he could have moved down a street full of inattentive humans and blended in, more or less. Mysancta and Zarathustra shared a fondness for pure shadow forms. They were animated pillars of darkness on the yacht's prow, apparently massless and occasionally prone to drifting slightly above the deck. Menuven was, as usual, a network of heavily modified vampires. Tonight it comprised only three such individuals; it had chosen to travel relatively lightly, with the rest of its hosts waiting in a Fira hotel at the edge of the caldera's eastern side.

Four other passengers waited at the back of the yacht. There was Lucita herself, still staked and unconscious, and Bishop Andrew to tend her. Her ghoul, Angelica Tranh, was in a lasting state of shock for the duration of Lucita's torpor, and the tailor Trasaric looked after her. Every so often—once or twice a night, usually—Angelica recovered full self-awareness long enough to feel the ongoing pain of Lucita's staking and burns, shriek, and pass out again. She spent most of her time in a trance state much like sleepwalking. Trasaric murmured softly to her; Timofiev had overheard it once, and greatly approved of the way the tailor told stories of the Sabbat's glories and the glories that could come to willing human servitors. The mortals would remain on board for the duration of the trial, and Andrew would take Lucita down.

Time to begin the ceremonies.

Timofiev stood at the forward-most part of the prow and faced the others. "Cardinals, lords, my brothers and sisters in the Blood, attend me." The others looked at him. "In the beginning of history as we reckon it, our Father in Darkness laid down the rules by which we should exist. He instructed us how to resolve our grievances. We gather tonight in accordance with his rules, that we may judge our sister in the blood. Let us go to the place appointed." Without further ado he stepped off and dropped into the warm Aegean waters. Splashes told him that the others were following.

The *Latter-Day Feast* had anchored fore and aft, and then the crew had dropped two more cables. Timofiev and the others sank down, pulling on the cables when necessary. Those with solid bodies enjoyed the usual vampiric lack of buoyancy and sank quickly, while those in shadow form relied on sheer will to shove themselves down. For the first part of their descent, moonlight and starlight gleamed in the water around them, but darkness soon claimed all. The vampires all relied on the senses other than sight to guide them after the first hundred meters.

Their destination came into their awareness gradually. It was as dark as the surrounding sea, but it reeked of fresh blood and the distinctive tang of preternaturally enhanced bodies. At 400 meters down, this ledge would remain dark even in the brightest day. Four yachts and two small cargo ships were lashed together and built over with superstructure to form a single edifice that remained the former noblemen of classical castles. De Polanco spoke softly with Zarathustra about great citadels they had known, while Timofiev searched for the marks showing the chambers prepared for this court.

Once he'd found them, he spoke again in formal tones (both in enunciated words and then in broadcast mental states, along with resonances echoing through the shadows tying them together). "Let us enter the place that is prepared for us, and make ourselves ready as we have done before." He led the way through open cargo doors into a liquid fuel compartment outfitted as the trial space. The raised panels covering emergency exhaust vents now supported a bench and row of chairs for the judges. A cargo crane base had been twisted and welded into a cage for the prisoner, with a central cruciform pillar to which she could be chained (or bolted, with bolts and bolt drivers thoughtfully left close at hand) and closely spaced bars ten feet from the pillar in all directions. Waterproof lights cast a harsh flat shadow-free illumination into the cell.

The members of the court arranged themselves in the seat: Timofiev in the center, with the two shadow-form judges on his left and the other two on his right. Andrew secured Lucita to the frame and then stood well back, against the far wall. If it were necessary, he could leap forward and subdue the defendant.

"Are we ready?" Timofiev asked. The others all nodded. "Then let us prepare the defendant." He held up a double-walled glass globe with rubber gaskets covering two openings. His hands slid in without difficulty. The fingernails of each hand sliced open the opposing wrist, and he let some of his blood drain into the space. When he withdrew his hands, the blood stayed inside. The other judges in corporeal forms also contributed some blood, as did Andrew. Once the globe was ready, Timofiev replaced one gasket with a smooth glass stopper, the other with a stopper to which a steel pipette was attached. Andrew put the glass inside the cell, where Lucita could see and reach it. He unchained one hand and stepped back again.

"Eldest, it is your place to decide how we will mask ourselves from the defendant," Timofiev said to Zarathustra. "Please set the tone for this court."

The shadow that was Zarathustra made an exaggerated nod, so that the others could tell he had understood and agreed. Without other visible gesture, he went to work. Darkness deeper than the benthal dimness didn't so much flow out of him as intensify itself throughout the area around the bench. Once they were properly cloaked, Timofiev extended a shadow arm into the cell. The bright light was uncomfortably warm, but not actually damaging. He pulled the stake out of Lucita's heart and lifted the vessel of blood to her lips. A vampiric reflex made her drink before real thought returned. In seconds she'd sucked the vessel empty. The worst of her wounds healed up then, and she looked around her for the first time in two weeks.

Thursday, 1 June 2000, 3:13 AM
Yacht *Latter-Day Feast*
Off the coast of Santorini, Greece

Awareness suddenly returned to Angelica. She felt as if she was having a heart attack and had been mugged by the soldiers of her childhood nightmares, but she could think and feel and sense and remember.

The last thing she remembered clearly was the hangar in Jiddah. Something had happened inside, something terrible had happened to Lucita, and then…Angelica didn't know. She had the sort of fleeting recollections she'd had in high fever. None of them added up to very much, and beneath them all was a steady whisper about the joys of abandoning humanity.

"Ah, you awaken to yourself."

Angelica turned to find herself facing a dapper little man dressed in the most peculiar suit she'd ever seen. It was cut something like a Victorian evening suit, but made of a velvet-like material that changed from purple to blue to black as the man moved. He was breathing, at least; this wasn't another vampire. His yellow silk cravat clashed both with the suit and with the silver jewelry around his neck and on his fingers. His expression was an equally peculiar mix of calm concern and an awesomely malevolent hostility. Angelica feared him as she'd feared Lucita and the other vampires at first, but with a sharper edge, knowing that here was a living man who had that darkness in his soul.

"Are you all right?" He spoke English with an unfamiliar accent—something European, she thought, but nothing she'd encountered. "Do you need assistance?" His twisted leer made an ugly contrast to the straightforward, almost kindly, words.

She drew breath and found it acutely painful. "Something…in chest. Hard to breathe."

"Ah, that's not you," he said matter-of-factly.

"Huh?"

"I say, that's not you. You feel the pain of the one to whom you are bound. She's had a stake shoved through her heart for days on end, and it takes a little time for that to heal. It will pass."

"What are you talking about?" Sure enough, she *did* feel the very worst of the pain fading. It was still agonizing, but she could at least concentrate and speak without gasping. "Where are we? Who are you, anyway?"

He made a very old-fashioned bow. "I am Trasaric, tailor to the Keepers, as it were. We are 422 meters above the spot where your domitor stands trial for her possible crimes against the integrity of her family in the blood. You are her ghoul, and as such you will share in whatever sentence is meted out to her."

Most of that made no sense to Angelica, but she could work out the key point: Lucita was in danger. Angelica was gradually realizing that she was on a boat floating on a bay with steep cliffs to the east and west. Was Lucita underwater, then? What was all this?

Trasaric studied her calmly. "You don't know very much about what's going on. Your domitor did not serve you well with information."

"Domitor?"

"Lucita. Your mistress. The one whose blood you've been drinking."

"Um, what?"

"Ahhh, I see. She really has kept you profoundly in the dark." He cackled. "Dark. Heh heh heh."

Angelica began to suspect that this would never make sense.

Thursday, 1 June 2000, 3:13 AM
The wreck of Liberian tanker ship *Emerald*
1,371 feet below sea level, Thera caldera, Santorini,
Greece

Lucita came to awareness very quickly, though not quite instantly. Her body had grabbed healing blood before she had a chance to consciously decide to do so, and she hated to concede the edge of decision-making in anyway.

She was underwater. That was the first thing she noticed. The water was dark even where it wasn't deliberately cloaked in vampire-made shadows, which meant that she was probably a thousand feet or more below the surface.

She was shackled. This was no hurried job, either. Someone had used good equipment to turn available material into an effective cage for her. The bars were far enough away that she couldn't draw shadow substance out of herself to pry them open, and the harsh lighting deprived her of any environmental advantages. A few exploratory tugs confirmed her expectations that the shackles had been designed with her level of strength in mind.

This was bad.

This was in fact very, very bad. She had no advantages at all beyond whatever lay in her mind and soul, and in her just-barely-recovering condition she was something less than sparkling.

A voice drifted out of the summoned darkness. "Lucita, childe of Ambrosio Luis Monçada, childe of Silvester de Ruiz, childe of Cleobolus, childe of Karotos, childe of Lasombra, hearken to our words."

It was worse than she'd imagined.

The voice continued, "You are on trial in accordance with the ancient practices. There is a sin of blood, and the Court of Blood must decide upon whose head the sin lies. Do you understand?"

She tried to speak but found her throat mangled and charred. It took another effort and that much more irreplaceable blood to heal the damage and let her answer. "I understand."

"You have declared yourself on many occasions the enemy of your sire and your clan. Your sire would have been well within his rights to challenge for our sanction of your destruction, but he always refrained. Now that he is gone, you are not shielded by his will, and it is the place of your superiors to decide that you ought to be held accountable. Now is the hour appointed for your trial. Do you understand?"

This was getting worse by the moment. Some elder Lasombra pressing a grievance for personal reasons would have been trouble; an elder acting out of what he, she, or it thought of as an impartial concern for the clan as a whole was more so, because the levers of personal favor wouldn't work. The principled were always harder to manage in a Court of Blood.

"You are accused of purposefully, with deliberation and calculation, destroying your sire. It is immaterial to this court whether you acted alone or with accomplices. We are not concerned with the actions of lesser clans. It is your responsibility to lead them, and we do not distinguish between acquiescence and initiation. Do you understand?"

"Yes."

"Describe for us the night in which your sire perished."

Lucita told the story, haltingly at first, then gathering force. She described how Monçada had exerted unsuspected control over her. She laid out what she knew of the Assamite mission to destroy the cardinal. After a pause to heal her throat again, she provided a technical account in occult terminology of Leviathan, the thing from the Abyss which Monçada had bound into the deepest levels of his haven, and the failure of the forces restraining it.

The judge drew out details from her, little nails of truth on which they'd make her lie down later. Had she collaborated willingly and of her own free will, to the best of her knowledge, with Fatima of the Assamites? She had. Had she exchanged blood with this Fatima before their attack on the cardinal's haven? She had. Had the cardinal unleashed his Leviathan without adequate means of restraining it, or of ascertaining that it would strike all and only his intended targets? She believed so. Had it become confused by the mingling of Assamite and Lasombra blood in Fatima? So it appeared. Had it turned then on the cardinal? It had.

The judges interrupted as she was about to embark on a clinical description of the terminal damage Monçada suffered. "That will suffice."

"Childe of Monçada, do you deny that you wished your sire destroyed?"

"No."

"Do you deny that such an act carried out without the sanction of these courts is itself punishable with destruction?"

"I do not deny that this is the practice of our clan."

"What explanation do you offer that might warrant a stay of execution right here and now?"

"A simple one. However much I wished him destroyed, the fact is that I didn't attack him. You can go through my memories as well as his surviving accounts to find that I warred against his underlings and resources and plans, but that I did not attempt to assassinate him."

Silence. At last, "That constitutes an acceptable defense. We shall pass on to the next charge, of your culpability on the night when in fact he perished."

"Again, a simple defense. Self-defense, which has always been recognized as valid. He released me long ago, but always claimed the right to continue treating me as the merest neonate. He initiated the attack upon me, both physically and mentally, and deliberately subverted my will. I was not capable of independent decision-making when the Assamites mounted their assault, I and behaved as the impaired creature he'd made me into. Had he left me in possession of my faculties, I would have been able to flee, or mediate, or do something other than strike in what seemed immediate preservation."

Silence again. "We will now ponder your words. Remain there." A cold chuckle sounded from somewhere in the darkness.

As a childe, Lucita had asked her sire why the Courts of Blood seemed to proceed so much more straightforwardly than the mortal courts of Aragon. Monçada told her, "The trial itself is not the trial. The real work—all the research and consideration—takes place beforehand. The only reason, really, that we take testimony at all is to make sure that we haven't overlooked anything. If we haven't, then the conclusion is foregone." She assumed now that she could hazard a very reliable guess as to the conclusion drawn, and waited for the inevitable announcement of her destruction.

Thursday, 1 June 2000, 2:40 AM
(3:40 AM Thera time)
Castle of Saint Rafael the Archangel
Sicily, Italy

Once again the summoning was complete. The cabal reveled in their growing prowess. Less effort now brought forth greater and greater power out of the Abyss. There had been no recurrences of that one encounter with the Antediluvian's voice (as they all thought of it), but these successes were clear sign of favor vested in the cabal.

Tonight they'd decided to range further east than before. Efforts at divination kept suggesting Aegean islands. Refinements in rune casting and the reading of entrails pointed to Thera, or Santorini as its people now called it. Very well, let darkness go where once fire had triumphed.

Thursday, 1 June 2000, 3:41 AM
The wreck of Liberian tanker ship *Emerald*
1,371 feet below sea level, Thera caldera, Santorini,
Greece

Lucita assumed, when the light began to dim, that the judges were responsible. It was a ploy of some sort, of course. As the glare faded there were more shadows within reach. It would exhaust her to dangerous extremes, but she *could* break free in not very many more minutes if this kept up. But they must know that. They knew enough about her history to gauge her abilities quite precisely. It must be a test of her behavior in a critical situation; her response would be a sort of testimony, or at least a witness to her character.

So it came as a surprise when a voice that hadn't spoken before said from the shadowed bench, "The defendant will refrain from the exercise of her powers while this trial is in progress."

"I am restraining myself."

"The defendant will refrain from such blatant falsehoods, and will restore the condition of lighting that prevailed until she began this act of insubordination."

"*I'm not doing it.*" She spoke more urgently. "Once again, probe me if you need confirmation. You've made it impossible for me to perform that kind of manipulation. I'd need much more blood than I have and much less distraction from confinement."

Silence. Then, "The defendant will submit to examination."

The chamber went completely dark in the moment that a judge's psychic probe struck. The probe was excruciating, like a metal spike straight into her forehead, made completely without regard for incidental trauma of any sort. "This court accepts the defendant's claim, and demands that if any outside party is here concealed, it reveal itself now."

Now Lucita was confused. That was a lot of work for a character test. The judges sounded genuinely confused by the situation. After a moment's reflection, she decided that confused ideologues were indeed worse than ones who felt themselves in control of the situation. She wasn't sure just how the trial could get any worse, and had the nagging certainty that she'd find out.

The Abyss wind broke out everywhere in the chamber at once. Everyone present recognized it. One of the judges shouted, "See that she doesn't escape!" The vampire behind her, whom she was aware of but hadn't yet seen, dove down from a high vantage point to brace himself against her chains, just in case anything started to give way. Turmoil around the bench suggested that the judges might be trying to layer defenses for themselves.

The first massive limb stretched through an opening at the top of the chamber. It wasn't the same sort of thing as Leviathan, or indeed like any Abyss creature Lucita had experience with, but there was no mistaking the essence of darkness animated by alien will. This was something from the Abyss…unleashed into the material world. Yes, the trial had indeed managed to get worse. The judges were silent, then started shouting a variety of wards along with commands to each other. "Strike!" "Barrier!" "Flee!"

The wind battered down the darkness hiding the bench, allowing Lucita to see her judges. She had time to recognize the ones in corporeal forms before fresh barriers went up. And she could see their shocked, surprised expressions.

One of the shadow-form judges glided out into the center of the chamber, pulling shadow arms out of every nook and cranny to wrap up the Abyss creature. It didn't work. There were now four limbs bracing against the opening to pull a yet-unseen body through, and their mindless contractions and expansions shredded the shadows under the judge's command. The judge continued to glide up, gesturing with tenebrous arms as if to pull the intruding limbs apart by sheer determination. Lucita suspected that the judge was working one of the obscure thaumaturgic paths she'd heard about that were allegedly capable of enhancing the clan's innate aptitude for darkness. It didn't work, either. One of the limbs rose, curled in a complex series of triple folds, and uncurled again with speed too great for Lucita to follow. The judge had no time to scream or otherwise communicate. Just, suddenly, it had no integrity of form anymore. Pieces of its body now drifted in the wind, flesh fading back in now that the will to be intangible was gone.

The other judges, exposed again as the Abyss wind continued to batter down their defenses, spread out from the bench. Cardinal Timofiev sent a mental shout in Lucita's direction. "Release her! We must not let an outside force destroy the defendant!" The vampire behind her picked himself up, shrugged ever so briefly, and quickly undid the locks and clamps holding her down. Lucita turned to see him, and recognized him as one of the pack waiting for her in the hanger back…however long ago it had been that they'd trapped her. She'd have liked to strike him down, but she recognized that this wasn't the time for that.

He shrugged again, and looked at her with a desperately applied neutral expression. "Can you do something to help?"

"I don't know. Let's try, at least."

The remaining shadow-form judge's voice echoed in their minds. "Spread yourselves evenly around the opening, and draw mundane darkness from your quadrant of the vicinity."

"Um, why?" That was Andrew, Lucita recognized.

"The light still burns, though we cannot see it. If we work together, we can liberate it, and let that light shine directly onto whatever it is still comes this way."

"Okay."

As the Abyss creature's body approached, the limbs— nine of them now—became more and more agitated. They struck glancing blows against Lucita, Andrew, and two of the judges, in each case leaving a bitter chill and sense of lethargy. Lucita was now altogether out of extra blood to burn, and had to rely on her basic physical competence. The others, she saw, were rapidly using up their own reserves, their actions becoming more sluggish. If this counter-attack didn't work, they'd soon lack the ability to do anything but perish in possibly interesting ways.

Maneuvering into position wasn't easy. The Abyss winds continued to strengthen, creating turbulent cross-currents. De Polanco was sucked altogether outside the chamber into open sea beyond, and had to exert every scrap of his superhuman strength to latch onto a dangling cable and crawl back. The pieces of Menuven clung to each other as best they could, using the basic principles of Tzimisce flesh-crafting they'd learned somewhere along the line to bond into a single unit, but were having difficulty maintaining coherence. They and Timofiev repeatedly slammed into the chamber's front wall. Timofiev seemed to be losing consciousness; he was bleeding from wounds all across his back and legs, and couldn't close them very effectively. Lucita saw him try to invoke his metamorphosis form without success—he simply couldn't master the mental acuity the transformation required.

The remaining shadow-form judge, the one Lucita didn't know but who seemed to be giving the orders, retained his (or her, or its, though he sounded male) calm. The currents eroded his strength as well, but he showed cunning and care in maneuvering past turbulent pockets, bracing himself when necessary, moving even a step or two when the opportunity arose. Gradually the judges, their aide, and their intended victim surrounded the opening into the Abyss. It wasn't precise or tidy, but it might do.

At the shadow judge's command of "Now," Lucita shut off her physical senses and concentrated on the sensation of drawing darkness into herself. She pictured the sea in its natural state, not filled with anything but water, simply free of sunlight. The preternatural darkness was like smoke and ash spread through it. She didn't realize that she actually opened her arms while exerting her will, commanding the darkness to seek union with a soul of darkness. In her was a home such as the material world could never offer, a place where what the world called sin and emptiness flourished. Around her she could feel the others doing the same, and doing it more effectively. Even the young stalker did nearly as good a job as she did, though he could scarcely be a tenth her age. She realized, and was not comfortable with the realization, that she had much to learn from her Sabbat cousins about this immersion in darkness, about *being* the night as well as *commanding* it. (Time for that later, she told herself, and returned to focusing on the task.)

All at once she felt the lights on her face. She opened her eyes to see them flared back into visibility. They'd gotten jarred in the turmoil and now pointed in all different directions, and all but one flickered and strobed as their wiring drifted in and out of connection. The one steady light was the one still in something like its original position, though its mounting bracket had twisted a quarter turn.

It pointed directly into the portal to the Abyss.

The creature's nine limbs dissolved immediately. Or rather they exploded. They rushed outward fast enough to create sonic booms within the water, seeking to spread themselves across enough darkness to retain their integrity. But the vampires had done their work well, and there simply wasn't anything but the natural absence of light to support the creature. Three limbs shredded and dissolved as they careened out of the chamber opening into the surrounding sea, and the rest fragmented into fear-laden viscosity spread across the chamber.

Then there came a sound or sensation completely unlike anything in Lucita's experience. Even Leviathan's destruction (if destroyed it had been) in Monçada's haven was less traumatic than this. Light poured into the lightless realm and briefly illuminated a vast irregular bulk, at least hundreds of feet across and extending an unknown distance away from the portal. Its highest curves were almost at the portal, and they shrieked in an inhuman agony as the light fell upon them. Alien emotions flooded throughout Lucita and the others, states of mind that owed no history to life or unlife in the material world. Lucita felt for a timeless interval like she might simply go insane under the weight of it all. Her mind reached for sensory organs that nothing material had, and filtered space and time through scales which had no meaning for her.

In the end, simple pain saved her. The trauma of compelled perceptions broke as the thing in the Abyss lost more and more of its internal coherence. Soon it was sending out only agony, and that was something Lucita understood. It wasn't enjoyable but at least it was comprehensible. She felt an urge to lash out at the source of the pain, to smash the lights and cast herself into the Abyss, and it took a great deal of willpower to stand fast.

Crashing sounds nearby drew her attention; she opened her eyes to see one of Menuven's bodies tear through its flesh bonds with its teeth and jump into the Abyss. Its extinction cry joined the Abyss dweller's sustained howl, for an instant. It even achieved a moment of independent self-awareness just before passing, recalling a life lived in an upper-class neighborhood in the southern end of Mexico City, Embrace after blackmail, rising through the Sabbat ranks, working on a comprehensive review of the Sabbat's successes and failures against the ancients, attracting Menuven's attention with disturbing conclusions, brought into the hive-mind to silence uncomfortable perceptions, thereafter lost to self…gone.

There was no telling how long the Abyss creature's dissolution took. The light burned through layer after layer after layer of uncreated substance, slicing apart timeless constructs of mind and will and passion, shredding the thing down into constituent particles of potential existence. At times the pain was almost as strong as when Lucita had burned in Jiddah, and lasted far longer. She didn't want to reward the assault with surrender and death, but it was hard. When the final sensations faded and the portal drifted closed, she saw that she was bone-white with tension, just as the others were. Very much longer, and they'd all have lost the ability to resist.

"Do you feel that?"

"Yes." "Yes." "I do."

"What *is* that?"

"Something has brought light into the Abyss." Gasps of shock answered the declaration. "

"What has made this happen?"

"I don't know. We must find out, and soon. Our Father in Darkness will not welcome the loss of one of His servants."

"What could it be? What could do this?"

"I don't know! You saw the omens yourself. The key to the success of the venture, they said, and you saw."

"I did."

"We must know." "We must." "We must."

"Send our servants. Let them explore and tell us what they see. And let us refrain from further summoning until we understand."

"Agreed." "Yes." "Agreed." "I concur."

shard

Thursday, 1 June 2000, 5:00 AM
The wreck of Liberian tanker ship *Emerald*
1,371 feet below sea level, Thera caldera, Santorini,
Greece

Timofiev couldn't recall the last time he'd been so tired. He drifted in the ebbing currents, trying to regain poise with only limited success.

This was a calamity, pure and simple. One and a third judges were gone forever; he could feel no trace of them anywhere, and felt confident they had ceased to exist in any form that might matter to him. And there was the awkward fact that the accused had been essential to their continued survival. In his review of the attack and defense, without her added strength it would not have been possible to drive the thing back and close the portal. The Father in Darkness had taught His children that success was the ultimate measure of worth. Those who could rule deserved to, and achievement justified effort. By tradition, Lucita's actions tonight were sufficient ground for court closure.

But Timofiev feared the thing that had come up, and very much wanted to know more about it. As he drifted, he sent his thoughts streaming through ripples of darkness to the other judges. "Eminences and worthy judges, I believe I have the proper course of action for this moment." He laid out his scheme and felt for the responses. Zarathustra listened passively, but did not object. The remaining units of Menuven were hot for vengeance and readily assented. De Polanco pondered longest, but agreed as well in the end.

Groggily, Andrew moved to reattach Lucita to her cage. Timofiev raised a cautionary hand. "No need for that, I believe, Bishop Emory. Let the accused stand free. She has earned the right." Timofiev was aware that she could see the judges, in violation of another tradition. He didn't care. None of them had the strength to conjure the shadow wall again, and just at the moment they all seemed to prefer a little distance from anything redolent of the Abyss. If it were really necessary, they could purge her memories later. Let tomorrows deal with themselves, in any event. "Lucita, childe of Monçada, are you prepared to hear your sentence?"

Lucita was dumfounded. The trial continued, after all that had happened? "I suppose I am."

"Lucita, childe of Monçada," Timofiev repeated, "this court has considered your actions and your decisions, and is prepared to render its judgment. Are you prepared to hear your sentence?"

Whatever. Lucita slipped exhaustedly back into courtly formalities. "I am."

"This court finds that you acted without justification in the matter of your sire's destruction. You willingly set aside your obligations as his childe and created the circumstances in which he felt it appropriate to act against you. The final travesty was your doing, however you may choose to construe your own decisions.

"The sentence of destruction is an appropriate one for such a case. But this court judges that certain extenuating circumstances apply, and that therefore another sentence is more fitting at this time. We shall lay an obligation upon you, and its successful completion will constitute adequate punishment. Your failure, if you fail, will be publicized as confirming evidence of your weakness; your success will likewise be publicized as vindication."

What? Lucita had no idea what the cardinal could have in mind. She'd expected not to survive until dawn. This was something unusual, coming from the mouth of one who shunned the unusual.

"This court sentences you to investigation. You are a traveler and a gatherer of secrets. Very well. You shall travel and gather secrets for us and for all your family in the blood. You will find how that thing of the Abyss came among us tonight, who unleashed it, how, and why. You will return to us in Mexico City with the answer, and you will join us in taking what steps seem warranted to our council when we understand these things."

"Suppose I refuse?"

"If you decline to accept this burden, tired as we are, we can destroy you on the spot. If you accept in word but not deed and attempt to pursue some other course of action once you are away from our scrutiny, you will become not merely outcast but enemy. We shall spare no effort to find you and bring to you at that time the punishment of destruction which you now escape. There is for you no future but the future of acceptance."

"I…"

The shadow-form vampire spoke to her for the first time. "Do not commit yourself lightly. Remember that the end is sometimes preferable to a fresh beginning, or so wisdom has it. If you cannot carry the burden, do not pick it up."

Lucita drifted silently.

The shadow-form vampire nodded at her contemplation. "It is well that you think. This is a moment when you stand at the crossroads. There is for us no path of light, but there are different darknesses, and you must consider carefully which is to be your home."

"Am I to become one with the Sabbat, then?"

Timofiev took charge again. "No, you are not. Should you choose to submit to the great rites, of course, you shall be as welcome as any of our kind who sees and accepts the truth. But we do not expect you to come to that realization. Your journey may well ally you with the Sword of Caine in its various parts, but you are not expected to allow it into yourself unless you freely choose to do so. We do not punish you at this time with the Vinculum."

That was something, at least. Though of course nothing would stop them from changing their mind later and subjecting her to the creation rites and rituals, at least she could put off that fear for a little while. "Do I search by myself?"

"We do not expect you to complete the punishment yourself. You shall choose companions suitable for each stage of your quest. We shall discuss these matters another time. They do not bear on the substance of your sentence. Lucita, childe of Monçada, do you hear and understand your sentence?"

"I do."

"And what do you say? Do you accept this sentence, or do you choose the release of destruction?"

"I accept."

Thursday, 1 June 2000, 5:30 AM
Yacht *Latter-Day Feast*
Off the coast of Santorini, Greece

"They're coming," Trasaric said without preamble.

Angelica jumped. It was the first time anyone had spoken in more than an hour, since the eruption or whatever it was had bubbled up from below. "Who?"

"All those who went below, of course. They must have completed their business."

A few minutes later, Lucita and the others did in fact bob to the surface. They were all wan and clearly exhausted, and the ship's crew had to help them onboard. One of the stewards brought vials of blood out of a storage locker. Each of the survivors drank nearly enough blood to fill a human body's vessels, and still looked more pale than usual.

Angelica studied Lucita fearfully. Sorrow and worry radiated from her mistress. Trasaric had explained to her that since she carried part of her mistress' essence in herself, she would continue to feel some of what her mistress did, just as (presumably) Lucita could tell the state of Angelica's soul. It would have been terrifying to learn that earlier, but now the fact of experienced devotion made it tolerable. And she could tell that her mistress grieved.

"What happened?"

"They decided how to punish me for my sins."

"What sins?"

"Later, later."

"At least tell me what we'll be doing now."

"*You* will be doing a great deal of flying, I think."

about the author

Bruce Baugh is the author of a great deal of material for White Wolf's Storyteller games and wrote two stories for the **Clan Novel Anthology**. **Shards** is his first novel.

what are we?

the damned
childer of caine?

the grotesque
lords of humanity?

the pitiful wretches
of eternal hell?

we are vampires,
and that is enough.

we are that which
must be feared,
worshipped
and adored.

the world is ours —
now and forever.

no one holds
command over us.

no man.

no god.

no prince.

VAMPIRE
THE MASQUERADE

WHITE WOLF
GAME STUDIO

THE RAGE CONTINUES...

ribe Novels 5:

hildren

f Gaia

Uktena

e Garou, the
stial werewolves
o fight to save
e natural world,
ve their backs
the wall.

Tribe Novel:
hildren of Gaia,
e storyteller
ies Havoc,
bbed of his
emories by the
yrm, fights to
come whole again.

Tribe Novel:
ktena, another
ngkeeper named
my Hundred-Voices
mes face to face
ith Lord Arkady,
e Silver Fang
cused of conspiring
ith the Wyrm.
an she turn him from
s destructive path?

March 2002

WEREWOLF THE APOCALYPSE